firefly

GENERATIONS

firefly

Big Damn Hero by James Lovegrove (original concept by Nancy Holder)
The Magnificent Nine by James Lovegrove
The Ghost Machine by James Lovegrove

GENERATIONS

firefly

BY TIM LEBBON

TITAN BOOKS

Firefly: Generations
Hardback edition ISBN: 9781785658327
E-book edition ISBN: 9781785658334

Published by Titan Books
A division of Titan Publishing Group Ltd
144 Southwark Street, London, SE1 0UP.

First edition: October 2020

1 3 5 7 9 10 8 6 4 2

A CIP catalogue record for this title is available from the British Library.

Printed and bound in the United States.

THIS ONE'S FOR THE NEWTs

Silas

Even asleep, he is more awake than most people. His body is suppressed, but his mind is extraordinary and can never be controlled. While he is held in suspended animation between one moment and the next, his mind still ranges beyond the confines of his prison. He plans and schemes, and every moment brings freedom that much closer. He has arranged for it to be this way. Once captured, and knowing that he would be put into suspension, he always intended to be found.

Set free.

The map leading back to him is out there, though Silas has some trouble trying to remember how long it has been since he sent it. His moments sometimes feel like seconds, sometimes years. He experiences a certain frustration, because he has so many things to do.

Once free he will better himself. He will bring his fury to bear upon those who sought to open his skull and stir his mind. He was their first subject—their lab-rat—and he is sure that more came after him. Maybe they were more perfect, but he thinks not. He is the original, and though changed for the better, still he wants his revenge for what they did.

Only someone like him—one of those who came after—will be able to read the map and lead others here. Then he will awaken.

A thin, hungry spider at the center of its web, Silas waits for the darkness and stillness to end. Once freed, he will wreak havoc.

Prologue

With his precious future held close to his heart, Private Heng Choi watched from a viewing port of the Alliance destroyer *Peacebringer* as doom closed in on them. Sirens wailed. Warnings echoed through gangways, ward rooms, and battle stations, and into escape pods there was no time to use. Service personnel ran back and forth, most carrying out their emergency duties as they had been trained, but in a barrack room across the wide hallway he saw several people crawling beneath bunks and curling themselves into the fetal position.

Heng laughed. They were following imminent crash protocol, as if hiding under a mesh bed would protect them from explosive decompression, the frozen draw of deep space, fire, crushing, crashing, pressure-blast, or one of the hundred other ways in which they were about to die. *Put your head between your knees and kiss your ass goodbye*, he thought, but gallows humor turned to sadness when he pressed his hand to his chest.

He felt it there, just inside his jacket, folded and vacuum-sealed within an airtight bag. He'd always known it was precious. He feared that so close to the end of his time, its knowledge and potential would never be fulfilled.

The terrorist ship, spewing atmosphere and beautiful, dancing fire from several holes in its hull, rolled toward them. A few optimistic cannon operators were pouring fire at its bulk, but the small explosions did little to halt its inexorable, terrifying advance. Heng couldn't help but feel a grudging respect for the terrorist ship's pilot, committing his vessel to a collision course as his final courageous act of defiance.

He closed his eyes, only opening them when the impact countdown broadcast to the *Peacebringer*'s crew reached ten seconds. He wanted to witness his final moments.

The impact sent him crashing against the viewing port, falling to the floor, then bouncing from wall to wall as the *Peacebringer* shuddered, ruptured, and broke. He expelled all the air from his lungs, yet the feared decompression did not come. His senses were in chaos. There were explosions and crunches, the screech of tearing metal and the screams of the dying. He smelled rancid air as the ship's treatment and recycling plant was shattered. Heng was knocked over again as several crew members were thrown against him by a nearby explosion. Their bodies shielded him from much of the blast, but he felt the warm kiss of blood spatter across his exposed face and arms.

He heard the repeating message to abandon ship, but he guessed that anyone who did go for the escape pods would be torn to pieces as soon as they launched. Outside, his whole field of view was filled with parts of the broken ships, blooming flowers of flame spewing from rents in the hull, and spinning, wretched corpses.

Heng stood again and hauled himself against the viewing port, one hand still pressed against the package in his uniform's inner pocket. *Is this all about me?* he wondered, and the idea struck him with the force of a disabled ship on collision course. He had been handed the map by a dangerous prisoner on his first ever posting as an Alliance soldier. It was his one and only journey beyond the Outer Rim, as part of a unit accompanying two unnerving blue-gloved Alliance science-types onto a strange, abandoned ship. The prisoner had caused a distraction, manufactured a chance encounter. *It's precious*, he'd whispered into Heng's ear, pressing the folded paper into his hand. Young, impressionable, afraid, Heng had not had any reason to doubt those words. He'd always kept it close, and realized now that it likely had a meaning and value way beyond money.

He heard more screams, more rending metal, and he realized that the *Peacebringer* had been knocked into a rapidly decaying orbit around the small planet they had been orbiting for several days. Their mission had been to broker a peace between warring clans on the planet, but what if that was simply a cover?

"What have I done?" he asked, but there was no one to offer a response. His heart beat faster, as if giving life to the strange map that he had never been able to decode. He had always kept it secret, hoping to profit from it one day. Perhaps that secrecy had been a mistake.

The ship began to spin.

The view from the port alternated between deep space, planet, and debris fields that spread and burned before his eyes.

Whatever questions he had left, he would die without knowing the answers.

Kathryn and her family watched the blazing ship spinning down through the scant atmosphere, shedding parts of itself that streaked away at differing angles, spewing flames and smoke as it roared its final, deafening scream of rage at whatever had brought it down.

"There'll be dozens seeing this," her father said. "We need to get there first."

Kathryn nodded and her brother did the same, but they all knew that the likelihood of them striking lucky was small. They never did. If there was an abandoned ship ripe for salvage, they'd arrive in time to pick over the dregs that were left. If there was a gas strike down in one of the deep ravines, they would get there in time to fill a few bottles of weak, crude stuff before the well ran dry. They roamed the surface of the planet looking for luck, but luck always remained one step ahead.

"It'll take too long to go home for the overlander," Kathryn said.

"We'd better run, then," her brother said, and to begin with they did. In the thin air, it didn't take long for them to slow, gasping and panting, to a fast walk.

The blazing ship had left a widening trail of smoke in the dark sky. It blotted out stars like a fresh brushstroke reimagining that part of the heavens. As they slowed from their optimistic run they heard the impact as the ship crashed into the distant Meadon mountain range. The horizon lit up with fire, casting a muted yellow glow across the mountainsides.

"Might not be much left," Kathryn said.

"There's always something," her father said. "Things we can trade or use ourselves."

"But the mountain gangs will reach the crash site long before us!"

"Then we'd better start running again!" They did as her father said, and although the thin air made their lungs strain, and her vision swam and became fluid, they ran through the pain toward what might be a source of much-needed salvage.

By the time they reached the crash site the fires had died down, the smoking wreck was all but silent, and the Meadon mountain gangs had indeed been and gone, taking with them anything worth salvaging from the remains of the Alliance ship. The debris field was crisscrossed with footprints, and laid out in a neat line away from the ship were the corpses of almost fifty Alliance crew. The survivors had been pulled from the wreckage and then executed.

She stared at the bodies. Some of them showed signs of terrible trauma from the crash—broken bones, severed limbs, bloodied wounds and burns—but every single one had holes in their upper torso from where they had been cut down by gunfire.

Her brother was the first to approach. He went to his knees and started rifling through the first corpse's clothing.

"No!" Kathryn said. "You can't! That's—"

"She won't care," her father said. He nodded toward the next corpse. "Neither will he. They might have money, ID tech, guns, even food. We leave it here to rot into the ground, or perhaps it benefits us for the next few weeks. It's really no choice at all."

"Even the mountain gangs don't steal from the dead."

"They *made* them dead!" her father said. "Only reason they don't take from them is they think the Alliance are unclean scum. Me… I just don't like them all that much."

Kathryn watched her father and brother searching the dead for ten minutes before joining in. Hunger had a way of winnowing through her morals.

The fourth body she searched was a middle-aged man, battered and broken from the crash and with three bullet holes in his chest. He had his right hand tucked inside his uniform, and as she pulled it out a vacuum-wrapped package came with it, clasped tight between his thumb and fingers.

She glanced around at her father and brother. They were immersed in their own searches, neither of them watching what she was doing. *They think I never find anything useful.* She started unwrapping the packet and it opened with a soft sigh.

Something inside sparked, just for a moment. It startled her. On first glance she thought it was folded paper, a last letter to his loved ones perhaps, but it seemed to contain tech. Maybe it would be worth something. She peeled the clear cover open and extracted the item, sitting in the mud and unfolding it across her knees. More sparks sizzled across its surface before dying down, and then it was just a piece of thick, waxy paper. The etched and inked designs were strange and difficult to make out.

"What you got?" her brother called.

"Nothing," she said. "Old drawing."

"Look for stuff worth something!" he said, before going back to searching another corpse.

Kathryn waved a hand his way without looking, frowning as she tried to make sense of what she had found. There was no obvious power source to the limp sheet—it must have been static from the crash—and the markings across both surfaces meant nothing to her.

She shoved the packet into her back pocket, then closed the dead man's eyes before moving on. His story was over. She wondered who he was.

Three days later Kathryn traded the packet for a pair of leather boots. They were far from new, but they were solid and fit her well. The weird old map had been worth nothing. She decided she'd made a good trade, and she felt smug when she told her father and brother so.

The man she'd traded with was called Martynn, and seventeen days later he was dead. He never heard the shot that killed him. The woman who pulled the trigger, Marcine Rume, had done so because she was paid to kill, and Martynn was the latest in a long line of men, women, and children—some of them bad people, some unfortunate innocents—who had died at her hand.

On the dead man's body she found three gold rings on his fingers, one silver tooth in his head, and a leather satchel containing a folded sheet of yellowed paper. Useless. She discarded the satchel and paper, and turned and walked back toward her ship. His body would rot into the land, and she had business elsewhere.

A few steps away from the body she paused, frowning. Just because she couldn't read what was written on the thick paper didn't mean it would not be valuable to someone else. Some people who'd never left the surface of a planet collected old rubbish like that.

She went back to collect it. The man's body was already attracting vermin, and high above circled three carrion birds.

Marcine Rume spent the next week at a brothel on one of the small moons of Bellerophon. She had money to spend, so the whores gave her plenty of time. They plied her with drink too, and when she fell into a drunken coma they went through her belongings. They were very careful about what they touched and stole. It was never wise to take money, because if they kept the woman happy she would give it to them soon enough. Personal effects would be missed. It was the small items that seemed to hold no importance that they looked for.

The whore who found and took the map was called Gemma. It was stolen from her a week later by a miner who worked the asteroid fields. He lost it in a fight with a fellow miner, and it dropped out of sight between two loose floorboards in a tavern.

Three weeks later a child found it, one of several who sometimes lived beneath the tavern scavenging for food and drink and gathering the few coins and notes that fell through the gaps. The child liked the map, and in his uncorrupted view its strange markings and symbols were quite beautiful, not befuddling. He didn't understand what it showed—in truth, he didn't realize that it was a map at all—but he appreciated the smooth silky feel of it, the old stale smell, and he was young and open-minded enough to see that though it meant little to him, to someone else this might mean the world.

Seven weeks after finding the map and hiding it away in a place only he knew, the child used it to buy food from a traveler passing through the town. His name was Deacon, an old man who had taken to wandering to preach his lessons of kindness. He showed this child kindness by giving him food of far greater value than the tattered, unreadable shred of paper he used to buy it.

Later that same day, camping just outside town and examining his new acquisition by the revealing light of a campfire, Deacon began to change his opinion.

In one of his distant past lives he had been a mercenary.

He knew a star map when he saw one.

1

"Why is it always me who gets to scrub the gorramn floors?" Jayne asked.

"Because you're best at it," Mal replied.

"Best? At scrubbin' floors?"

"It's those muscles you're building up from you and the Shepherd liftin' weights."

"Huh. Right. I guess that's a joke."

"I'm having no part of this," Book said.

"No joke, Jayne." Mal leaned on the walkway handrail and looked down into the depressingly empty cargo bay.

"So why can't Book do it? He's got the same muscles."

"Book's busy."

"Doin' what?"

Mal sighed.

"I'm busy filling my time with study and contemplation," Book said. In truth he was going through a case of books they'd ended up with after their last real job, moving a rich family from one moon to another. Mal had communicated with them following the job to say that a crate had somehow been left behind, but the reply had been as he'd expected—"fifty million miles is a long way to go for some books." The Shepherd had been delighted, and ever since he'd spent an hour or so each day going through the case. He claimed he was looking for volumes worth money to collectors. Mal was pretty certain he was just reading them all, leaning back against the crate with a contented smile on his face. He didn't mind. Anything that kept a member of his crew busy in this painfully slack period was fine by him.

Which brought him back to Jayne, and the floor.

"Well then, why can't Kaylee be floor scrubber this time?" Jayne asked, just as Kaylee entered the bay from the rear of *Serenity*. She was wearing overalls and carrying a small object that sprouted snipped wires and cables. Her face was smeared with oil, her hair tied in a bun, and she appeared unaware of anything apart from the strange item in her hands. It seemed to Mal as if it belonged inside some creature.

"Because Kaylee keeps us flying," Mal said. "The ship's her baby and she looks after it. Learn to service the grav drive, then maybe we can talk."

Jayne dropped his brush into a bucket of water and stood, and Mal groaned. He knew it would come to this eventually. They were all aware that they were just filling time—even Kaylee, who by her own admission was servicing parts that didn't really need the attention—but so far the underlying tension in the ship had been vented in good-natured banter with only an occasional barbed comment.

If trouble was going to come from anywhere, it would be from Jayne.

"What about Wash?" Jayne asked.

"Wash flies the ship."

"The ship flies itself."

"Even when the ship is flying itself, Wash is making sure it's going the right way."

"Inara."

"You really wanna ask a Companion to scrub your floor?"

"Zoë, then. Or the Doc. Or the girl. Why do I gotta do it?" Jayne looked around, as he always did when River was mentioned. He'd been wary of her since the incident with the carving knife, and even though she seemed to be much more levelheaded nowadays after their visit to Ariel, he was always nervous in her presence. In truth, Jayne's nervousness meant that Mal was often on edge around River too. He might be antagonistic and arrogant, but Jayne was one of the hardest people he knew.

"Because I told you to," Mal said. "You polish your guns anymore and you'll wear 'em away."

"Yeah, well, maybe I'll just jump ship and you'll have to scrub the gorramn floors yourself!"

Mal tried to come up with a response, and failed. Jayne was right. None of them had been paid in some time, and with the ship's supplies of food and booze rapidly dwindling, he had to expect cussing and moaning from the crew. Jayne weren't no surprise, but he'd come across Zoë and Wash whispering with each other just the day before. Not an unusual occurrence in itself, but their sudden change in demeanor and tone upon his arrival had made it obvious they were talking about him. Simon and River kept pretty much to themselves, as usual, and Book seemed content with his old tomes. Inara, he knew, was getting itchy feet, and it wouldn't surprise him if she left for another appointment sooner rather than later. Even Kaylee wasn't her usual sunny self. She'd mentioned a couple of times lately about wanting them to spend some time in a decently equipped port, or a space dock where she could perform a more thorough overhaul of *Serenity*. Usually she was happy just spending time on the ship.

"You missed a bit," Kaylee said, glancing down from the walkway at the cargo-bay floor. Jayne pulled a face and aimed a rude gesture her way.

"I ain't jokin'." She pointed past Jayne. He frowned, turned to look, and Kaylee laughed.

Jayne plucked the brush from his bucket and lobbed it at her. She ducked just in time, grinning.

"Let's eat," Mal said. "All of us together. I think it's time for some honest talk."

"Honest, like when do we get our back pay?" Jayne asked.

"Back pay?" Kaylee asked, looking at Mal.

"In the mess," Mal said. "Now!"

It was time to come up with a plan to find some work. It wasn't all about the money, it was about staying purposeful. It was about keeping his crew sane, and safe. Mal was their captain, they looked to him to provide, and there were only so many times Jayne would agree to get on his knees and polish the gorramn deck.

"Maybe Inara has the right idea," Jayne said. He scooped a third spoonful of energy supplement onto his plate, glancing at Mal as he did so. They'd agreed that they were all on rations of two spoons per meal until they resupplied somewhere. Mal blinked at him but said nothing. The fact that he was having to pick his battles, even with Jayne, meant that this had gone on for too long.

"Inara has every right to come and go as she pleases," Mal said.

"Good time to leave when we've become a bunch of no-hopers," Jayne said.

"I have an appointment," Inara said. "I take advantage of good opportunities the same as the rest of you."

"Good rich opportunities, I'll bet," Mal said.

"I prefer to think of them as people of means," she said, smiling at Mal. Her smile always did something to him he wasn't used to. It confused him. And the last person in the crew he'd want to pick up on that always seemed to be the one who did.

"I doubt she'd have you even if you could afford to pay," Jayne said. River giggled at that, causing a moment of shocked silence around the table. The girl didn't usually laugh at anything, or if she did it was something none of them understood.

"It was bad luck we had to dump the pods," Zoë said, and Mal wished she'd changed the topic to something else.

"Bad luck on the Spider Slugs inside," Inara said.

"We had an Alliance cruiser closin' in," Mal said. "If they'd boarded us—"

"Still don't know how anyone can eat those gorramn things," Jayne said, spooning a mass of paste into his mouth. "I mean, they're slugs. As big as my arm!" He shivered. "Euch."

"They're a delicacy on Londinium," Book said. "One good-sized slug costs fifty credits."

"You're speakin' as if you've tried them," Kaylee said.

Book shrugged. "Once or twice. Actually… once. They taste as bad as they look."

Jayne was looking back and forth between Book and Kaylee. "But fifty credits *each*?"

"Why do you think I was so ready to smuggle them?" Mal said.

"And we dumped 'em in deep space?" Jayne shook his head. "We could have hidden the pods. This ship's got more hiding places than… than somethin' with lots of hiding places."

"They didn't come on board," River said. "They were sailing, that's all, sailing on by."

"We weren't to know they weren't aimin' to board us," Mal protested.

"You never asked." River stirred her food but didn't eat any. She stared down at the patterns it made on her plate, and Mal wondered what she might be seeing. Something other than energy paste and rehydrated potato, that was for sure.

"I appreciate everyone's patience," Mal said. "We've been here before, lookin' for work and missin' out on commissions by a few days."

"Or a few million miles," Zoë said.

"But we'll pull through if we hold together. One big score and we'll forget about this."

"A familiar refrain," Book said.

Jayne scooped up more paste to add to the remnants of his meal. "Take me a long time to forget about this." It didn't taste of much, but it provided essential vitamins and calories. Simon had recommended supplementing their meals with it ten days before, and since then it had become a constant.

"I hear you on that one," Mal said.

"Evening," Wash said. He sat beside Zoë and started spooning food onto his plate. "Oh, yum. Potatoes and goo for dinner again."

"We were just discussing its culinary merits," Zoë said.

"Merits?" Wash looked around at them all, one eyebrow raised. "What'd I miss?"

"Mal telling us how much those Spider Slugs were worth," Jayne said. "And where our next score is comin' from."

"Yeah, about that," Wash said. "I might have an idea." He forked food into his mouth and succeeded in chewing without pulling a face. Mal admired him for that.

"So share!" Kaylee said.

"Golden's Bane." Wash smiled, green paste between his teeth.

"That another type of *gǒu shǐ* food?" Jayne asked.

"It's a place," Wash said, looking around the table. "Don't

tell me none of you have heard of it?"

"Rings a bell," Mal said, tapping his fork on the table. "So where and what is it?"

"It's a mining town on Zeus's fifth moon," Wash said. "Or rather, it's a valley on that moon, and there are buildings scattered either side of the valley's river for a mile or so. Wouldn't really call it a town."

"Why not?" River asked. She seemed suddenly interested. Mal still found it mystifying what might grab the girl's attention. Simon didn't appear to know either, much as he pretended to understand her. Must have been tough, losing your sister like that, then getting her back different.

"It's just… a rough place. Buildings appeared when they found gold in the hills, then when the gold was all mined out the place remained. Prospectors who went there with no money and found nothing couldn't afford to leave. Over the years it's built something of a reputation as a way station for criminals and miscreants. I went there once, years ago, when I was piloting a small transport ship for a mining facility on Aberdeen. They traded with the town for a while, buying a lot of the old mining equipment in return for farming gear, seeds, water filtration plants, that sort of goings on. Not somewhere I'd even hoped to visit again."

"Not to your usual standard of civility?" Zoë asked.

"Could say that, sweetheart. The place was a dump. No law and order, no real system of rule other than local gang lords warring back and forth through the place. I was there four days and there were three murders, one in the tavern I was drinking in. I realized it was the butthole of the 'verse and left the next day."

"I'm liking the place more and more," Jayne said, grinning.

"Mal?" Zoë asked. He'd been thinking, and her saying his name jogged a memory he wasn't too pleased to recall.

"Lassen Pride," he said.

Zoë looked up, surprised, or maybe shocked.

"What the hell is Lassen Pride?" Jayne asked.

"Who, not what," Zoë said. "Mal and I fought with him. He was…"

"Not a good man," Mal said. "The killin' suited him, and after the war stopped, he didn't."

"So what's he got to do with Golden's Bane?" Wash asked.

"It's where he went when he retired," Zoë said.

"From killin'?" Jayne asked.

"So it's purported," Mal said. "But it's also said he got into the smugglin' business. If we're close, and Wash knows the lie of the land as well's he claims, maybe he'll be a useful contact."

"You were friends?" Book asked.

Mal gave a forced grin.

"Friendly enough," Zoë said.

"Yeah. He didn't try to kill either of you," Jayne said, and he chuckled.

There was silence around the table. When Mal caught Zoë's eye he saw a glimmer of uncertainty there, and suspected it was reflected in his own. He couldn't afford that. A captain shouldn't be uncertain. He pressed his hands to the table and stood.

"Let's pay a visit," he said. "Pride might find us some work."

"By 'work,' I assume you mean questionable employment that might eventually require my expertise?" Simon asked.

"We always start out hoping not," Mal said. "How things turn out is rarely of our making."

"If I may," Book said, "I believe I'll be sitting this one out."

"Sitting it out?" Mal asked. He caught a glance between Inara and Book and he sat back down, slapping his hand on the table. "Spill."

"Nothing to spill," Book said. "I've asked Inara if I can accompany her to her appointment. She's going to a space station in orbit around Ghost, and there's a fine book trader there who I believe will pay handsomely for three of the old Bibles I found in the crate."

"How handsome?" Jayne asked.

"That's what I'm going to find out."

"You know that crate belongs to *Serenity*," Mal said.

Book held out his hands. "And I'd be more than happy to donate any proceeds to her. I could even use them to pick up the supplies we're in need of."

"So we go to Golden's Bane and mix it up with this Pride character, and you go to a library," Jayne said.

"And if I make some money, and you still find no work, Inara and I return with food," Book said. He glanced at Kaylee. "And spare parts."

"And booze," Jayne said.

"Goes without saying."

"I'm not fond of my crew being split," Mal said.

"Split the crew, double the chance we make a score," Book said. "And these books, Mal… they're rather precious."

"You mean more'n money," Mal said.

Book nodded once.

"They're just books!" Jayne said. "Maybe we can burn 'em, keep warm."

"Not being a book lover, I'm not sure a gentleman like you would understand," Book said.

"So educate me."

"We've tried," Mal said.

Jayne looked around the table at them all, then snorted.

"So when do you leave?" Mal asked, looking at Book but directing his question at Inara. Whenever she left *Serenity* on an appointment he felt a cool sense of loss. Part of it was seeing her leave, part knowing what she was going to do. One day maybe he'd tell her, but sometimes he felt they'd been doing the dance for so long that might never happen.

"Right after dinner," Inara said.

Jayne slammed down his spoon with a clatter. "You call this dinner?"

Kaylee didn't like the sound of Golden's Bane, at least not how Wash had described it, and she knew him to be solid and dependable and not someone prone to exaggeration or embellishment. She didn't like the sound of Lassen Pride. She didn't like Jayne's increasing agitation, pacing the ship like a caged wolf, snapping at anyone who even looked at him the wrong way, nor that Inara and Book had flown away, leaving the ship lighter two crew, one shuttle, and a whole lot of character. Most of all, she didn't like not having the gear she needed to tend to the ship. *Serenity* was flying sweet and clean, but only because she'd had plenty of opportunity to service, tweak, and fine-tune the systems. She could do with a new gravity drop tube, and two of the lateral stabilizer foils were starting to chatter and shake, especially when they were flying into or out of an atmo. But these were new buys and refits, not repairs, and as usual there was no money.

At least they now had a destination in mind. She loved *Serenity*, more than the rest of the crew combined—more even than Mal, and she thought Mal knew that too. But she also sometimes craved time on solid ground, with rock or dust beneath her feet and air to breathe that didn't carry the faint taint of carbon filters and yesterday's memories.

And then there was Simon. Being in such a confined space increased the pressure between them. *Serenity* was not a large ship, and the whole crew was likely to bump into each other whenever they went wandering from their private rooms. She wished she could just be brave and kiss him, but even after so long she was worried that she had read the situation wrong. She had no doubt that Simon was attracted to her. He made that clear, though not as clear as she'd like.

Her worry that she'd read things wrong was all about River. Simon was committed to his sister. He'd given up a promising career for her, rescuing her from the Alliance butchers who'd done whatever nasty stuff they'd done to her, and now he was looking after her as best he could. At least he'd begun practicing medicine again, but Kaylee doubted treating gunshots or knife wounds was the type of medicine he'd really trained for. On Ariel he'd found some of the answers he'd been seeking, and his treatment of River had eased her unpredictability some.

She thought she knew Simon, but perhaps all she knew for sure was *Serenity*.

"Maybe it's just you and me forever," she said.

"What's that?"

"Mal!" Kaylee jumped and spun around. She'd thought she was alone in the engine room. She often became so embroiled in *Serenity* that she didn't hear when people approached, or didn't allow her senses to notice them. Maybe that was what it was like being in love.

"Didn't intend startlin' you. Thinking on Golden's Bane?"

"Yes, just that. Sounds like a charmin' place, full of sweet folk and no peril whatsoever."

"It's necessary," Mal said. "We need a job, and we all need a break from each other too. Few days' shore leave—"

"Need me to stay with the ship?" Kaylee asked.

"You don't have to."

She shrugged. In truth, she hadn't really thought about what she'd do when they landed.

"Just to let you know we're approaching, best to buckle in. You know how the old girl rocks and rolls when we're in atmosphere."

"Sure, Mal. And talking of which…"

"Lateral stabilizer foils, for sure. First thing on my list once we bring in some credits."

"Thanks."

Mal left, and Kaylee unhinged the buckled seat against the bulkhead wall. Before sitting down she tapped the engine casing and said, "Be a good girl and set us down in one piece."

The vibrations started, and the stabilizer foils began to whistle and whine.

"You weren't wrong," Kaylee said. "What a dump."

"I like it," Jayne said.

"Yeah, it's lovely," Zoë said. "Maybe they've got a Jayne statue somewhere."

"My reputation goes before me."

"I sincerely hope not," Wash said. He'd brought them down on a level escarpment above the river and the town straddling it. The valley was deep, its sides steep, and to land any lower would have been dangerous. Setting down close to the town might also have stirred up dust and mud, and the last thing they wanted to do was annoy the townsfolk. They were here to try to get work, after all.

"So who was Golden?" Simon asked.

"Huh?" Wash grunted.

"If this place was his bane," Simon continued, "who was he, and what went wrong for him?"

"Erm… must admit, I don't rightly know."

"Nothing to worry about here," River interrupted, "as long as you stay away from the orange."

"The orange?" Mal asked. River stared down into the valley.

With *Serenity* clicking and cooling behind them, the crew stood enjoying solid ground beneath their feet, and the gentle breeze on their skin. The air smelled dusty but fresh, with no signs of any heavy industries close by tainting it. There were a few smoking chimneys scattered among the random buildings, but there were also lots of trees and plenty of green further up the hillside.

"Looks like whoever designed this place dropped the buildings from a height and anchored them where they fell," Kaylee said.

"It's not too pleasing on the eye," Zoë said, "but I smell cooking meat. Or is that just me?"

"Not just you," Mal said.

"Smells like pork," Jayne said, and started walking downhill.

Kaylee closed her eyes and breathed in, and suddenly the idea of staying with *Serenity* didn't seem so appealing. She couldn't remember the last time she'd eaten fresh barbecue.

When she opened her eyes again, Simon was standing right in front of her. He smiled.

"Can I buy you dinner?"

"If dinner is half a roast pig in a loaf of bread, you surely can!"

Wash closed up the ship, and as the seven of them headed down the rocky slope toward town, Kaylee glanced back. It wasn't often she saw *Serenity* from the outside, and she constantly surprised her with her beauty. Some thought she was an ugly ship, but Kaylee saw sweeping lines, delicate curves, and a restrained power that only she really knew how to let loose. *Serenity*'s grav drive was part of her own beating heart. *See you soon*, she thought.

River walked ahead of her and Simon. The girl was on her own, looking around with interest at the trees and shrubs, the rocks, the familiar and unfamiliar birds and small animals scampering through the canopy and along lower branches.

"What do you think she means about the orange?" Kaylee asked.

"Often it only becomes clear after the event." Simon shrugged.

"Which is in itself useless. I wish she'd give us sense instead of riddles."

"I wish lots of things."

Unseen by the others, Simon took her hand.

Kaylee squeezed back. "Maybe Golden's Bane is where wishes come true."

2

Close to the edge of town they found the source of the mouthwatering smell. Two men and two women were tending several halved metal barrels filled with charcoal, turning slabs of meat laid over griddles and mesh. Coals sizzled and spat, and the jumping flames ignited dripping oil and fat.

"We've landed in dust and found our way to heaven," Jayne said. His mouth was watering, every sense set on fire. He already had his hand in his pocket, fingering the few coins he'd brought with him from the ship. He wasn't as poor as he let on—back in his cabin he had several stashes of rare metals and stones stored away in various hidey-holes—but he had enough with him for a good meal, several bottles of whatever their poison was here, and a night with a couple of whores.

Tomorrow could look after itself.

"My ears are open to the sounds of cookin' pork." Jayne nodded to the barbecuers and pointed at several chunks of meat. "That one and that one between two bread loaves, and a chunk of that cheese too," he said.

"Just arrived?" the woman asked. She was maybe sixty, short

and thin, wiry and strong. Her gray hair was cut close to her scalp, and several of her teeth were missing. She might have lived on any of the frontier planets or moons.

"Within the hour," Jayne said.

"You're from that ship we saw land up on the north barrens."

"That's us," Jayne said. "Traveled a while, walked downhill. Been hungry for a long time."

"Mighty sorry to hear that," the woman said, smiling. She piled his food on a slab of slate and handed it over. "Try some of my nuclear sauce," she said, tapping a bowl and spoon.

"Nuclear?"

She laughed. "It'll burn your balls off, space cowboy."

Jayne liked being called a space cowboy. It wasn't the first time, and it wouldn't be the last. He'd already clocked that most people here carried weapons, and he was sporting one of his favorite guns, a six-shooter modeled on an original design from Earth-That-Was. Maybe if they pulled in some business here he'd buy himself another hat.

He scooped a spoonful of sauce and dribbled it onto his meat. When he saw a couple of the other cooks watching, he took a second, slower spoonful.

Mal chatted with the cooks while the rest of the crew ate. Jayne dug into his second bowl. The captain was a fighter, no doubt about it, but soft as hell. Gabbing away with the old folk when he could be listening to Jayne. It weren't even like Mal was some bigwig general in the war, all full of fighting knowledge. He'd just been a sergeant. Ain't nothing about being a Browncoat that helped anyone. Just took food out of their mouths, what with the *xi niu* Alliance always seeming on their tail. Jayne had stepped in more than once to fix the captain's problems.

"Find us anything?" he asked through a mouthful of succulent barbecued meat.

Mal sat beside him with his own plate of food. "Maybe," he said through his food. They were all enjoying the meal, even that loopy River. She stared at the water flowing by as she chewed, and Jayne chuckled to himself as he considered throwing River in.

She still spooked the hell out of him, and it wasn't anything to do with the scar across his chest. Her confused mumblings often coalesced into warnings, only some of them came too late.

However long they spent in this place, he'd look out for anything that might be "the orange."

"So?" Jayne asked.

"Oh, you'll like it," Mal said. "You'll all like it."

"Don't tell me you've got us work before we even hit the town," Zoë said.

"We ain't transportin' cattle again," Jayne said. "My boots ain't smelled the same since."

River giggled. It was a sound that seemed to match the tinkling flow of the water.

"I ain't that quick," Mal said. "But those fine cooks did tell me the best place in town to find the sort of work we might be lookin' for."

"Smuggling," Wash said. "Dodging the authorities. Occurrences with fists and guns."

"Not necessarily. They don't know of Lassen Pride, but the place they described is the sorta place he'd frequent."

"Tell me it's the saloon," Jayne said.

"It is indeed the saloon. Which is also the local brothel."

Jayne sighed in satisfaction and looked up to the sky. It was sunny, clear of clouds, and it was good to be breathing clean air again. "Then let's not keep the whiskey and the ladies waiting," he said.

* * *

"Well, that took longer than usual," Zoë said.

"You think he does it on purpose?" Wash asked.

"I don't think so," Mal said. "I think it's just his face."

"To be fair, I do on occasion want to punch it." Zoë drained her glass, slammed it on the table, and picked up the bottle to pour them another shot.

Jayne was across the other side of the saloon, arguing with a woman whose partner he'd just laid out with one slug to the jaw. Others in the large saloon watched the exchange, and Mal noticed several hands creeping closer to weapons.

Zoë had noticed as well. Her casual drunkenness was a sham, and she was as ready for trouble as him. But Mal was pissed that Jayne had brought attention on them. They'd turned heads when they'd entered anyway, but conversation had soon risen to its previous levels, and the atmosphere in the saloon was calm, even friendly. This was a place used to entertaining strangers, and probably thankful for their money. That should have made things easier for them.

But not if Jayne started fighting.

"Damn it," Mal said. He stood and downed his drink, then walked slowly across the room, careful not to nudge into any tables or those seated around them.

"He with you?" one man asked.

"Yeah, he's with me."

"Ornery fella, ain't he?"

"He is," Mal said. "Rumor has it his mother loved him."

"I ain't his mother."

Mal looked the man up and down. He was overweight, bald, with two teeth in his head and a milky, blind eye crossed with a knife scar.

"That, you most certainly are not."

The man nodded at Jayne. "You better calm him down or there'll be trouble."

Mal touched his brow and moved closer to the fray.

The man Jayne had floored was back on his feet, holding his jaw and groaning. Jayne took a step back when the woman jabbed him in the chest, then he caught Mal's eye.

"Ain't my fault," he said, but Mal ignored him.

"Please excuse my friend," he said. "We had a bumpy landin' and he took a blow to the head. He's somewhat agitated."

"He ain't goin' with any of my girls after that," the woman said.

"Fair enough," Mal said, and when Jayne went to protest he held up a hand. "Drink, Jayne. Eat. Make merry. Just stay away from the ladies."

Grumbling to himself, Jayne stalked off to the bar.

"Meantime, while your friend's keeping occupied, there's a card game starting over in the corner," the woman said. "You play switch and draw?"

"I have done."

"Then let's go. We need one more player, and I hear you and your crew are looking for a job."

"You heard that." Mal frowned. They hadn't yet approached anyone, partly because he wanted to suss the lay of the land and see if Lassen Pride was still here, but mostly because they all wanted to relax a little before turning to work.

The woman grinned, and the creases around her eyes and lips were filled with laughter. Mal liked her instantly. That didn't happen very often.

"Mal Reynolds," he said, holding out his hand.

"Gentle," she said.

"Your name or your manner?"

"Depends on how much I like you. Shall we?" She nodded toward the far corner of the saloon and Mal followed her to the table. She glanced back at the man still nursing his bruised jaw.

"Derrik, bring us a bottle of the good stuff."

"One thing, Gentle, if I may?" Mal asked before they reached the table.

"You may."

"Do you know a gentleman by the name of Lassen Pride?"

She paused, and he saw the coolness in her eyes, and something else. Fear? Surprise?

"Did once know him," Gentle said. "And I'd never've called him a gentleman. Don't matter now, though, 'cause he's in the ground."

"Pride's dead?"

"And the world's a better place. You knew him?"

"Long time ago," Mal said, and he shrugged. "Ain't surprised he got hisself killed."

"Did I say he was killed?" Gentle asked, arching an eyebrow.

Mal smiled.

"Guess I didn't have to. Come on, Mal Reynolds. Let's play cards."

Mal sighed, wondering whether Lassen's death might mean that their chance of getting work on this rock was less than ever. But he didn't wish to portray any outward lack of confidence. He nodded to Zoë and Wash, and they each raised a glass in return. With Jayne at the bar with a bottle and another bowl of food, Mal hoped it might just settle into the calm, easy evening they all desired.

There were already two men and two women seated at the table, drinking and conversing. Mal thought at least three of them knew each other. The fourth, an old man with a kindly face and an open smile, listened instead of talking. He didn't know the others. He'd be the last one Mal would scope out as a cheat.

"This is Mal," Gentle said, "he's offered to complete our sextet."

"Excellent!" one of the women said. "So now we can start this gorramn game at last!"

Mal nodded to the others and sat opposite the old man. The woman who'd spoken was a fellow traveler—he could tell from her attire, her attitude, and the paleness of her skin that she spent much time aboard a ship. The other man and woman appeared local. The old man he wasn't sure about.

"Pleased to meet you all," Mal said. "And thanks for lettin' me join your game."

"Thanks for agreeing to let me win all your money, and more," the traveler said, and she laughed. She was shuffling both decks, one in each hand, expertly cutting and splicing the packs without even watching what she was doing. She wore a leather vest with no sleeves to hide wildcards. Her hair was long and tied back from her face, so she was obviously confident that she'd reveal no tells. If any of his opponents were going to cheat, it was her.

"The game's switch and draw, freeform rules," Gentle said. "You can team up but then your winnings are split. Everyone happy with that?"

"I never play in a team," the card-shuffling woman said. "But maybe I'll make an exception for you, Mal."

"You got me at a disadvantage," he said, uncomfortable at her familiarity.

"And that's how I like it." She slammed both packs down on the table. "So who wants to cut?"

The old man cut both packs and the game began.

It had been a while since Mal had played switch and draw. Over the first four divisions he lost twenty pieces of platinum, and the pile in front of the woman was already beginning to grow. She played with a willful abandon, taking risks where Mal wouldn't even consider doing so and winning more often than not. He wondered whether she had her own ship, and if so what she used it for. She interested him, but she might also be competition for any potential work.

"Feeling good," the woman said, revealing her second hand and sweeping her winnings toward her.

"Oh now, Holly, you'll wipe us all out before dinner," Gentle said.

"Now you've given away my advantage," Holly said.

"Holly," Mal said. "Holly." He touched his chin, frowning as he looked at her. "Nope, I've never heard of you."

This time her flash of anger was real and it remained.

"Mal was asking after Lassen Pride," Gentle said.

"Huh," Holly said. "That piece of *gǒu shǐ.*" She lost the next hand to the old man. His expression didn't change as he stacked his winnings.

More drinks were brought, and Mal slowly got into the game's rhythm. He used the next few divisions to feel his way around the players, throwing games to see how much they gambled and bluffed, and what turnarounds and sacrifices they were willing to make. The old man was the most consistent player, and Mal reckoned his age had given him an almost perfect game face. He couldn't spot any tells in the old man's expression or manner, other than the fact that he seemed to take a drink whenever he believed he had a winning hand. But that in itself could be manufactured as a bluff.

After seven hands they paused for a break. Gentle called over more drinks and some food, and as she stretched in her chair, Mal sidled a little closer.

"There's no work here for the likes of you, Mal," Gentle said.

"Huh?" For a moment he thought he'd misheard her. He glanced around the table at the others. None of them seemed to be paying any particular attention, which meant that some of them most certainly were. Holly was counting her winnings, making a point of not looking at them.

"Sorry to disappoint."

"Lassen had a pretty cozy smugglin' racket going on from here, so I understand," Mal said.

"And a year ago you'd have found work with him. But now, Golden's Bane is hanging on by its fingernails. Since Pride died, the smaller local gangs have been at each other's throats, and any smugglin' done is small-scale. People're more mistrustful than ever of givin' work to strangers." She glanced across the saloon at Jayne. "Especially ones that bring trouble."

"An' what about you?"

She glared at him. "You think I'm wealthy? You think me or any of the girls would be here doing this if we had money?"

"Doubt it."

He glanced across the table at Holly. She caught his eye and looked away again, counting her winnings a second time.

"An' you'll only find trouble there," Gentle whispered.

"Story of my life."

"She's a merc, with no problems workin' for the Alliance."

That gave Mal pause. Any brush with the Alliance might have been a problem, especially with Simon and River in tow.

"You'll finish the game?" Gentle asked.

Mal looked at Zoë and Wash. They both raised eyebrows at him and he shrugged slightly. "Never start somethin' I don't intend finishing," he said.

"Good. Second round is always the most fun. It's when everyone plays on what they think they know about everyone else. I like a few surprises."

Gentle wasn't wrong. The next hour *was* full of surprises. Holly lost most of her previous winnings in one fiercely contested hand, the balance passing across the table to Gentle. The other man and woman were wiped out and left the table grumbling, and Mal saw a couple of severe-looking women keeping an eye on them in case they caused trouble.

He also saw his crew watching the game as they drank and ate, and they weren't just keeping an eye out for trouble. They were watching him, waiting for him to find what they needed.

Toward the end of the game, Mal was dealt two solid hands and he went to work. The tells he'd carefully nurtured fooled the old man and Holly, but Gentle read him like a book and all but cleaned him out.

Mal was in too deep now. He ignored Zoë's glare. To abandon the game before its natural end would show weakness of character, and that was something he had no desire to project.

Luck shone down with the final hand. He cleaned out Holly, who glowered but remained at the table to see the game's end. He won ninety pieces of platinum from Gentle and negated her hand with a brilliant turnaround. And then it was just him and the old man.

"Come on, Deacon," Holly said, using his name for the first time. "He's just a space pirate, prolly bad as Lassen Pride, and I put that turd in the ground."

Mal held in his shock. Just.

"And I'm just a traveler preachin' kindness," Deacon said. "I'd have become a pirate years ago if I could afford a ship." He frowned at his hand, then sighed. "I've got no more platinum or valuables, Mal, but I don't want to give up this game. Will you take other payment?"

"What've you got?" Mal asked.

The old man, Deacon, brought a backpack up from beneath the table and rooted around inside. He pulled out what Mal first thought was a book, but when he placed it on the table he saw a folded piece of thick paper contained in a clear packet.

"Picked this up a while back," he said. "Never been able to understand it. Maybe you can."

"What is it?"

"Some sort of star map."

"To where?"

Deacon shrugged. "If I could work that out, maybe I'd be in no mind to gamble it for a few pieces. But it's all I have left of any worth."

Mal reached for the map, and just as he touched it he heard a sharp intake of breath from his left. Holly. He glanced at her but she was looking at her fingernails, biting and picking at them. He dragged the map across the table close to him, and watched her glance at it again from the corner of his eye.

"Sure," he said. "But I get to call."

Deacon nodded. Mal called. Deacon laid out his cards and they were two solid hands. But Mal's were better.

"Damn it. Guess I'll never be a pirate," Deacon said, and he raised his glass at Mal with a smile.

"Thank you all for the game," Mal said. He stood and pocketed the handful of platinum and other stuff he'd won, leaving the map sitting on the table. He saw Holly half-rise and tense. Then she caught his eye, and saw his other hand resting casually on his pistol's handle. "And thanks for this," he said, picking up the map. "It'll keep me occupied when I'm sittin' in my ship without any work."

Gentle smiled at him and shrugged. "Sorry, sweetheart."

"Not your fault," Mal said. "Thanks for the hospitality. And the food was shiny."

He turned away from the table and tucked the folded map into his jacket's inside pocket. For a second it felt strange—warm, tingly, almost like it held a static charge—and he paused close to Wash and Zoë.

"So?" Zoë asked.

"Wash, tell Jayne to finish his drink. We're leavin'."

"What's up?" Zoë asked.

"Plenty," Mal said. Holly was dangerous, likely freelancing

for the Alliance, and she'd taken an interest in him and what he'd won. That meant he had an interest in it too.

"So we got some work?"

"Nope. No work."

"So what *did* you get?" Zoë asked. They both stood, and Mal caught Zoë glancing over his shoulder. "Oh," she said.

"She lookin'?" Mal asked. "The younger one, not the Madam."

"She's doing everything *but* looking this way."

"Right. The old guy?"

"She's talking to him. A deep talk, if you ask me. So, you going to tell us, Mal?"

"I won somethin' from the old man that she wants."

"She expected to win it from him?"

"I don't think she even knew he had it. But when she saw it…" He opened his eyes and mouth wide in feigned shock.

"What is it?" Wash asked.

"A map."

"To what?"

"I have no idea. That's why we're leavin', and sharpish. I have a feeling Holly isn't on her own, and she claims to have put Lassen Pride in the ground. An' Gentle said she's likely an Alliance merc. So get Jayne, Zoë and I'll round up Kaylee, Simon, and River. Then we take our leave of this place. We don't want it renamed *Serenity*'s Bane."

Zoë touched his arm. "Mal, this isn't like you."

"Just bein' cautious," he said. "No use putting ourselves in danger. There's no work here, but if I've somethin' of worth in the map, we need to keep it. An' if she is an Alliance merc, mayhap she has pictures of River and Simon."

"Now she most pointedly *is* looking our way."

"Wash? Out the back door with Jayne. We'll meet you by

the food vendors. Quick as you can."

"She's calling someone, wrist communicator," Zoë said. "*Wŏ men wán le*."

"Time to leave."

"River, what's the orange?" Kaylee asked. "Because if it's perilous for us we need to know."

"Shhhhh," River said, and she moved her hand back and forth before her face.

"What's that?" Mal asked.

"I don't know," Simon said.

"Kaylee, ask again," the captain said. "If we're walkin' into something, it's best we know about it."

From the minute Mal and Zoë came looking for them in the small outdoor market, Kaylee had known something was wrong. None of them could say what, exactly, but Mal was on edge and alert. Zoë said it was to do with someone in the saloon.

They were walking along a rough path next to the river, passing an array of buildings—homes, shops, storage barns. Half of them were fallen to ruin or boarded up, and those still occupied were mostly in a poor state of repair. They'd arrived in the town on the other side of the river, and Kaylee, Simon, and River had crossed to find the market. She'd experienced sensory overload in the chaos, a familiar feeling when exiting *Serenity* after a long flight, but one that she never quite got used to. An array of smells, sights, and sounds flowed around and through her, and she'd reveled in the scent of spice and flowers, the colors of knitted hats and woven mats, and the diverse group of hardy people who'd made this rough place their home. Kaylee now carried a shoulder bag with some fresh fruit, root crops, and a good selection of dehydrated food, and Simon had managed to find a few common medicines to restock the ship's supplies. It wasn't much, but if rationed with the supplies still on the ship, it'd keep them going for another few weeks.

"There's a bridge ahead," Zoë said.

"River, the orange?" Kaylee asked, prompting her for an answer.

River did that strange thing in front of her face again. "Shhhh."

"No matter," Mal said. "Over the bridge, meet Jayne and Wash, then we're back to the ship and away."

"Then we follow the map to a big bucket of treasure," Zoë said, one eyebrow raised.

"Map?" Kaylee asked, and Mal only shook his head.

"Precious sun…" River whispered. Only Kaylee heard. She didn't have time to ask what she meant.

Several figures emerged from behind a tumbled-down shop. They wore dusty, torn longcoats, pale green hats, and they carried heavy wooden clubs or knives. It was obvious that they'd been waiting.

"Over the bridge," Mal said. "Nice, slow, easy. 'Til we have to run."

"They've brought knives to a gunfight, Mal," Zoë said, touching the weapon on her belt.

"Let's not start blasting away just yet," he said. "Simon, River, you first."

It was a small footbridge spanning the waterway, wide enough for two or three people at a time and supported on heavy stone columns. The water broke and splashed around these columns, and as she stepped onto the wooden bridge after Simon, Kaylee caught something from the corner of her eye. She paused and looked closer, down into the water. There was something there. It wasn't just the river's flow but a shape moving against the current. Something *alive*.

The water was orange with the dust it carried from surrounding areas.

"Mal—" Kaylee said, and then there came a shout from the bridge's opposite end.

"Six more of us on this side," the woman said. "No need for any nastiness, Mal. Let's just settle this and we can both move on."

"Settle what, Holly?" he said. "Thought all the settlin' was done at the card table."

"You know what I mean," she said. She walked onto the bridge, and behind her several other men and women stood nursing clubs and knives.

River and Simon, Kaylee thought. But Holly hadn't even spared them a glance. If she was an Alliance-employed mercenary, they didn't appear to be her concern.

"So what is it?" Mal asked.

"Precious sun…" River whispered, and she turned and came to Kaylee, hanging on to her and shivering.

"Hey, hey, nothin' to be worried about," Kaylee said, but she didn't really think that. She thought there was plenty to be worried about. Mal and the others could hold their own in a fight, but what worried her most was how River might handle it. She was already acting strange, more agitated than before. She had no wish to see the girl turn once again into that killing machine that was buried deep inside, behind her general weirdness and sense of vulnerability.

"It's nothing to you, that's what," Holly said. "Deacon had no right putting it into the game. In fact, he stole it from me."

"See, that's where I stop believin' you," Mal said. "And where I start thinkin' you're an Alliance merc."

"Don't rightly care," Holly said. "Not about them fugitives, neither." She nodded at River and Simon. Her voice was lower, quieter.

"Behind us, Mal," Zoë said, and Kaylee glanced back to see the figures closing in on them, weapons swinging down by their sides.

River stopped shivering, and her fast breathing eased into a more normal rhythm.

Kaylee eased the girl away, no longer wishing to be close to her. But what she'd expected to see—that distant humor, an almost soulless depth to her eyes as she prepared to kill—was absent. Instead she was lost, staring into an unknown distance with her mouth slightly open and arms limp at her sides.

"This doesn't need to escalate," Mal said. "You can see we're carrying guns."

"You think we're not?" Holly eased her coat aside to show the six-shooters resting on either hip. "I never draw without shooting."

"A good rule to live by." Mal glanced back at his crew, and Kaylee recognized that look. *Be ready.*

"I won it fair and square," Mal said. "But let's say you wanted to buy it from me. What do you think a fair and reasonable price—"

"I'm not buying, I'm taking," Holly said.

"Back to your employers?" Mal asked.

Holly shrugged. "I might negotiate with them first."

Where are Jayne and Wash? Kaylee thought. "Simon," she whispered, and Simon came and held on to his sister. Kaylee hated fighting, and was the first to admit she wasn't very good at it, but she was as prepared for trouble as any of them. She had to be, being part of *Serenity*'s crew.

She was starting to wish she'd stayed on her ship.

Holly sighed, a mite theatrically, Kaylee thought. "Gonna count to five," she said. "Five…"

"That's counting *down* from five," Mal said. "You aiming to count *to* five, you generally start at one."

Holly froze for a second, and Kaylee actually saw any remaining good humor drain from her, like a fire extinguished in a surge of water. Then she gave a small nod and the trouble began.

Zoë dashed behind Kaylee and faced the heavies coming from that direction, while Mal crouched, one hand on his gun, the other ready to ward off an attack from the front. The footbridge constrained them, but it also meant that the attackers could only come at them two abreast. Which, Kaylee realized, didn't really help them that much at all.

"Keep her safe," Kaylee said to Simon, and even as she turned around she realized how redundant that comment was.

Zoë ducked a club, kicked out, and popped one guy's knee. He went down screaming. His buddy jabbed with his knife and Zoë deflected his arm, pivoted, grabbed his wrist, braced it against her own, snapped it. He screamed too, and his knife bounced from the bridge and fell into the river.

More splashing sounds. *Those things*, Kaylee thought. *They'll know about them.* "Mind the water!" she said, but she wasn't sure the rest of the crew heard. She ducked down behind Zoë and picked up the dropped club, then stood and lifted it back past her shoulder.

Zoë sidestepped as a woman came at her, and Kaylee slammed the club across her arm. She winced as she heard the crack of bones breaking.

Zoë kicked out, tripped the woman, and as she crouched Kaylee saw what was going to happen. "Zoë!" she said, but Zoë was already shouldering the woman toward the handrail. Unable to hold on with her broken arm, the woman flipped over and dropped into the water below.

Kaylee heard the splash and one short, terrified shout, and then she saw a sudden wash of red merged with the dull orange waters flowing downstream.

She glanced behind her. Simon and River hugged in the center of the narrow bridge, River still staring into space. Beyond, Mal was taking on two men, ducking, kicking, punching, sucking in his gut to avoid a slashing knife, headbutting a man and sending him to his knees.

Beyond Mal, past Holly and two of her goons at the end of the bridge, Wash and Jayne were sprinting toward them, unnoticed by anyone else. *We just have to hold out another few seconds*, Kaylee thought, and then Zoë banged into her and sent her sprawling. She rolled and came up onto her knees, one hand swinging the club around. A man was standing astride Zoë, knife raised in his right hand. His coat flapped open and showed an array of knives on his belt, and his face was crisscrossed with pale, ugly scars.

Kaylee stretched forward, and as her club connected with his hip, Zoë drove her boot up into his crotch. The impact was so hard it lifted him from his feet, and he groaned and folded double, falling forward. Zoë rolled to the side and his head struck the bridge.

Kaylee shoved him away, and he curled into a ball, rocking back and forth and holding his bruised balls.

Mal shouted out behind them, and Kaylee rose and turned, terrified at what she would see. Mal crouched and held on to his arm, but Kaylee knew he was not really wounded. His shout was a distraction.

At the bridge's far end Wash pointed at Holly, Jayne stormed forward and grabbed her in a bear hug from behind, and Kaylee saw what was about to happen.

"Jayne, no!" she shouted, but he either didn't hear or chose not to take heed. She knew he was no fool, especially when it came to combat, and Wash had pointed out the leader of this gang. To bring the fight to a halt, Jayne was trying to take the head off the snake.

He marched her toward the colored river, Holly kicking at his shins and slamming her head back into his face. Jayne's head rocked back and his nose exploded red, but his rage was stronger. Ignoring the pain and the blood he dropped her and heaved her forward.

Kaylee saw the terror in the woman's eyes—*She knows, she's been here long enough to understand*—but she was already overbalanced. She teetered on the water's edge and then fell in.

The flowing surface broke in a dozen places around the splash caused by her body, and they all saw the gnashing teeth and spiked spines of the eel-like creatures that bore down on her. Holly surfaced once, the flow carrying her under the bridge and downstream. She stroked for shore, and Kaylee actually thought she might make it.

Then she was tugged beneath the surface, the water foamed, and another slick of death spread and was carried away on the orange.

"Told you," River muttered.

The violence paused on either end of the bridge. Holly's heavies glanced at each other, then one of them held his hands up, palms out.

"She weren't payin' us enough, anyways," he said, and he backed away from Zoë. The others followed suit, and a minute later the *Serenity* crew were left standing on the bridge and shore, the only sound the flow of the deadly river.

Jayne was looking particularly smug. "Can I go back and finish my business now?" he asked.

"Do you always just have to kill them?" Mal asked.

"Huh?"

"So what, Wash points the way and you home in like a huntin' dog? Didn't you even think I might want to talk to her?"

"Er… you're welcome?" Jayne gestured at the gang retreating back into the town.

Mal shook his head, went to berate Jayne some more, realized it was lost on him. "We all good?"

"Oh, we're all just shiny," Kaylee said. Zoë clapped her on the shoulder. Simon smiled at her. River was looking around as if nothing had happened.

"Guess we know what the orange is now," Mal said.

"And we know to get the hell away from it," Zoë said.

"Back to the ship, and smart," Mal said. "This map's far from worthless, but I wanna get away from here sharpish."

"Oh, yes," Kaylee said. "Time to flee this rock."

"I'm still waitin' for a thank you," Jayne said.

Wash and Zoë hugged, and they all started uphill toward where they'd parked the ship. Kaylee had already had enough of the fresh air and wide-open spaces.

"Goodbye, orange," River said. "Hello, precious sun."

3

Jayne didn't like the fact that he'd saved them all from a whoopin', and yet all he got was grief for killing that gorramn woman. Weren't even like it was intentional—he wasn't to know the stream was filled with nasties. Ãiya!

"Not a good way to go," he said.

"Not good at all," Mal said. "Ouch!"

They were in the medical bay and the Doc was sewing up a slash on Mal's forearm.

"So, this map?" Jayne asked.

"Who knows?" Mal shrugged and winced again. "Guy I won it off obviously didn't know its worth, otherwise he'd not have thrown it into such a small pot. No idea where he came upon it, but he was a traveler who'd been some places. A real mix of clothing, collection of tattoos on his hands. Soon as he bet the map, that woman Holly changed."

"Changed how?" Jayne asked. "Her eyes lit up? Like, greedy?"

"At first she just went blank. Putting on a bluffer's face, but that in itself gives away plenty."

"S'pose she knew what it was."

"An' perhaps she didn't think she had what it was worth to buy it from me."

"Huh." Jayne frowned. "But she had at least eight people in her crew, and they were just the ones we saw."

"That's what I was thinking. Someone like that would have money."

"You've got six people in your crew, and you're broke." Jayne grinned.

Mal snorted. "We done here?" he asked.

"I believe so," Simon said. "Keep it clean and it should heal just fine."

"Your sister seems to know somethin' about this map," Jayne said to Simon. "I just came from the mess and she's sittin' at the table starin' at it."

"What is she doing exactly?" Simon asked.

"Like I told you, just starin'," Jayne said. "Kaylee reckoned she was pretty feisty back in Golden's Bane. That's nothing new, but the map's calmed her somewhat. She's just… looking."

"We should get up there," Simon said. He glanced at Mal, who nodded and waved him away. When Simon left the medical bay, Jayne and Mal followed.

Up in the mess, when Mal saw her sitting at the table he realized it was more than intrigue. The girl was gorramn hypnotized.

And the map was no longer silent and still.

"Everyone to the mess!" Mal shouted. On the bridge Wash heard him, and he put the call out through the tannoy. Mal heard boots on metal as the rest of the crew converged, but he couldn't take his eyes off the girl, and the map.

She was touching it with the fingertips of one hand, and sparks danced across her knuckles from the weird swirls and lines. It wasn't a map in its truest form, but rather a merging of drawing, symbols, and strange sets of numbers and letters that could have been code, or perhaps coordinates.

"What the hell?" Wash asked as he came down from the bridge.

"Simon," Mal said, and the Doc sat in a chair beside his sister. He held her in an embrace, careful not to touch the sheet or knock her hand away from it.

"River, what's happening?" Simon asked softly.

Kaylee appeared behind them, having had the furthest to come from the engine room, and Mal heard her draw in a sharp breath.

"You know what that is?" Jayne asked her.

"Me? How would I know?"

"You're the mechanic."

"I know engines and ships, Jayne. Not… whatever that is."

"Anyone?" Mal asked.

No one replied. Zoë stepped closer, and the others gathered around the table.

"Doesn't seem to be doing anything dangerous," Zoë said.

"I left it folded and in the clear wallet," Mal said. "D'you open it up, River?" Her eyes didn't even flicker.

"River, we need to know what this is," Simon said.

River smiled, took her hand away and sat back, then looked directly at her brother.

"You know what it is, silly. It's a map."

"A map to where?" Mal asked. "And to what?"

"Here and there, through the 'verse," she said. She tapped her fingers on the table, but the map had ceased sparking. She leaned in against Simon and closed her eyes.

"Oh, don't go to sleep now," Zoë said.

"Leave her for a spell," Mal said. "It's that I'm interested in."

"It's sorta beautiful," Kaylee said. "Those sparks, anyway."

"None of you are worried about that thing?" Jayne said. They all looked to him. "It could be dangerous. Maybe she's started a process in whatever it is. The stuff drawn on it might be a distraction, somethin' to keep us intrigued, while it ticks away and explodes, or releases a gas. Or sends a signal to someone trackin' us!" Jayne backed away from the table and looked around as if the Alliance were about to bushwhack them there and then.

"How paranoid are you?" Wash asked.

"I ain't paranoid," Jayne said, "I just know the whole 'verse is out to get me."

"I don't think there's any harm to it," Zoë said. She looked closer, drawing her knife and sliding it across the table, lifting the corner of the map. No sparks emerged, and it moved like a normal sheet of paper. Thicker than some, perhaps. "Looks like it's waxed paper of some sort, pretty heavy. Thick enough to hide some tech inside."

"Inside a sheet of paper?" Mal asked.

"Maybe Alliance nanotech," Zoë said.

"I've seen something similar," Simon said. "When I was training, there were labs developing synthetic skin that contained some sort of tech."

"Why would you want skin with electronics inside?" Jayne asked.

"For the military," Zoë said.

"You're saying that's a flap of skin?" Kaylee asked.

"Synthetic," Zoë said. "Honey, can you get the star charts up on a tablet and bring them here?"

Wash nodded and went back up to the bridge.

"You see something?" Mal asked.

"Not yet," Zoë said. "But unless we start looking, this map'll lead us nowhere."

Wash returned with a tablet, and Zoë aimed it at the map and took a picture of the part that looked like some sort of star chart. They all huddled around behind her and looked at the image. Nothing seemed to match to any of the 'verse maps stored on the tablet.

"Not surprised," Jayne said.

"I'll take the nearest likeness then search manually," Zoë said. She sighed. "This may take some time."

"I got nowhere to be," Wash said.

"Then sit your cute behind next to me and help me scan," Zoë said. "When we finally find—"

"Precious sun," River said, eyes still closed. She was frowning now, twitching, no longer asleep. "Hidden in a dead and scattered planet. Dancing through the ruins. Loaded with…" Her eyes snapped open. "Loaded with old, old people."

Zoë reached for the map with her knife again, sliding across the table closer to River without touching it herself.

"Help us," Mal said. "River? It'd be good to know what you see in the map."

River looked at Kaylee and smiled, her face lighting up. "I see the precious sun."

"Plenty of precious suns in the 'verse," Mal said.

"Only the precious *Sun Tzu* hides in a scattered planet. And oh, I need to go there. Need to go." She closed her eyes again, but reached out and touched the edge of the map. It sparkled, light motes flowing across its surface and up her finger until they dispersed across the back of her hand. "He's singing to me."

"I know those words," Kaylee said. "Sun Tzu."

"So what is it?" Mal asked.

"Hang on. Hang on." Kaylee closed her eyes and frowned, thinking hard. Then her eyes snapped open again. "Oh my! *Sun Tzu*. Inara told me about it one day when she was fixin' my hair. It was a ship, or so the legend went."

"What legend?" Mal asked.

"Inara said the *Sun Tzu* was supposed to be one of the Generation ships that brought the survivors from Earth-That-Was," Kaylee said.

"And Inara knew that how?" Zoë asked.

"She couldn't recall where she'd heard the name," Kaylee said. "You know Inara, meets lots of people."

"Five centuries ago," Wash said. He looked at the map along with everyone else.

"They were pretty amazing ships," Kaylee said. "Think of all the tech. Old-Earth stuff, just sittin' out there in a ship lost for hundreds of years. The raw materials themselves in a boat that size would be worth a fortune! And it's said they used gold coating on some of the components of their old computers."

"Think of the loot," Jayne said. "Some of those Earth-That-Was antiques bring a hefty sum on the dark market."

Mal shivered. That sadistic bastard Niska had been a collector of such stuff. But Kaylee and Jayne were right. A ship like that, and its contents, would be worth a good sum. It was also a treasure trove of history.

"Always had a fascination with those ships," Mal said. "My folks first told me about 'em, and for them it was nothin' more than an adventure story. Fact is, it's a tale of horror."

"How so?" Zoë asked.

"It was humanity on the run," Mal said. "Desperate an' almost hopeless. Runnin' from Earth-That-Was, and the air they'd poisoned, and the ground they'd turned too toxic to grow food. These people were lookin' for a new frontier, and leaving behind everything they knew. They came searching for hope, never knowin' what they'd find." Mal trailed off, and for a few seconds the crew were silent, each of them considering his words.

"Wow," Kaylee said.

"Just think of all the bottled booze from that long ago," Jayne said.

"Trust you, Jayne," Zoë said.

"That'll be some good whiskey," Wash said.

"Don't wanna drink it. Wanna sell it to fools like you."

"So what do you think, sir?" Zoë asked Mal. "Worth taking a chance?"

"I think we got nothing to lose," Mal said. "From our run-in with the unfortunate Holly, seems the Alliance is lookin' to recover this map. That gives us more'n a good reason to follow it, to see what they might be hidin'. Heard rumors of Alliance ships flyin' that far out, but never saw no reason to wonder why. Now I do—perhaps they know the *Sun Tzu*'s out there, and they're guardin' it. Just imagine a whole ship from way back when. We have to see if it's real."

"I haven't seen River this focused in a while," Simon said. "I trust what she's saying, but I'm not sure we should go."

"Why not?" Mal asked.

"She's anxious, troubled about this, but…"

"You trust your sister?" Mal asked, but River answered for him.

"You all trust me," River said.

"I say we go," Mal said, and he looked around at his crew.

"We've got nothing else goin' on," Zoë said.

"Yeah," Wash said, "and we stocked up some on Golden's Bane, and we got food and water to last us there and back, long as you ain't mindin' that food substitute for a while."

"Kaylee, how's the fuel situation?" Mal asked.

"We're tickin' over fine," she said. "Ain't the levels I'm worried about, it's the wear 'n' tear."

"We'll get new parts. If this is real, and the ship's still in one piece, mebbe it'll be the find of the century."

"Now all we've got to do is figure out how to read that thing," Wash said.

"Oh, that's easy," River said, and she picked up the map in both hands. Fine tendrils of light zigged and zagged across its surface, and her eyes went wide. "I can read it simple. I see a sun, and planets and moons, and a moon that isn't a moon anymore. Just follow me. I know the way."

4

"She's hardly slept for seven days and she looks as fresh and lively as ever."

Kaylee couldn't argue with Simon. She had been keeping an eye on River since they left Golden's Bane, and she seemed more animated than she had in a long while. Right now she was in the cargo bay watching Mal, Zoë, and Jayne cleaning and repacking some of their equipment, weapons, and empty storage containers. Part of it was killing time, but they were also preparing for what they might find once they reached the coordinates and location indicated on the mysterious map, details of which River had communicated to Wash so that he could program their flight computer. Kaylee could hear River mumbling and giggling to herself, and she wondered whether her presence was troubling the others too.

"She's excited about where we're going," Kaylee said.

"If they're the correct coordinates," Simon said.

"Why would she lie?"

"She has a damaged mind."

Simon had spoken about his sister like this before, and Kaylee didn't like hearing it, even though all evidence pointed to it being true. River was not the same as when she'd been born. At the Academy, the Alliance had changed her, digging into her mind with multiple surgeries and other arcane procedures, and might have made her into something else entirely.

"It's nice to see her looking so well," Kaylee said, and she didn't have to glance at Simon to see the doubt on his face.

"We're all relying on her," he said. "Right now it's River who's steering this ship. Even you, trying to find out more about that map... so have you found anything?"

Kaylee paused before looking up from the map. It was flat on the mess table before her, an array of tools and instruments set around it. Over the past few days Mal had let her try to penetrate its mechanics and workings, on the proviso she didn't do anything to damage it. She'd worked on it a couple of hours per day, in between maintaining the ship. She didn't want her ship to think she had greater interest in the map, though she'd never voice that aloud. *Serenity* was her girl, and she was as bright and alive as most of the people Kaylee knew.

"I've found out hardly anything," Kaylee said. "It's a real work of art. I think it's printed on some sort of conductive material, possibly the synthetic skin Zoë was rememberin'. There's nanotech of some kind in there, but it's very high-end stuff, and I just can't find any way to communicate with it. There's a series of impressions, or printings, and they change in phase with each other, but again I can't make out enough from them to come to any conclusions. Comparin' the coordinates River gave us with the star charts we have on board, I can just about figure some of the locale where she's takin' us. It's way out past the Rim, mostly uncharted an' further from the core than *Serenity*'s ever been."

"Mal seems to think it's worth it," Simon said.

"Oh, so do I! We only just have the fuel reserves to get there and back, but don't think I'm scared of travelin' that far out, Simon. It's exciting! All the things we might see or find if it really is a Generation ship."

"I don't know an awful lot about those ships." He seemed almost embarrassed at the admission, and Kaylee wondered why he'd left it so long to say anything. Perhaps because he'd been waiting for a time when it was just the two of them alone. She hoped so.

"Really? You were never taught about them in your schooling, or by your parents?"

"Not in an Alliance school," he said. "I know some of the legends, but Earth-That-Was is hardly ever mentioned once you're living in the light of the White Sun. The Alliance regard themselves as the center of the whole human galaxy, and the story of how our ancestors all came from elsewhere is not something they're fond of entertaining."

"Wow. That's so… *ignorant*! Were you never curious enough to find out on your own?"

"Not for a long time," he said. "Not until now."

Kaylee sat back in her chair, stretching her back from where she'd been leaning over the map. It was nice to have Simon to talk to on his own, and good to divert her attention from the map for a while. Much as she was limiting her time examining it, she had found over the past couple of days that it was taking up too much headspace, even when she was back in the engine room. She was usually very good at compartmentalizing her activities. She worried that the map, and its strange tech, had formed something of a hold over her.

"I've always loved stories of spaceships and travel, since I was a little girl," Kaylee said. "Some of what I know is from schoolin', but most is from me jus'… askin' around, I guess. Speakin' with likeminded folk. So, the Generation ships… they were really amazing creations, but they weren't the first. When our ancestors knew they had to leave Earth-That-Was, they sent a load of terraformin' ships on ahead to settle the planets and moons around the White Sun. That took years, some say decades, and while that was happening the Generation ships were being built. This was many centuries ago, remember, when knowledge and available tech really shouldn't've made them possible. There's an idea that war advances technological know-how more than anything else, but way back then it was the loomin' extinction of humanity that forced big advancements in engineerin' and tech. After what they'd done to Earth-That-Was, poisonin' its seas and skies an' all, our ancestors had a choice—flee their world and survive, or stay behind and die."

"Story I heard is that people had used up Earth-That-Was and left it an empty shell."

"That's pretty much it. Changes to the climate, resources all used up, air so stinky you'd die if you breathed it too long. So many'd already died, and time was runnin' out. So they left. There were over two hundred Generation ships, so they say, all built in orbit by different nations or groups of nations, but all sharin' the know-how to construct them. That's what made it possible. More'n the scientific or engineering knowledge, it was the willingness to work together that allowed it to happen. Some of these ships were bigger'n I can imagine, that's for sure. There's tales of one called the *New Tianjin* which was three miles long, a mile wide, and carried fifty million people."

"That's... mind-boggling. Way beyond anything we can build now. Even the largest Alliance cruiser is a fraction of that size."

"Why'd you think I always found the stories so interestin'? Anyway, the ships were all shapes and all pretty big, and the people on board were asleep for their long journey. They carried massive great holds full of equipment, too, old-style planetary and terraformin' tech ready for when they arrived, just in case the ships they'd already sent on had broken down, I guess. Most ships had a human crew who lived and sometimes died en route, looking after the ships and those sleepin' in them. A few were fully automated. They were all comin' here, to the 'verse."

"It sounds amazing," Simon said.

"Don't it? I'd love to get a chance to see it all. The drives they used to travel so far, the technologies to build such big ships, the life-support systems they must've built. And then there's the suspended animation stuff. It's used in the 'verse, sometimes, but it ain't reliable, and ain't used that much. They put a whole world to sleep, ready to wake 'em up again when they found a new world." Kaylee's smile faded a little, and her voice dropped. "But that's where some of what's told, and some of what's understood to be true, tend to drift apart somewhat."

"How so?"

"Well, the shiny tales you might be told say that all the ships made it here, the 'verse was established, and humanity lived happy ever after."

"Or not so happy, for some."

Kaylee shrugged. "Wars and conflict and nastiness, true, but humanity survived. But the truth is a little darker, I reckon. These tales are mixed, and maybe mixed up in the tellin'. Some say only about seventy percent of the ships made it to the 'verse. Others reckon only thirteen ships in total survived the journey."

Simon looked shocked. "No wonder such history isn't taught. So what happened to the ships that didn't reach here?"

"Some vanished completely, never to be seen again. Maybe they're still travelin' somewhere, their human cargo still sleepin' and dreamin'. I like to think one or two of them found somewhere else to end their trips, and maybe even now there are humans far, far out there, people we'll never see and who don't know anything about us."

"That's... disturbing."

"You think? I think it's kinda shiny. Guess what you think about it depends on which way your mind swings." Simon blinked and Kaylee looked away, worried that she'd offended him.

"You said some vanished," he said. "What about the others that didn't make it?"

"There're loads of stories about 'em. It's said that one crashed into one of Heinlein's moons when it arrived. Another was hit by an asteroid close to the end of its trip. And one… this is really grim, you sure you want me to go on?"

"Only if you want to."

"Hmm." Kaylee pulled a face. "One ship finished the journey years after the others, and there was no one left alive on board. There'd been a war. It looked like it'd gone on for years, and the ship was a mess, inside an' out. All battered and burnt up, and with the bodies of millions rotting in their pods or scattered around in warzones inside the ship. But the *Sun Tzu* is one that made it here," Kaylee added hastily, seeing Simon's face. "None of the other ships remain, most were broken down and used to build smaller ships back in the early days, space stations, and the metals and other materials were used to colonize the planets. It was always intended that way, to give the travelers a good shiny start. That way I guess they wouldn't have to think too much about mining and manufacturin' 'til they'd really established comfy homes and communities."

"But the *Sun Tzu* wasn't broken down," Simon said.

"Seems not. And now we're going to see if it's still out there. It's so exciting!"

"It sure is. I just wonder why there's a map to the ship, with Alliance tech in it. And why only River can read it."

"I've wondered that too," Kaylee said. "And the fact it's an Alliance map…"

"You're *sure* about that?"

"I'm sure no one else I know has tech like this."

Simon nodded slowly but said nothing more.

"We'll be fine," she said. "If it really is out there—"

"If it's there, the Alliance never meant anyone to find it."

"But you were so keen for us to come," Kaylee said.

"Because of how animated River was. Now, the closer we get, the more agitated she gets. But I don't think Mal's one for turning around, do you?"

"Definitely not," Kaylee said, and she thought, *I wouldn't be either. Not for this*.

She felt a chill down her spine when Simon turned and left. She looked at the map. It was a tease, knowledge laid out before her but still unreadable, unknowable, except to River.

"It'll all be good," she said.

"See the sleepers!" River said. "See them walking, hear them singing. Such beautiful songs."

One glance from Mal and Simon held his sister's arm and guided her gently from the bridge. She was wearing them all down with her heightened state and her apparent lack of sleep. They'd been following the map—at least, following River's open translation of the map, while linking it as best they could to their somewhat fragmented star charts for areas beyond the Outer Rim—for over twenty days, and her behavior was becoming more and more erratic. There was never anything threatening in what she did, but the bursts of excited chatter were tiresome. Sometimes they were gorramn troubling.

Now she was talking about sleepers. Considering the ship they were coming to find, such talk pricked at them all in different ways. *But the ship's old and empty*, Jayne had said. *There wouldn't be anyone still asleep on board. Right?* Mal didn't see how there could be, but the girl's comments seeded unsettling thoughts in his mind. He knew that not every Generation ship that left Earth-That-Was had made it to the 'verse, and even though the *Sun Tzu* was reputed to be one that had didn't mean it had disgorged its cargo once it arrived. It didn't mean everyone on board hadn't died.

Maybe she's talking about ghosts, Kaylee had said one mealtime. *A ship that old, who knows what's on board?*

No such thing as ghosts, Wash had said, but for a while everyone ate in silence, thinking their own thoughts.

"According to the charts, this planet doesn't have rings," Wash said. Apart from Simon and River they were all on the bridge, watching through the viewing ports as Wash guided the ship toward the planet they had come to find. Uninhabited and unsettled, it orbited billions of miles distant from the Blue Sun, way beyond the orbit of the gas giant Burnham, too far out from the Core to be considered worth naming. It was almost too small to be called a planet, but too large to be an asteroid. Could be that no one had ever set eyes on this piece of space rock before.

Finding an old, dead ship in orbit here would not be an easy task, but that had just been made a million times more difficult by their discovery that the planet had a plane of debris around its equator. Overgrown asteroid, dwarf planet, fractured moon, whatever, something had broken up in the pull of its gravity and the resulting mess had settled into an uneven orbit. If the *Sun Tzu* was here, and had found itself pulled into that same orbit, it would be almost impossible to find. Either that, or it would have been smashed to smithereens. Maybe parts of what made up these rings were fragments of one of the legendary ships from Earth-That-Was.

"We've come this far," Mal said. "Let's get into orbit fifty miles above the widest extent of the rings, see what we can see."

"What about the map?" Zoë asked. "Maybe there's something on it that'll reveal a closer coordinate for the ship."

"We've been trying that for days," Mal said. He was troubled by how much they were still relying on River's reading of the map. Kaylee had examined it, in fact all of them had taken a look, but it was only the most unpredictable member of *Serenity*'s crew who could gain any sense out of it. "River's lost interest in the map. It's brought us this far, and she seems happy enough with that. Take us in, Wash. Nice and slow. Zoë, keep watch on the scanner for any space debris in our way."

"Autoscan should find that," Zoë said.

"I'd like a pair of eyes too."

"You do realize how dangerous this is," Wash said. "I mean, if I had to put it into context, I might compare it to jumping the ship through a star's corona, or landing on an asteroid, or maybe—"

"Danger is your middle name," Mal said. "Come on, show us why you're the best pilot in the 'verse."

"I don't claim to be that," Wash said, glancing at Zoë for support. "I've never claimed to be that."

"Get us through this alive and you can." Mal tapped him on the shoulder, not too hard. Wash was already steering *Serenity* closer in toward the planet.

Mal, Kaylee, and Jayne stood back to let Wash and Zoë do their thing, and to observe their approach. It was really quite beautiful. Mal never grew tired of looking out into the void. In deep space the differences were more difficult to perceive, but they were there if he looked carefully—a comet tail a million miles away; an asteroid field; a star's light pulsing through space dust or quasars spinning out their history. Closer to planets and stars there were endless things to see, and sometimes the views changed hour by hour, even minute by minute.

This close in, it changed with every beat of his heart.

The planet was small, gray, barren, and bland, lacking an atmosphere and pocked with impact craters. They were drifting in to stay ahead of the terminator once in orbit, using the natural light to help spot anything artificial that might be adrift in the scattered rings. Light from the distant Blue Sun filtered through these rings, and the closer Wash took them the more that light was split into individual wavelengths by moisture, dust, and ice. It wasn't often Mal saw a rainbow in space, but when he did it brought home how stunning it was out here, and how small and meaningless he really was.

"Whoa," Jayne said. No one else spoke. Mal guessed perhaps they were all feeling a differing version of the same thing.

"Taking us closer," Wash said after a while. "Zoë?"

"I'm looking," she said. She had her face to the scanner, hands shielding her eyes on either side. "Just a bunch of rocks."

"There'll be thousands of miles of these rings," Jayne said. "How do we know the ship's even here?"

"Map brought us this far," Mal said. "We can scan open space while we're followin' the rings. Anything in an alternate orbit will be picked up once we've done a few adjusted orbits of the planet. My guess is, if the ship's been hidden out here by the Alliance, this is where it'll be."

"Hidden?" Jayne asked. Wash also glanced at him, eyebrow raised.

"So far out here, no sense believin' otherwise," Mal said.

"Right," Kaylee said. "That map weren't made to be easily read."

"'Cept by that headcase River," Jayne said. "Let's hope her freaky cleverness finds us a ship filled with riches."

"That and more," Mal said.

"More'n riches?"

He didn't bother replying. The view was too stunning for small talk to detract from it. He crouched in front of his captain's seat low to the portside viewing window, breathing lightly so that his breath did not mist the glass, and for a few moments all his small worries and concerns were swept away. The rings around the planet were ice and rock, glimmering in the splashes of rainbow light, seemingly flickering as they tumbled, turned, and spun. *Serenity* was still miles above the upper extreme of the rings, but they were wide enough to form the large part of their view, the individual elements mostly too small to be visible.

"Okay, we're about sixty miles above the rings," Wash said. "We go any closer and imminent death will be... imminent."

"Any trace of a ship?" Mal asked.

"Got nothing," Zoë said. "Maybe it's on the other side of the planet."

"Maybe it's *on* the planet," Kaylee said.

"But the Generation ships were massive, weren't they?" Wash asked. "A mile long, or more? No way you could land something like that."

"Not on a normal-sized planet, maybe," Mal said. "The gravity would break it apart. But this is more like a moon."

"If that's the case, it'll be tough to find," Jayne said.

"But not impossible," Zoë said. "Just very, very time consuming."

"Let's stick to the plan," Mal said. "Now we're in orbit, all eyes outside. Zoë will stay with the scanner, the rest of us look for anything out of the ordinary."

From back in the mess they heard River's voice, and it was almost as if she was singing.

They performed one orbit of the small planet and saw nothing on any of the scopes. Wash slowed them down so that they began drifting against the direction of the rings, passing above them at a relative speed of two hundred miles an hour. While Zoë remained glued to the scopes, Mal went back into the mess.

The others were still there, River and Simon sitting in easy chairs and not talking. River held her knees to her chest and stared at her hands, thumbs slowly moving to perform circles around each other. Mal watched her for a moment, then grabbed the map from the table and sat down opposite them. Simon looked at him expectantly. River didn't even appear to notice he was there.

"We've come close, but we need to know more," Mal said, holding out the map to River. "You brought us here. If we've got this far and we don't find the *Sun Tzu*, it'll all have been for nothin', and my ship and crew are cravin' something other than a wasted journey."

Mal stood and placed the map over River's knees and folded hands. She glanced up at him then down at the map, her fingers still describing their slow movements beneath it, causing it to rise and fall.

"Precious *Sun Tzu*," Mal said.

"Yes!" River said. She dropped her legs and held the map up in both hands, presenting it up to the light as if she could see through it. A sheen of tiny sparks fizzled across its surface and fell away like shattered ice.

"If it's anywhere close to the rings it'll have been pulverized centuries ago," Simon said.

"Could be you're right," Mal said. "But whether the Alliance placed it here or found it here, they didn't seem to think that'd happen." He was looking at River as he spoke. She scanned the map, moving it up and down, left and right, and her eyes were wide and filled with wonder. She saw the map differently from anyone else in the crew. She recognized something wondrous in its strange swirls and curls.

"Mal!" Zoë called from the bridge. "Better get up here."

River changed. From excited and wide-eyed she became meek

and afraid, throwing the map to the floor and curling up against Simon. He took her hand.

"Be careful," Simon said as Mal dashed for the bridge. He thought it was strange, and perhaps he should be saying the same to Simon.

"What is it?" Mal asked as he entered.

"Got a ship," Zoë said. She was bent over the scope, left hand tweaking a dial to adjust search parameters. "I think it's Alliance."

Mal caught his breath and blinked away his surprise. "Weren't expecting that."

"You and me both," she said.

"This doesn't sit well in my precious, sensitive flesh and bones," Wash said.

"So what's the story?" Mal asked.

"It's a long way off. Scope picked up an old drive trail, but definitely Alliance, probably a destroyer rather than one of the big cruisers."

"No regular Alliance patrol come out this far," Wash said.

"I said I'd heard whispers here 'n' there about the Alliance comin' this far out from the Core, and in this sector," Mal said.

"For the *Sun Tzu*," Wash said.

"I reckon."

"Oh, that's just great," Wash said. "Trouble follows us. It seeks us out. Trouble is my middle—"

"Wash," Mal said. "Fly the gorramn ship." He scanned the readings and leaned on the back of Wash's seat. "Ease our speed, and take us in closer to the rings."

"I was afraid you were going to say that," Wash said. Reducing speed, he dropped *Serenity* closer to the plane of smashed rock and ice encircling the mysterious planet.

"So, turns out there must be something here worth stealing," Jayne said.

"Much as I endeavor not to agree with you most times, I agree," Mal said. "The Alliance has a reason for sendin' a patrol out here. Zoë, how old's the trail?"

"Difficult to say. I'd reckon less than ten days. After that, trace of a gravity drive tends to drop away."

"We're goin' closer to the rings?" Jayne asked when he saw what Wash was doing.

"We're more likely to stay undetected that way," Mal said. "Meanwhile, I'll get Simon to work on River so maybe she can—"

"Hold on to your behinds," Zoë said. She was bent over the scope again. "Got another ship."

"Alliance?" Kaylee asked.

"Not this one. No drive trace, either. This is close enough to see, and it's like nothing I've ever seen before."

"Sounds like our baby," Jayne said.

"Ease up," Mal said firmly. "Slow and gentle, Wash. Get us there in one piece, but gentle steps, and not too close for now. Just so we can see."

They all huddled around Wash as, guided by Zoë, he skimmed *Serenity* close to the planet's rings, aiming for a point of light in the far distance.

As they drew nearer a long, thin object manifested from the vastness of the Black, reflecting weak light from the distant star.

"*Sun Tzu*," Mal said. "We found you."

From the dining area, River screamed.

5

I'm where I was always meant to be, and suddenly I'd rather be anywhere else.

River reaches for Simon and he holds her. He's her one safe place against a cruel 'verse that seeks to bind her, blind her, and make her its own, whereas in reality the whole 'verse could be hers. Simon doesn't understand, but he helps so much. Without him she's not sure what would have become of her. Some of the others help her, and some are sweet, Kaylee especially. Sweet and innocent of so much, every one of them.

She sees how Kaylee looks at her, though. She doesn't like her fear, because she would rather *no one* be afraid of her, and she knows the crew are in danger because they protect her. After returning to Ariel and letting Simon look into her mind, she sometimes fears herself.

Sometimes, River tries her best to live in the present and make do, molding herself into something new—a full human being, a good person—even though the trips and flips her brain undertakes makes that difficult.

Now, here, she is looking to the future.

A man sleeps on this ship. He has brought her here to him.

Even from billions of miles away, she knew that he was just like her. Mutilated. Tortured. Bettered.

Precious *Sun Tzu* waits for them all, and like her, the ship is not as it seems. It is a relic not as hollow, and not wholly as old, as it appears. She's been led here, maybe even lured by the sleeping man, and though in some ways she wishes herself anywhere else… there's also a part of her that relishes what is to come.

She wonders if this is what it feels like coming home.

Usually Kaylee preferred being back in the engine room, listening to the heart of *Serenity* as she powered through deep space. Sometimes if that heart fluttered or strained she would perform some form of mechanical surgery to make her well again. She was as bound to *Serenity* as the pulsing heart of her gravity drive. Out of them all, perhaps Wash might come the closest to understanding. If she was conjoined with the ship's heart, then he was the manifestation of its senses.

Now, though, she much preferred being on the bridge. Wash urged and lulled the ship to his wishes, expert hands guiding it close to the staggering spread of the planet's rings and toward the shape gradually appearing in the distance. This was something none of them had ever seen before, and the silence on the bridge was heavy and filled with wonder.

"Beautiful," Kaylee said.

"Will be when we get closer," Jayne said.

"I'm still worried about that Alliance destroyer," Wash said. "You know what destroyers are for, right? The clue's in the name."

"No sign of it now," Zoë said. "It's been and gone. Like any routine patrol. We might've just been lucky enough to arrive between sweeps."

"Probably just looks like it's gone," Wash said. "It saw us coming and has powered down until we wander into its killing zone. Whatever, we're flying toward an ancient, legendary ship that supposedly ceased to be five centuries ago, and there's signs of an Alliance ship having been here on the edge of space. I think— and I'm sure you'll be stunned by my deductive powers, and I thank you all in advance—but I think the two might be linked."

"So I've said," Mal said.

"Right! So. Let's go."

"We've come this far," Mal said.

Wash shook his head. "Seriously?"

"We'll move in closer, check it out." Mal looked around at them, settling on Kaylee. *Like he's inviting an answer*, she thought, but she wasn't sure what her answer would be.

"The Alliance knows it's here!" Wash said.

"But they're not here right now, far as we can tell," Mal said. "Which means they ain't expectin' anyone to find this ship, cos they hid it good and safe. Which in turn means there's more of a reason for us to be here too."

He looked out at the distant ship again. They were approaching slowly, drive silent, skipping close to the rings to hopefully avoid detection from anyone scanning the local area.

"And there's River," Kaylee said.

"And there's River," Mal repeated. "She's been somethin' of a mystery since she came on board, and I'm startin' to think some of that might be resolved here."

"She's agitated," Kaylee said. "I might even say scared."

"Simon reckons she's excited. And she can surely read the map. There's some sort of link I'm eager to uncover, and I know you are too."

"Me?"

"You're more pally with her than any of us."

"Guess I am," Kaylee said. There was also the allure of the *Sun Tzu* and what it represented. She'd like nothing more than to get on board and check out all that old tech and equipment. The mere prospect sent a shiver down her spine; she was looking across miles of space at a piece of ancient history.

As they closed on the ship it became clear that it was way beyond the rings, settled in an orbit nearer to the planet than the inner ring—and safe from any collision damage from any of the floating chunks—yet still close enough to be sheltered. It was obvious that its orbital positioning was a very deliberate act.

"Kaylee, you seem to know a lot about these ships," Mal asked.

"From schooling and my own interest, but I'm guessin' a lot of what's known is flighty guesswork. The arrival in the 'verse was a time of confusion, and the last thing people had time for was recordin' their actions for posterity."

"Not something I was too concerned about when I was getting my education," Jayne said.

"You were educated?" Mal asked.

"Ha ha."

"Inara told me of the most popular stories, from Jordan Cluley and Jess Ray," Kaylee said. "They give some quirky personal insights and plenty of sciency goings-on about the ships, but nothing too techy. It's said Cluley was a food farmer on one of the ships, and she died before reachin' the 'verse, so most of her writings concern soils and aquaponics. And Jess Ray was insane."

"Maybe you can write your own account now," Wash said. "*Kaylee's Guide to Legendary Ships*. Maybe we can make that our mission from now on, Mal? Going to the most dangerous an' inhospitable places in the 'verse to find empty old wrecks."

"Take us closer, Wash," the captain said.

Kaylee felt a flutter of excitement in her chest as Wash guided them above the rings and closer to what they all assumed to be the *Sun Tzu*. River had stopped shouting, at least, and apart from the usual sounds on the bridge—the gentle, constant hum of the ship's engine, a buzzing and creaking from Wash's control panels and flight seat—all was silent. Even Jayne didn't have any quips. The sight was stunning and humbling.

"Keep your eye on that scope, Zoë," Mal said. "Don't want no surprises."

"That would be nice," Wash said. "I'll run a book on whether we get any nasty surprises here or not. Any takers?"

No one replied.

Kaylee could not tear her eyes away from the viewing windows. As they closed on the *Sun Tzu* more detail began to emerge. The first thing that became clear was that the ship was huge. Not just big, but massive, its scale difficult to discern with little to compare against. She had no doubt it was larger than any vessel she'd ever seen. She'd always known that the Generation ships had been big, but as details became clearer on this old vessel she saw just how expansive it was, more so than any of the Alliance cruisers she'd ever seen or heard of. Over a mile long, maybe a lot more, it was a long, blocky rectangle with equal-width sides, and built with no nod to aesthetics. Its rear end flared into a box shape to incorporate a heavy thrust structure on each of the four sides. Its front was flat and snub-nosed, and each long surface was ridged and speckled with structures, depressions, and protrusions whose purposes were unclear. Even though size was difficult to relate to in space, the ship dwarfed *Serenity*. It felt like they were closing on another planet rather than something built by people. Wash flew them closer and closer, and weak light from the distant Blue Sun caught each aspect of the *Sun Tzu* as it performed a gentle, slow revolution around its long axis.

"It's beautiful," Kaylee said, and although the vessel was ugly and entirely functional, the word held true.

"It's a wreck," Wash said.

"I'm sure you won't look so shiny when you're five hundred years old," Kaylee said.

"No, I mean it's a wreck. Can't you see? Look along the side facin' us now, a third of the way from the rear end."

"Is that a shadow?" Zoë asked.

"Hull breach," Jayne said. "Great."

"And it's not the only place," Mal said. "I see at least one other. Zoë, how are we looking?"

"No signs of any vessel in the vicinity," she said. "Whatever Alliance ship was here is definitely gone now."

"I still don't like it," Mal said. "But we've come this far. Take us in, Wash, nice and slow. And keep one hand on overdrive. First glimmer of anything amiss and we get the hell out of here, and no looking back."

"I'm with you on that," Wash said.

"I'll prep the suits," Jayne said nervously. "How many?"

"Four," Kaylee said before Mal could answer. "River should be here, and Simon with her."

"I was thinkin' the same," Mal said. "And Wash needs to stay with the ship."

Wash glanced at Zoë, and she nodded. "Be ready to rescue me, baby," she said, but Kaylee knew she was only trying to make Wash feel better. He always preferred remaining as *Serenity*'s pilot. They were lucky he was the best any of them had ever known.

"Looks like it's really been in the wars," Zoë said as they drew closer. Wash took them slowly from bow to stern, keeping station a couple of miles out, and Kaylee couldn't help but agree. The vast ship was long neglected, battered, apparently breached in several places, and visible on one side as it continued in its gentle roll was a large, open wound, a crater revealing the heavy structural elements of the interior, blackened like burnt bones. Around this ugly hole the metal hull was scorched black and deformed.

"How did that not rip the ship in two?" Mal asked.

Kaylee's stomach was sinking. With damage like this visible from a couple of miles out, the chance of the ship being in any fit state to board was lessening. They had come all this way to find a hulk, and it wasn't the time it had taken or the lack of reward for their journey that upset her. It was the loss of everything that might have been.

"What the hell happened here?" Wash said.

"I'm just hoping it was long ago," Zoë said. "That's a heavy impact from a serious weapon."

"We still investigate," Mal said. "We've come this far and—" He'd glanced back at them and now he froze, looking past Kaylee and Jayne toward the entrance to the bridge.

Kaylee turned but she knew what she would see. River stood braced in the doorway, one hand holding either jamb, and Kaylee didn't think she had ever seen anyone looking so afraid.

"It feels like coming home," the girl said.

"You have to keep her out of the way," Mal said. He'd already spoken to Wash about this, but Simon was a different matter. He was the only person Mal really thought could do it.

"I always do. As much as she'll let me."

Mal nodded. Shrugging on his overlayers to wear beneath the space suit, he glanced at the girl pacing the dining area. She was scared and excited, and projecting emotions that were difficult to pin down, for her as well as them. One moment she cried, the next she laughed. There was no doubt the proximity of the *Sun Tzu* was causing that, and pretty much everything about this situation, and everything out of her mouth, was making him wonder if they should turn tail and flee back the way they'd come.

"Good," he said. "I have the feelin' you might have to keep us safe from her too."

"River wouldn't do anything to harm the crew," Simon said.

"Most times I'm mainly confident of that being true," Mal said, "though I've gone up and down on the issue since you came aboard. But right now ain't most times."

"Maybe," Simon said quietly. "I'm not at all sure *what* right now is."

"Then we'll go and see," Mal said. "River needs to stay here. The ship's old and it's seen some action, and there's a fair to good chance all of it is vented to space."

"I'm not sure that would stop her from trying to come."

"So you *prevent* her from tryin'. You're the one person she always listens to, and she needs to stay here. If there's something dangerous on that ship, last person we want meddlin' with it is your sister."

"I'll watch her." Simon paused, awkward, as if he had something else to say.

"Spill," Mal said.

"Something about that ship has her wired," Simon said.

"Yeah, I've noticed. Even more so'n usual."

"I'd be grateful if you could find what that might be, Mal. I mean, I know your business and what's probably forefront in your mind, but we found the ship because of River."

"Rest assured I'm not just lookin' for treasure from Earth-That-Was," Mal said.

"Thanks. I can't imagine what it could be."

"I'm tryin' not to."

* * *

When Mal reached the main airlock in the front cargo doors the others were already suited up, bulky helmets hanging by straps on their backs ready to be pulled on. Jayne was carrying the gun he called Boo in a clipped holster on his leg, and on the other side a heavier weapon, a shotgun Mal wasn't aware he'd named but probably had. Zoë also wore her sidearm, and that was a comfort as well. Kaylee refused to carry a gun, but Mal noticed a tool belt around her waist.

"Wash is taking us in," Mal said. "For now he won't dock, not until we've gone over and found somewhere suitable and safe. He'll match the *Sun Tzu*'s pitch and yaw and get us in close. Once *Serenity*'s airlock's open, I'll go across with a line, and when I secure it, you can all clip on and follow me over. Questions?"

There were none.

Mal always felt a flutter of excitement and fear when he prepared for a space walk. On *Serenity* there was a sense of scale. Every view on board ship had a limit, a horizon to contain you even if your eyes were closed. Sometimes he sat in his small, sparse cabin with his eyes closed and tried to meditate, removing himself from the world he found himself in along with whatever troubles were bothering him at any particular moment. Even if he could not rein in his troubles, he always felt swaddled by the ship, hearing his breathing echoing from walls and feeling *Serenity*'s gentle, persistent rumble.

Now he was about to drift free of that embrace.

The airlock cycled, and as the outer door opened Mal moved to the edge and stared out. He paused there for a moment, and sensed no impatience from his three crewmates and friends. Of course not. They were all feeling the same thing.

He pushed off gently. Mal was instantly alone, and all he could hear was his breathing. It was faster and shallower than usual, and he tried to settle it down. Ahead of him was the bulk of the *Sun Tzu*, and beyond it the pale gray curve of the planet it had been orbiting for who knew how long. Around him was infinity, that deep darkness that felt both endlessly light and staggeringly heavy. Everything that made him Malcom Reynolds had not existed before he was born and would cease when he died, and floating in this inhospitable place was the greatest reminder of his own impermanence.

The *Sun Tzu* seemed even larger when not viewed from inside *Serenity*. It filled his field of vision, and with its strange protrusions and time-scarred fuselage turning from light to shadow and back again as the vessel spun, its deep age intimidated, its size filled him with awe. It was unlike any ship he'd ever seen, and the knowledge of its origins—the certainty of how far it had come—was humbling.

"This is one ugly-ass chunk of battle-scarred metal," Jayne said over the com.

"Oh, Jayne," Kaylee said.

"What?"

Mal chuckled. "Once we're all down we'll head for that sticky-outy thing at two o'clock. You all got it?"

"Yeah, I see," Zoë said. "You thinkin' there might be a hatch there?"

"No idea, but we need to find a way in."

"Why not go in through one of the damaged bits?" Kaylee asked.

"It might come to that, but I'd rather find a hatch or external docking area." Mal gripped the suit's small control unit in both hands, and he gave a gentle tap that fired compressed air from its vents. His forward motion was altered to the right, he corrected slightly, then settled into the slow trip across to the *Sun Tzu*. It would take less than a minute, and he was already judging his relative speed to land safely against the structure.

Wash had leveled them with the ship and matched its spin, and it was a strange sensation seeing the view beyond changing as they all rotated—the planet, the rings, open space, and then the planet again. It made Mal feel queasy, and he was glad when he closed on the hull. He slowed his approach a little, then searched for something to grab on to when he hit. The surface was surprisingly smooth, so he used one of the suit's vacuum-seal units on a short leash. Attaching to the hull as soon as he hit, he lengthened the leash enough to be able to stand and use his boots' magnetic soles. He connected the line that trailed from *Serenity* and the others clipped on and floated across. Soon the four of them were standing together on the great *Sun Tzu*, the ship from Earth-That-Was. No one said anything for a while as they took in their surroundings. *Serenity* hung above them, and beyond was the slowly turning vista of rings, space, planet.

The view toward the bow of the *Sun Tzu* was obscured by the protuberance they'd aimed for, and Mal was disappointed that there was no evidence of a hatch or airlock anywhere close by. Back toward the stern they could see the first signs of the large damaged area, blackened structural components pointing out from the ship like cracked fingers or broken ribs. This one side of the ship was so vast that there had to be some sort of opening for them to try to negotiate.

"We could split up, two forward, two back?" Zoë asked.

"Let's stay together for now," Mal said. "We'll head aft. Hopefully by the time we reach the explosion site we'll find a way in. Wash, how're things looking up there?"

"Nice and warm and comfortable in my chair, thanks, Captain. I've just made a cup of coffee and am seriously considering some cake."

"Since when did we have cake?" Kaylee asked.

"I only said I'm considering it," Wash said. "It's torture."

"Scopes clear?" Zoë asked.

"Oh, whoops."

"Wash," Mal said, voice low.

"Of course they're clear," he said. "If they weren't I'd have told you. Might even have waited for you to get back before getting the hell outta here."

"Keep in touch," Mal said.

"I'm watching you from on high," Wash said, and Mal looked up toward *Serenity*, but the cockpit glass was opaque so he couldn't see Wash, and starlight glimmered from its surface and turned it into a mirror. Jayne threw the pilot a rude gesture anyway.

They started along the ship, Mal leading the way. He tried to concentrate on the hull ahead of him, but his attention was drawn to the constantly changing panorama around them, and the deep, cold lure of infinity. It was a strange thought knowing that this vessel had been built trillions of miles away, and had come such an inexplicable distance on its travels. It chilled him to consider what the people who'd built and crewed it had been like. They had been humans, yes, just like him and the rest of his crew, but they'd also come from a vastly different world and background. Their histories were beyond imagining, and so desperate that they had been forced to flee those old lives and search for something new.

"Mal, over there on the left," Kaylee said. "You see that?"

"Looks like a… blister?" Jayne said.

"Yeah," Zoë said. "Some sort of viewing pod."

It was difficult to discern scale with nothing to add reference. When they arrived at the protrusion it was to find it perhaps the height of a person and twice as wide. It was made of some sort of glass or polymer, and Mal was frustrated to find it was impossible to see through. Its inner surface was obscured, possibly by dust. He pressed the faceplate of his helmet against it and shielded his eyes, but he could still not see inside.

"We can't just cut or blast it open," Kaylee said.

"Why not?" Jayne asked.

"Because if this part of the ship is still pressurized it'll explode outwards, pierce our suits, and we'll fly off into space."

"Like that Early dude," Jayne said. "Like to think he's still out there, floatin' about."

"I vote we all stand back and let Jayne blast it," Zoë said, and Kaylee chuckled.

"Yeah, well, still waiting for your bright ideas," Jayne said. "Should've gone straight for that blast zone like I said."

They moved on, down the length of the ship toward the flared back end. And though they searched for ways in that would not risk any potential depressurization launching them into space, they found nothing.

"We should get back to *Serenity* and fly her around the ship," Kaylee said. "If Wash brings us in close enough we'll eventually find somewhere good and easy to access."

"That's surely the safe bet," Zoë said.

"That ship might be full of loot, why concern ourselves with safe?" Jayne asked, and Mal turned to look at them all. *Eventually doesn't cut it*, he thought. *Not with an Alliance destroyer somewhere out there.*

"I don't want to tarry," he said. "Let's take a look at the blasted area. Maybe there is a way in."

As they closed on the damaged portion of the ship, Mal turned over all the known facts and tried to form a theory about what had happened here. Maybe the *Sun Tzu* had reached the 'verse and then been struck by a meteor. Perhaps there'd been a malfunction when whatever sort of star drive those old Earth-That-Was explorers used fired to slow the ship down on their approach. A revolution on board, sabotage, an accident, or perhaps they'd arrived years or decades after the first ships, and those original settlers were keen to keep the place to themselves. Accident or intentional, the explosion had crippled the ship. But he was pretty certain it hadn't happened here, in this planet's rings.

The *Sun Tzu* was hidden away from prying eyes. Shielded within the embrace of the strange rings that encircled the planet— and he'd never seen or heard of rings surrounding such a small planet before—it was too perfectly placed, its orbit too balanced, to have ended up there by accident. Whatever the Alliance had going on here, they'd moved the ship here themselves.

"Wash, follow us over," Mal said.

"Quick escape," Zoë said.

"Escape from what?" Kaylee asked.

"Whatever nasties are inside the ship," Jayne said. "You heard the girl singing her usual crazy song. Sleepers, she was saying, I heard her. Maybe she means zombies. Those people brought from Earth-That-Was all been sleeping for so long, we go in there now and wake them up and they'll be hungry for Kaylee flesh."

"Bottle it, Jayne!" Mal snapped.

"Guys, sounds like you're having fun down there," Wash said, "but meanwhile River is going pretty damn wild up here, and I'm not liking this at all. I'm shutting and locking the bridge door."

"Sure, lock it tight," Mal said. He understood why Wash was doing so. One nudge from the mad girl, one distraction if Simon lost control of her and she ran onto the bridge, and Wash might steer *Serenity* into the *Sun Tzu*.

They soon reached the first part of the ship's blasted area. The hull was rumpled for a good distance, deformed by whatever impact or explosion had caused the damage, and they had to tread carefully so that their magnetic boots maintained a suitable fixing. The going became uneven, and looking at their feet was a welcome distraction from the slowly turning view from the spinning ship.

"It's bigger than it seemed from above," Zoë said. "Much bigger."

Mal looked along at the ruined hull. What they'd taken to be a small zone of damage was actually hundreds of feet across, and it stretched almost the entire width of the ship's hull at that point. He was amazed the vessel's back hadn't broken.

"This is recent," Jayne said.

"You're sure?"

"Sure I'm sure!"

None of them disputed Jayne's opinion. He might have been a jackass sometimes, but he wasn't always quite the fool he made himself out to be. The fact that he was still alive paid testament to that.

"That changes things," Zoë said.

"Not really," Mal said. "The *Sun Tzu* didn't come to rest here on her own. And there's the map. The Alliance put her here for a reason, so maybe that damage ain't what it seems."

"In and out," Zoë said. "Quick as we can."

They edged forward and soon reached the first rips and tears in the hull. It had been blown apart and peeled back, the structure turned into vicious spikes and serrated edges ready to rip their space suits at the first wrong move. Beyond the tattered and torn metal was a shallow crater in the otherwise flat plane of the ship where a chunk of the fuselage had been blown out into space. Ragged ends remained. Hollows seemed to pulse and shift as the light continued to change, shadows growing and shrinking again, and the tattered remnants of structure and superstructure appeared fluid in the stark coldness of open space. It almost looked like a wound in a shivering, living thing.

Mal was just about to order them all back to *Serenity* when Kaylee let out a gasp of surprise.

"What the hell's troubling you now?" Jayne asked.

"Over there," she said. She was pointing across the crater toward the far edge, and for a terrifying second when Mal looked, he thought she had seen something alive.

It's moving, writhing, squirming to get out and at us, and maybe it's one of the sleepers River is raving about. From the corner of his eye he saw Jayne's hand going to Boo in its holster.

"That looks new," Zoë said, and Mal realized he'd been seeing light and shadows dancing again, absorbing starlight and hiding from it as the ship slowly turned.

"Yeah, well, that's because it *is* new," Kaylee said. "Rest of this ship is old as can be. We're walking on something built on or above Earth-That-Was, and that's got me giddy so I can hardly see. But that over there isn't somewhere that's been blown up. That's something that's been fixed."

Mal looked closer at where she was pointing, and it was as if knowing what he was searching for brought it into focus. Embedded in the wall of the metallic crater, fixed in and around protruding steelwork and broken pieces of ship, a dull gray surface presented a flat, undamaged facade.

"Another, over there," Kaylee said. She moved forward toward the hole, climbing over a ridge of melted and re-formed metal, and looked around the wide pit's edges. "And another. Four that I can see, and I'm gonna bet there's more."

"What the hell is this?" Jayne asked. "Someone's been here before us? Got away with all the loot?"

Mal heard a muttered curse in his earpiece and wasn't sure whether it was Zoë or Kaylee.

"This is more than just salvage," Mal said. "Don't you see that by now?"

"So what else is it?" Jayne asked.

"Someone's made it look like this ship is dead," Kaylee said. "Maybe this hole was an accident, maybe it wasn't, but there's been enough repair work done to make me wonder if we'll even need our suits inside."

"You're kidding, right?" Jayne asked. "Who'd bother to repair this old hulk?"

Kaylee glared back at him. "You do realize what this old hulk is, right?"

"You thinking what I'm thinking?" Zoë asked.

Mal nodded. "That the Alliance has more to do with the *Sun Tzu* than just checking up on it now and then."

"Yeah."

"Wash, need you to do a scan on the ship for us," Mal said.

Wash's voice crackled in his earpiece then settled down. *Serenity* was holding station above them, its shadow sweeping past them every few minutes as the *Sun Tzu* turned.

"What sort of scan?" he asked.

"Heat sources," Mal said.

"You mean like tech or engine activity?"

"No. I mean like life signs."

6

I'm as still as a point in time and traveling at the speed of light.
Simon still has her huddled up against him, and he is warmth and comfort and familiarity, but never safety. She has not felt safe for a very long time, and that is perhaps the root of everything that goes through her mind and comes out confused and befuddled. She knows for sure that the others do not understand her. She rarely understands herself.

Even when everything has a clarity that seems to outline and define the whole universe. Even when she thinks she can count to infinity with one breath, or name each star, or solve the deepest of puzzles while still laughing at one of the few memories she holds dear. Even then, she does not really understand.

Understanding is coming. It's close. She isn't sure how she knows this, but the knowledge is as certain as her own name, and that's something she has never let go.

I am River. I flow from past to future. I renew.

Like a molecule of water within a river, she has spent so long moving randomly that she has lost herself a thousand times over. Simon tries to rescue her. But though he has struggled to discover

91

what they did to her, and developed treatments and medicines, he has never managed more than to hold her on a true path for a short while. She takes those moments to catch her breath, but strangely when they occur she wishes for the randomness again. Being lost is no bad thing when reality—being found—threatens to bring her so much pain.

They found me. They did this to me.

Memories of the time before Simon rescued her are like fleeting images of a former life. When they come during sleep they take the form of nightmares; when she's awake, they're flashbacks filled with horror, and terror, and they propagate a rage that she hopes one day will dissipate at last.

She's restrained in a chair. People in white coats and black masks hover around her, pushing needles into her skin, watching as she convulses. They take notes on portable computers, and when she cries they collect her tears and take them away for testing.

She is flat on a table, unable to move, and she senses the delicate whisper-touch of surgical implements in her brain. There are no nerves there, but still she feels them digging through her life.

She is alone in a room. It's warm, there's food and a comfortable bed, the walls are soft and white, but it is still a cell.

She hates those memories, and prefers when they're lost in the flow.

Now, she is speeding up. Given mass and energy by the man who has drawn her here, her movements no longer feel random. *Silas is real.* Back in the Academy he had been a myth between her and other prisoners, a story about the first test subject who rampaged. The Academy put him down and started again, with her and with others. They took lessons from their failure. *He really, really exists, and they didn't put him down at all.*

Now, he wants to be free, and I'm the one to free him. And perhaps...

Purpose is a grand thing and it has her in its grasp. Her velocity builds. Sitting motionless with Simon, her mind is traveling so fast that she can hardly draw breath.

Perhaps in freeing him, I will also free myself.

Typical, Mal thought, *we finally find something that might be worth a fortune and someone's been here already.*

For him, these new structures all around the blast hole could mean only one thing—someone had already found the ship, which meant that anything of worth might have been taken.

He floated gently above and behind Kaylee, Zoë, and Jayne, tethered by his suit's umbilical. Kaylee was convinced that the tech used to repair areas of the blast site was Alliance, and that hardly came as a surprise. It put them all on edge.

But though there were signs that the Alliance had already plundered the wreck, it would take years to search everywhere on board. Mal was still trying to get to grips with the ship's staggering size, and he was certain that even if some stuff with salvage value had been cleared out, there would still be plenty to find. *Serenity* was a thousandth the size of the *Sun Tzu*, and she had hidey-holes and nooks aplenty. There was still hope. Once Kaylee managed to bypass the security built into the new airlock they'd be inside, and then he could get searching.

"How's it going?" he asked.

"Not as easy as I hoped," Kaylee said. She was working at a panel beside a doorway built into the new bulkhead. Loosened wires drifted and waved like a nest of worms, and she attached gadgets to them, twined and twisted, undid them again.

"Keep ready," Mal said.

"I *am* ready," Jayne said. As soon as the door opened he'd

have them covered, in case there was anyone waiting for them on the other side. Mal didn't see how there could be. Wash had scanned the ship for heat sources and found none. No life signs, no leftover radiation from working tech. Just cold, empty nothing. This ship was dead.

"Got it," Kaylee said suddenly. "Just let me decipher the entry code and—"

The doors slid open. A surge of escaping air hit them all, and Kaylee fell back, dropping her tools and striking the broken metal behind her before ricocheting and spinning up and away, feet kicking out as she sought to stamp down with her magnetic boots.

Mal tweaked the vents on his suit and slammed into Kaylee before she could drift away from the ship and out into space, grabbing her ankle with one other hand.

"Get control of your suit," he said.

"Got it. Got it." She was breathing hard, and he saw her wide eyes through her faceplate.

He felt the jerk and surge as Kaylee caught herself, then he let go and she drifted back down, away from the opened door and to the right. Jayne was already covering the opening, and Mal also drew his gun. If they fired they'd have to use suit thrusters to counter the recoil.

"What's happening down there?" Wash asked.

"Excitement," Mal said. "That's all. Don't worry yourself up there in your nice warm seat, Wash."

"Airlock," Kaylee said. "I tripped the door before I deciphered the entry code, purging the compartment."

"Just lucky the inner doors are closed," Mal said.

"Lucky. Yeah." She nodded at him. "Thanks."

He nodded back, then engaged the motor on his umbilical to drag him back down to the ship. He landed in front of the open doors and shone his headlamp into the revealed airlock. It was barely large enough for the four of them, and it filled him with a surge of hope. If the Alliance had built airlocks this small, they hadn't intended to move a lot of material from off the ship.

Kaylee went first, taking out her spare toolkit, and she got to work on the inner door controls.

"Just, er, shut the outer doors first, yeah?" Zoë said.

"Thanks for the advice," Kaylee said. "Talk among yourselves."

Silently, Mal waited.

The artificial gravity as they entered the airlock was a strange feeling. One moment they were floating, the next their feet snapped to the floor. Mal disengaged his magnetic boots and they remained firmly set, though he felt lighter than usual. On *Serenity* the gravity was a by-product of the ship's drive. On the *Sun Tzu*, inside the hull, the ship's gentle spin helped keep them pulled down to the deck. It was another sign that the Alliance had placed the ship in this orbit, and location, very deliberately.

Jayne took point beside Kaylee. The outer doors slid shut, and after Mal ensured that their comms with Wash were still working, Kaylee flooded the airlock with atmosphere from inside the ship. Zoë tested the air with her suit's onboard computer and announced it cold but safe to breathe.

"But keep suited up 'til Kaylee's opened the inner doors," Mal said. "Just in case there're more defense mechanisms."

"If they wanted no one to board, they'd have set explosives," Jayne said.

"Maybe just a deterrent," Kaylee said.

"Since when have the Alliance been subtle about their desire to blow people apart or blast 'em into space?" Mal asked.

The inner doors slid open, and they all swayed as pressures balanced.

"Welcome to the *Sun Tzu*," Kaylee said. "We're about to go back in time."

"We're about to become rich," Jayne said.

"Wash, we're in," Mal said. "Hold station, but keep alert. How's River?"

"Odd as ever," Wash said.

"Tell us something we don't know," Mal said. "I meant what is she doin'?"

"Odd things," Wash replied. "Singing a bit, shouting. Last time I asked she was folding paper into weird shapes."

"Huh?" Zoë asked.

"Combative origami," Wash said. "She's really quite good."

"Just watch those scopes," Mal said. "First sign of anything approaching, we haul ass out of here."

"This is quite something," Jayne said. It was dark and cold inside, and they turned on their suit lights, the combined illumination flooding the space before them. It had sustained damage from the blast, but the corridor leading away from them was intact, walls scarred and scorched, ceiling blackened by fire. Their suit lights penetrated partway along the corridor, swallowed into darkness further in.

"There's hardly anything to see," Zoë said.

"We all feel that?" Mal asked.

"Yes," Kaylee said. "How can we not?"

A sense of wide, deep space. The sheer scale of the ship crushing in around them. Unknown potentials ahead, depending on which turning they took, which levels they explored. And surrounding it all, a humbling sense of history, time stretched and experienced, centuries long-passed impressed into the structure of the ship.

"Gives me the rutting willies," Jayne said.

"Let's stay sharp," Mal said. "Anything amiss and we head back here. Kaylee has the airlock's codes, right, Kaylee?"

"Right. Maybe it's best you all have them." She sent the codes to their suits. Mal heard a soft chime as his acknowledged receipt.

Jayne ran his hand across a sign set into the wall, smearing off a fine layer of frost and dust. "Huh—this sign's in English too—only it's different."

"Old Earth-That-Was English. Guess they still had to write in both languages back then," Mal said. "Anyhow let's head out. Jayne, Kaylee, you two go aft. Only bring back things small enough to carry in a hurry, and manhandle out through those new airlocks. We're lookin' for old collectible stuff, anything we can sell to those interested in such things."

"Why we headin' aft?" Jayne asked.

"Because that's where the engine room is!" Kaylee said, slapping his shoulder.

"Engines," Jayne said. "Shiny."

"Kaylee has an eye for tech that's worth somethin'. We don't know much about the ship's layout," Mal said. "Zoë and I will try to work our way around or beneath the damage and head forward, see what we can find. Keep comm channels open and check in every ten minutes. No risks."

Jayne grunted.

"No risks, Jayne."

Jayne flipped open his faceplate and then slid off his helmet, letting it hang down his back by its straps. He took in a deep breath. When he exhaled it condensed before him in a shower of tiny ice particles. "No risks."

Mal was about to berate him when Zoë interrupted.

"Well, he ain't dropped dead. I'd say we're good, Mal."

"I knew that," Jayne said. The others took off their helmets and let them fold and hang behind their suits. They took a few deep breaths to adjust to the cold. They were nervous, turning on every suit light and shining them around at the damaged and scorched surroundings. "I *knew* that!" Jayne insisted.

"We'll meet back here in two hours," Mal said. "In that time we should get a feel for whether it's worth stayin'."

"Two hours ain't nothin'," Jayne said. "You've seen the size of this ship. We could spend two days on board and barely scratch the surface."

"Two hours, Jayne," Mal said. "Wash says there's no life signs aboard, so we ain't gonna stumble into any Alliance troops. But this is just a recce to see what's worth takin', gather up a few bits an' pieces. Then we'll reconvene and decide how to proceed. Pointless just blunderin' about without a plan, and we need a real picture of what we've found here. I know they're cumbersome, but keep your suits on. There's no tellin' how unstable this ship's structure is. And watch out for each other."

"Don't worry," Kaylee said, "I'll look after him."

"Right," Jayne said.

They headed off, and at the end of a short corridor they came to a junction. Jayne and Kaylee turned left, and Zoë and Mal took the right passageway. Mal kept one hand on the gun in its waist holster, because something about this ship definitely wasn't right.

Maybe it was the icy darkness, old and heavy. Maybe it was the sense of deep, turbulent history contained within these steel walls, echoes from humanity's mysterious past, and the idea that people from Earth-That-Was had walked these corridors long centuries ago.

Or maybe it was the feeling that they were being watched.

* * *

Kaylee was excited and afraid at the same time. It was a combination she'd become used to traveling on *Serenity*. It was also a sensation she often felt when she was alone in River's company. Experiencing it now, on this amazing old ship, was no surprise.

As she moved forward, though the fear and cold remained, they also made room for something else—a true sense of wonder. Until this moment all her concentration had been focused on approaching and entering the ship, and their mishap at the airlock was still fresh in her mind. Now, she could let that restrained fascination root and take hold. She was on the *Sun Tzu*, and all around her was a deep sense of an incredible, almost legendary past.

For her, any real treasure on board this ship would be the Earth-That-Was technology. She felt surrounded by a history that might take her a lifetime to examine in detail. She saw old screws with tool marks on their heads, and wondered who had affixed them. She saw bolts with their edges sheared, and thought about the person who had last turned them, and their hopes and dreams and fears. They were centuries away from her from a world she could barely comprehend, yet in some ways she felt close to those people—mechanics, builders, workers, and engineers with scars on their hands and grime beneath their fingernails. Sheets of metal walling held firm together. Lighting and ducted services speckled and lined the ceilings, dead now, but still filled with a potential of life. The surface facade of this vessel was visible and solid, but she wanted to undo these screws and bolts, dig deeper into the ship, and make sense of the old technologies that had brought the *Sun Tzu* so far.

Jayne didn't feel it. That was obvious, and she was not surprised, but she didn't think any of the crew felt quite the way she did now. Agendas were different, she knew that, and though making money was what it was all about for most of them, for her, coming here had been all about the *Sun Tzu*. If she tilted her head and half-closed her eyes she could almost hear the voices of those who had come before. "Our ancestors walked these corridors," she said. "Ain't that thrilling, Jayne?"

"I'd want a quiet word with mine," he said. "Ask 'em why they didn't set me up better."

"Huh?"

"With more money, and position, and such."

"But can't you feel it? A sense of wonder?"

"Sure. Wonderin' where all the good stuff is."

The corridor jigged left and right. They passed several doors, all of them closed, and they tried every one. Locked. Jayne tried kicking one open, grunting as he bounced back against the wall.

Kaylee stared at him. "Plenty more places to explore."

"Locked doors means there's something worth taking inside," Jayne said.

"Or maybe it just means 'Private, keep out.'"

"Same thing."

By the time the corridor opened out into a wide, circular area with other corridors leading off, most signs of damage from the explosion were behind them. The fireball had not reached this far, and the bulkheads were no longer rippled and deformed. It was still dark and cold, their suit lights causing shadows to jitter and dance in hollows in the walls or along some of the mysterious corridors leading away from this junction. The ceiling was domed, and as Kaylee glanced up and around her lights picked out designs carved into the curved metal. There was no uniting feature or style in these names and symbols. They were not instructions or official diagrams. It was graffiti pure and simple, people from half a millennium ago having left their marks, perhaps as a way to pass time on their long, incredible journey. She found it melancholy, and quite beautiful.

"So which way now?" Jayne asked. "I could spin a coin."

"That way," Kaylee said, pointing across the hallway. "Toward the engine room."

The next corridor was wider, with doors more regularly spaced on either side. Some of them hung open, shadows slinking back inside as they approached, and at the first few they paused to peer into the rooms. They were small crew sleeping quarters, not much larger than those aboard *Serenity*, with beds and cupboards, tables and chairs. They were sparse and mostly empty of personal belongings.

At the end of this corridor the space opened up into another domed, circular room, but this one was different. Larger than the first, it was still filled with furniture, and its purpose quickly became surprisingly familiar—a saloon. Curved around the wall for a quarter of the room was a genuine wooden bar, behind which dusty, faded mirrors clung to the walls, and empty liquor bottles were fixed upside down, contents long-since evaporated through dispensing optics.

"Reckon I'll find some unopened bottles behind there," Jayne said, and he went for the bar. But as Kaylee looked around and saw what hung on the walls around the rest of the room, she gasped. She forgot Jayne, and the bottles he sought, and pretty much everything else. For a few seconds when her heart beat in rhythm with those who must've talked and drunk and laughed here so many years before, she took in the images, and felt tears at the corners of her eyes.

"Jayne," she whispered. "Look."

He looked. "Pretty pictures," he said.

"Paintings of Earth-That-Was," she said.

"So?" He went back to leaning over the bar, searching for his precious bottles.

So... Kaylee thought, but she couldn't answer, and saw no point attempting to. You either felt it or you didn't, and Jayne didn't.

"Amazing," Kaylee breathed. She walked slowly around the

edge of the room, like someone looked at paintings in the finest gallery on Londinium. Every image was amazing. Each world shown was wondrous, and gave an idea of the incredible star system Earth-That-Was had been a part of.

A tall spire, speckled with lights that looked like stars, set in a wide, flat city.

A massive stone pyramid in a desert, sand-colored and tattered from exposure to the elements.

The sprawl of a vast city with buildings reaching for the sky; the endless spread of a jungle, with trees taller than any she'd ever seen, flocks of birds spotting the deep blue sky, a moisture misting above it to form clouds.

A boat on a vast ocean. A winged aircraft, surfing the clouds on one of the Earth-That-Was worlds or moons. People on a beach, smiling at the sun. People everywhere, so many people, all of them now dead. Something niggled at her mind as she walked from image to image, reaching out but never quite touching the paintings. As she came to the final picture—a photograph taken from space, showing the blocky mass of a Generation ship with the gorgeous blue and white jewel of Earth-That-Was in the background—the truth hit home.

"These are all one place," she said.

"Huh?" Jayne said. He was sitting on the bar, an upturned, empty bottle in his hand.

"All these pictures, Jayne. Earth-That-Was wasn't a system, like I always thought. It was just one planet. It was all our worlds in one, and every place in the 'verse started there."

"So?"

Kaylee smiled and shook her head. He'd never understand. She stared at that final picture and felt a sadness tugging at her insides. Even if Earth-That-Was remained, in whatever poisoned and damaged form it existed in now, she'd never see it.

She placed her hand flat against the wall next to the picture, and the cool metal pressed back.

"Let's go," Jayne said, heading off into another corridor. "This *hūn dàn* place is empty."

Kaylee sighed and followed him. She felt the weight of the *Sun Tzu* heavy all around her, and even though she'd never see what those pictures represented for real, the ship was still here. She'd like to take it apart bit by bit and revel in the way it was put together, delve down into its mechanical guts like a tapeworm.

They passed along another narrow hallway and Jayne stepped through the second open door into the small room beyond. Kaylee followed, and while Jayne rooted around for loot, she took a picture frame from the wall. It showed a tall woman in a strange uniform, a man standing beside her, and two small children. The woman rested a hand on each kid's shoulder and the man's arm was around her waist. They looked happy. The photograph had been taken in a garden, and behind them was a wide vista ending in a range of low hills. Perhaps just over those hills was the city with the tall spire. "You think this is worth anything?" Jayne held up a coffee mug that was half a millennium old. On its side was written, *Dangerous If Empty*.

"This is amazing," she said, showing him the picture.

"What's with you an' all those pictures? Seen their like before."

"Not like this. We've seen holos and approved pictures, but this is… personal. This is love, in the place we all came from."

"Maybe I can trade it on Jubilee," Jayne said. "I know someone who knows someone who runs an old restaurant, all their crap's from back in the day. Tables, plates, all from Earth-That-Was. Or so he claims." He turned the mug back and forth in his hand. "I think he's talking *niǔ shi*."

"They might be our actual ancestors," Kaylee said. She held

the photo up and compared Jayne to the man and woman. They looked somehow more proud and more sad at the same time. She wondered who they had been, what they had done, and whether their dreams and ambitions had been realized. The *Sun Tzu* had reached the 'verse, after all. Maybe these peoples' descendants were alive and thriving.

"'Made in the USA,'" Jayne said, reading the print on the bottom of the mug. "What the ruttin' hell is a USA?" He dropped the coffee cup and picked up something else. It was a book with a faded cover and pages yellowed and stuck together by time. "Remember what the Shepherd said? This could bring a pretty sum."

"What is it?" Kaylee asked, still holding on to the photo. The woman might have read it when she was trying to fall asleep at night. The man might have read it to his children.

"It's a book."

"I know that, silly. Which one?"

"What does it matter?" Jayne looked at the cover and frowned, turning it this way and that, then flicked through the pages. "Can't hardly understand it, anyway. Rich folks on Anson's World buy old books to line their walls. Makes them look intelligent. Don't matter to them which book it is." Jayne stuffed it into his backpack and started searching through drawers in an old wooden cabinet.

Kaylee felt suddenly sad watching Jayne sorting through this forgotten family's belongings. She wasn't sure why—they were beyond knowing, and she'd stolen her fair share of things in the past—but she felt unaccountably close to them, as if looking into their photographed eyes could make them see both ways.

"You'll be carrying stuff worth next to nothing," she said. "Leave it here. We've only just begun searching, and we'll find plenty more."

"Like what?"

"Old tech," Kaylee said. "Engine room stuff. It's said they

used gold in some electrical units way back when, and that'd bring a pretty price."

"You just want to get all gooey looking at the ship's nethers."

"Maybe, but could be I can salvage some bits and use 'em on *Serenity*," she said. "And there's a fast trade in old ships' drive parts among collectors."

"Where? In your grease-monkey conventions?"

Kaylee shrugged and left the room. She felt much better outside in the empty, featureless corridor, less of an invader, and Jayne soon joined her, backpack over his shoulder.

"You really love this old stuff," he said as they started walking. "Don't you?"

"If it's worth somethin', that's shiny."

"This is where we *came* from, Jayne. This is our history. Everything in the 'verse, all the wars and disputes, the settlements, the planets we've terraformed, the societies we've built up and seen fall by the wayside… all that started with these ships arrivin' here hundreds of years ago."

"Huh," Jayne said. "Haven't really dwelled on that side of things that much."

"Why do you think it's worth so much?"

"'Cause people like old stuff." He looked around. "Guess 'cause they were clever too."

"Clever how?" Kaylee said.

"To get here. Build these ships."

"Right, yeah. So clever that they polluted their own planet so much, they had to flee." She wondered what was left of Earth-That-Was. The 'verse had come into being because their ancestors had had to leave, but perhaps some of them had been left behind? Maybe Earth-That-Was really did still exist in some form, a poisoned, toxic place where only a hardy few survived. They'd never know of her, not like she knew of them. That was beyond strange. That was just plain scary.

Kaylee led the way along the corridor, ignoring the few doors that hung open because she didn't like the feeling of being an intruder.

"I thought this was a ship full of sleepers," Jayne said.

"Stop trying to spook me." She thought of River, and the strange things the girl had been ranting about the ship.

"I'm not! I mean, everyone on board was all cozy and sleeping for the journey from Earth-That-Was to the 'verse. So why the cabins?"

"These Generation ships had crews," Kaylee said. "The *Sun Tzu* is a mile long and ten million tons, so there's plenty to go wrong, 'specially on a journey that lasts for decades or even longer. They needed people to maintain and work the ship and its systems, and look after those sleepers who'd only 'spect to wake when they reached a new home."

"The 'verse," Jayne said.

"Yep, the 'verse. It's reckoned some crew were even born on board, worked, and died inside these walls. Never saw no sky but the Black. Never felt ground under their feet." Jayne fell silent, and she hoped he was thinking about the same thing as her. Imagining being born on the ship, growing up here, serving your life as an engineer or computer technician, meeting someone and falling in love, having a family, growing old, dying. All on board. For some people, this ship had been their whole world. Their past, present, and future. Their forever.

She loved *Serenity* as well as she loved people, and a lot more than most, but she couldn't imagine spending her whole life on board.

"It's creepy," Jayne said.

"Sure is."

"I wonder what the Alliance were doing here?"

Kaylee wondered that as well. As they moved deeper into the

ship, and further toward the stern, she looked for signs of recent activity. The airlock they'd entered through, and the other new structures and bulkheads that had been built around the area of damage to the ship's hull, had been obvious new work. Since leaving that location she'd seen nothing similar.

What she did see were examples of old tech she'd only heard about from a few of the deep space pirates she'd come across since hooking up with *Serenity*. Blank, dusty screens hung in the junctions of corridors, possibly the old eyes of the ship's controlling computer. There was talk they'd even had a form of artificial intelligence on these old ships, advanced, almost magical technology lost in the early, rough days of the 'verse. They came across a wide corridor with several platforms scattered in haphazard fashion, and Kaylee guessed they'd been moving floors, flitting crew back and forth along the length of the ship. For everything she saw that she could identify, there was something else she could not—round glass globes protruding from walls, their inner surface dusted opaque; a series of large winged shapes hanging from corridor ceilings, plastics molded to resemble wood with no discernible use; open doorways with strange chain curtains. She wanted two weeks to explore the wonders of this ancient ship. She had less than two hours.

The captain's voice crackled in their comm. "Wash, we lookin' good?"

"All shiny here. I'm having a second hot chocolate, and the Doc is currently trying to stop his sister from running herself into an early grave."

"How is she?" Kaylee asked.

"Same as ever. She's in the cargo bay running back and forth... and back and forth... But the chocolate is fine, to say the least."

"Nothing on the scopes?" Mal asked.

"Just the deep, soul-destroying nothingness of endless space."

107

"You sound edgy," Zoë said. Kaylee smiled. Trust Zoë to hear through Wash's quips to an underlying tension.

"So would you if you had to listen to this," he said. "She runs, he shouts, she sings, he pleads. It's a mite troubling."

"We'll be back soon," Mal said. "Two hours or less. Then we get our *gŏu shî* together and reassess. Kaylee, Jayne, all good with you?"

"All shiny here, Captain," Kaylee said.

They passed through more darkened accommodation levels and found themselves in a series of wider, more functional corridors, all built to a curve around a huge inner space.

"No security," Jayne said on the open comm channel.

"What d'you mean?" Kaylee asked.

"If there was something on board worth stealing, the Alliance would have protected it," Jayne said. "Dammit."

"Don't bank on that," Zoë said. "We're way out beyond the Rim here. Maybe they thought hiding the ship like this was enough."

"But the map?" Jayne asked.

"Somethin' covert," Mal said. "Somethin' they lost that shows the way here."

"It's like a treasure map!" Kaylee said, and Jayne's eyes lit up.

As they moved on, their suit lights illuminated the corridor for many paces ahead. The wall to their right was high and convex, and the further they went the more eager she was to see what was on the other side. There were no doorways or viewing windows that way, and whatever space lay beyond the wall appeared vast. She almost felt the weight of the space contained within there, and the silence made it seem even more loaded. As if it was waiting for them to discover it.

When the corridor came to an end against a tall bulkhead, the door leading beyond half-open, it was Jayne who saw the second doorway set into the wall to their right. This one was closed and cast so perfectly that it showed barely an outline. It was only their shifting lights that created shadows enough to discern the junction between door and wall.

Heart beating faster, Kaylee set her decoder against the door, held there by magnetic tape, and used a listener to try to pinpoint where any electronic locks were engaged.

"Good solid door like that might mean somethin' worth seeing beyond," Jayne said.

"Seeing or stealing?"

"This is salvage, not theft."

"Could mean the nuclear heart of the ship," Kaylee said. "It's said these old ships used fission reactors, real unstable if left uncooled. After so long the reactor coolants might've leaked or fizzled away to nothing, leavin' behind a nice stew of instant death."

"Oh. Great."

"Don't worry, I'm scanning for any dangers." She viewed her wrist scanner and phased it through every wavelength and range. *Any dangers we know of, at least*, she thought. There was no telling what might be on board this ship that had fallen into humanity's past, lost to memory and myth—strange tech, dangerous compounds, toxic ideas. There was only one way to find out.

Jayne expected this door to open on riches that would set him leaping with joy. She hoped it would slide open to reveal a room filled with wondrous tech and mechanical workings. Treasures for them both, in different ways.

When the door whispered open into the wall, the space beyond contained neither.

Kaylee had never seen so many corpses.

7

"It's a pity we can't just take the whole ship," Zoë said.

"Yeah, right. Fly it right back into the heart of the 'verse."

Mal paused and glanced at Zoë.

"You're serious."

Zoë shrugged and looked around. They had worked their way around the damaged areas and headed toward the bow, and they had arrived at the remains of a food production center. It was a wide, low room, with row upon row of tables where plants had once grown. They were gone now, rotted away to dust and occasional delicate, stick-like remnants.

Mal was haunted by the implication of this room, its use and scope. It had been designed to feed a crew of hundreds or thousands over many years, decades, even centuries. No one knew for sure how long these ships' journeys had lasted from Earth-That-Was, but the scale of the undertaking was epic. To uproot a whole society—virtually a whole species—and shift it trillions of miles through interstellar space was beyond his comprehension. Doing so without knowing for sure whether there would be a habitable home at the end was the ultimate in desperation.

They sure must've messed up their old planet good and proper to come this far searchin' for someplace new, he thought.

Their arrival in the room had caused a subtle shift in the atmosphere. The remaining plants fell apart in small wafts of dust, like slow-motion breaths finding cold and spreading until they vanished from view. The fecundity of this place was a distant echo. Just like the crew, and just like the millions of people who had been transported here in suspended animation. This dark, empty, cold place was like a memory being revisited once again, still dead but laying itself open to view. Mal imagined *Serenity* as equally lifeless, and it made the sight painfully sad.

"Takin' the whole ship back's a thought," he said. "It's like a museum. Maybe it's our duty to take it back so others can see it."

"Duty, Mal?"

He shrugged. "We'd charge admission. But it's a foolish notion."

"That ever stop us before?"

"Huh." Mal often entertained these wild but brief flights of fantasy. The idea of flying the *Sun Tzu* back to the Core was delightful, perhaps with *Serenity* leading her in, planets and moons turning out to welcome their incredible return. Delightful, but ridiculous. The Alliance would stop them a hundred times before they made it to the Outer Rim. They had gone to efforts to make the ship their own, and they had ensured it remained safely hidden away.

Besides, the chances of it being serviceable were remote. However much of a natural Kaylee was with engines and mechanics—sometimes, Mal thought she and River had more in common than anyone thought, only Kaylee's instincts and talents were of a more practical bent—this was something else.

"Maybe in our dreams," Zoë said. "But that doesn't mean there won't be stuff here that can make us rich."

"Right," Mal said. "The captain's name plate would be nice, for starters. Star charts from their journey. Planners and logs. Imagine that tale, handed down from captain to captain as one grew old and another took over. The places they must've passed through. The sights they must've seen. I'm sure Jayne's looking for treasures, but sometimes treasures ain't what you might expect."

"Remember Niska?" Zoë asked.

"You suppose I'll forget him in a rush?"

"He had a fine collection of memorabilia from Earth-That-Was. Him and people like him would pay a small fortune—"

"Rather not deal with his like again, if it's all the same to you."

"He did have a certain charm." Zoë smiled.

"Let's haul our asses through this place, get closer to the bridge. I've an inkling that's where we'll find something of worth." Mal glanced at his watch. "We've been forty minutes. Time to turn back soon and regroup, but we've a picture of the geography of the ship now. Maybe Wash can engineer a docking, and we can spend some days on board."

Zoë shivered. "Spooky," she said.

"For sure, but we've seen nothin' yet that'll do us harm."

The ship spooked him, but fascinated him as well. Just like River.

"Wash, how's the girl?" he asked.

"Just as weird as ever."

Weird as ever, Mal thought, but that wasn't quite true. She was *weirder* than ever. The *Sun Tzu* had her stirred up, and coming here had been as much because of River and her ability to read that map as anything else. Without her they'd have never found the ship. He remembered his promise to the Doc that he'd search for whatever had made River so keen to come here. He couldn't help think it might not be something good.

"Maybe it's safe to bring her on board now," Zoë said, and Mal was surprised once again at how she seemed to read his mind.

Fighting together, almost dying together, had given them a bond that would never be broken, no matter what the future brought.

"Maybe I'll ask Simon to bring her," he said.

"I'm not sure Simon will have a say in it."

"How do you mean?"

"I mean he's looking after River, but sometimes I think it's her looking after all of us."

Mal didn't answer that. It was a strange thought, and disconcerting, but a form of that idea had implanted itself in his subconscious some time ago, and it still returned to trouble him on occasion.

Beyond the hydroponic area their lights revealed another set of new blast doors. They were obviously retrofitted, and they opened to a touch on their control pad. They were thick and heavy, welded into the solid bulkheads of the ship. Their style and construction did not match the rest of the *Sun Tzu*, and construction marks and fixing points were obvious.

"More Alliance control panels," Mal said.

"Yeah," Zoë said. "I've been thinking on this."

"Me too. I got nothing."

"They've done their best to make the ship still look like a derelict, while protecting the interior."

"How do you figure that?"

"That blast zone we came in through. Jayne thought it was recent, and could be he's right. Maybe that wasn't something that happened long ago, when the *Sun Tzu* first arrived in the 'verse, but intentional destruction to make the ship look dead. And these doors—and I'm willing to bet there are more in other directions, all away from the damaged area—are to isolate the damage from the rest of the ship."

"It's a big effort for them to go to."

"Some things are worth such an effort," Zoë said.

They moved on, and a few minutes later they arrived at a set of open doors leading into a large hold area. They shone their lights around the wide space, and Mal caught his breath.

"Whoa," Zoë said.

"Looks like they came ready for some travelin' and explorin'," Mal said.

The hold was filled with vehicles of all shapes and sizes, colors and designs. Lined along the wall to their left were six large, bulky and identical trucks, and Mal guessed these were military transports of some kind. They were built for strength and reliability, not aesthetics. Elsewhere, other wheeled cars sat side by side, tied down to the deck and packed in between with blocks of a compressible material that had grown hard and brittle over the centuries. Some of these vehicles presented their back ends to Zoë and Mal.

"What's that say?" Zoë asked. She knew Mal had a smattering of old Earth-That-Was English.

"Ford," he said. "Same name on all of 'em."

"Guess our ancestors weren't too imaginative about naming their transports," Zoë said.

"Right." The hold presented a sad sight. Whatever had happened at the end of the *Sun Tzu*'s journey, its passengers hadn't had a chance to unload this part of its cargo. Some vehicles remained where they'd been loaded and tied down, but shining their lights through the assembled ranks, they could make out a few jumbled areas where cars and trucks had rolled, flipped, and crashed down on each other. So much effort had gone into building and loading, all for naught.

"Seems kinda wasteful," Zoë said.

"That it does," Mal said. "More Fords over there. And those army-lookin' trucks are all… General… Dynamic."

"They gave their vehicles ranks?"

Mal shrugged. "Guessin' that's the case."

"Mal," Kaylee's voice came over the comms. "We've found something." Mal could hear the tension in her voice. And perhaps the fear.

"What have you found?" he asked.

"Bodies," Kaylee said. "Lots of bodies."

Jayne had seen his fair share of corpses, and he'd been responsible for quite a few of them. This was something else. This was death on an unimaginable scale.

"I wonder if they went into those things wearing their jewelry," he said, and Kaylee turned and shoved him in the chest. He staggered back, hands held out. Kaylee had tears in her eyes, and rage, but when she saw his expression she stopped and froze.

"Jayne…" she said.

"Yeah." They handled things in different ways.

She shivered with shock. "Cryo pods. The Alliance uses them sometimes, but it's glitchy tech, never been fully developed. It's always said Earth-That-Was knew more about this sort of thing than we ever will, 'cause desperation drove 'em to it."

"Must be worth a lot, then," Jayne said. The ranks of suspension pods marched into the distance, away from the small doorway and corridor they had ducked through and leading left and right, radiating out in stacked curved rows that encircled a distant central area. A low level of lighting—the first sign of active power they'd seen in the ship—glowed from countless points on the high ceiling, forming a regular constellation that drew together in the distance, along with the racks of ordered pods, to add a dizzying perspective to the huge space. The far extremes were too distant to make out in the gloomy illumination. Jayne reckoned there were at least fifteen levels of pods on the complex stacking system. Frost speckled every metal surface, as if a fine layer of snow had fallen from the high ceiling. In places stalactites hung down from the framing, glimmering in their torchlight, like fiery spikes. The cryo units were made of clear material—glass, plastic, or some sort of natural crystal, he couldn't rightly tell— and some still contained their occupants.

Just a few paces from him was the first of the dead bodies. He couldn't tell what sex it had once been because the pod had failed, and the person was a shriveled husk. Skin clung to its skeletal remains, hair long and tangled, face pressed to the pod's side with mouth open in a silent, endless scream. Others close by also still contained their subjects. Some were lying on their backs with wires, pipes, and cables still attached to them in various places, having seemingly died in repose. A smaller number were in a tangled mess. A couple had clawed hands raised before them, as if they had still been scraping and banging at the clear, impenetrable lids when they had eventually died.

"All those people," Kaylee said, and her voice broke.

"*Lão tiãn yé*. Long way to come to die like that," Jayne said.

The chamber was so large that the pod structures in the distance became a blur, so much so that Jayne thought there might be some sort of haze on the air.

"Weird that the lights are still on," Kaylee said. "Still power."

"Wash, did you pick up any power traces?" Jayne asked.

"Nothing obvious," Wash said. "You got power down there?"

"Sorta," Jayne said. "Still keeping my suit lights on, though."

"Could be they used some sort of natural luminous material," Kaylee said. "But after so long it wouldn't still be active."

"What else you got?" Mal asked.

"Cargo hold," Jayne said, and Kaylee glared at him. "What?"

"Thousands of suspension pods," Kaylee said. "Some still contain bodies."

"Don't touch anything down there. If there's a power source that Wash hasn't picked up, no one else will detect it either. Let's leave well alone."

"So many bodies, Mal," Kaylee said.

"It ain't the dead that concern me."

In silence, Kaylee and Jayne stood and stared around the vast space. It was difficult to take in. Jayne reckoned there were ten thousand pods in that one place, maybe more. He guessed there were many halls like this throughout the ship.

"I wonder what went wrong," Kaylee said.

"Maybe nothin'," Jayne said.

"How do you figure that?"

"Most people are gone." He pointed at an empty pod. "Might've been my great-great-great grandaddy in there, and he survived and got out, went to land on Osiris to build his new life, meet my great-great-great grandmommy and plant a seed in her. And centuries later there's me."

"The wonders of evolution at work," Kaylee said.

"So nothin' went wrong for most of them," Jayne said. "Some might've died during the journey. Others when they got here." He trailed off because he knew it didn't make what they were seeing any easier. They were looking at part of the human story from before the 'verse was populated. Deep down he knew that fact was more precious than any riches he might find on board, but back in the world he wouldn't be able to sell stories, or make a windfall from his memories. He needed something solid to profit from this jaunt.

He wandered closer to one of the lower pods that still contained a body. The pod was likely worth a gorramn fortune, but there was no way to lug it back to *Serenity*, not right now. Maybe when they got back together he'd press the captain to let them stay for a while, and then he could figure a way to load up one of the empty cryo units. Looked just like a clear coffin to him, with wires and techy gizmos. But from what Kaylee said, it might be worth a sweet sum to those in the know.

The corpse inside was small and shriveled, resting on its side with one sightless eye staring out at him. Even this close he couldn't make out whether it was a man or woman, or even a child. Unexpected sadness tugged at him. Whoever this had been back in the Solar System, they'd willingly loaded themselves into this thing with the dream of a brand-new life accompanying them down into sleep.

Then nothing.

He moved closer. Looked at the corpse's fingers, ears, throat. Damn it, no jewelry. Maybe there was a room somewhere in the *Sun Tzu* filled with stored valuables from the millions of people carried within its belly.

"Jayne," Kaylee said.

"Just wonderin' about this one's story," he said.

"Jayne!" Her voice was more urgent this time. He turned around and she had her back to him, staring at the doorway they'd entered through.

Staring at the tall, thin shape standing there.

As it shifted, Jayne reached for the gun on his hip. His movement was instinctive and rapid, muscles working faster than conscious thought, and when he saw the threat in the figure's altered position he replied in kind, squeezing Boo's trigger even as he drew the gun from its magnetic holster, exerting enough pressure so that just as the barrel rose and pointed at the figure, the gun fired. It jumped in his hand and he stepped forward, squeezing again as he reached for Kaylee, snagged her jacket with his fingers, tugged her back and down. The figure spun and fell back, and Jayne stepped past

Kaylee and crouched, firing one more time as the shape attempted to crawl back into the shadows.

This was when Jayne came alive. This was his world, his reality, his most comfortable circle of existence, and he never felt more at ease with himself than right then.

His mind started to catch up as the smell of the discharged weapon reached his nostrils.

"Jayne!" Mal shouted in his ear. "I heard gunfire."

"Hold up." Jayne moved forward, and without taking his eyes from the fallen shape he asked, "You okay, Kaylee?"

"I'm good. Be careful!"

Jayne grunted. He turned slightly so that the full glare from his suit lights flooded the narrow corridor. He already knew what he was going to see. The sight of light glinting on metal, the sound of soft muffled tracks, the subtle taint of spilled hydraulics on the air. A second later he was close enough to see, and his suspicions were confirmed.

"Alliance sentry drone," he said. "Older model, but still effective, given the right advantage."

"Drone?" Mal asked. "Wash, how come you didn't make it out?"

"Must've been powered down," Wash said through the comms. "Hang on. Oh."

"Oh?" Mal asked.

"Yeah, oh. Or rather, erm, if you'd prefer."

"Don't oh and erm me, Wash!"

"Just tell us," Jayne said as he knelt beside the drone. He'd fired three times and hit his target every time—one bullet through each of its head sensors, one shattering its composite spinal column. Its legs moved feebly, multi-way tracks scraping against the floor, but its central control hub was smashed. It leaked fluids, and most importantly its main sensors were finished. Whoever was keeping tabs on this thing wouldn't know what had hit it.

But they would know *something* had hit it.

"Seventeen traces now showing throughout the *Sun Tzu*," Wash said. "None of them are you guys—I've got your suit transponders plotted. These are less friendly spots of light on my scanners."

"Locations?" Mal asked.

"Two close to you and Zoë. Jayne, you and Kaylee look pretty clear for now."

"Lucky us," Jayne said. He spotted the weapon dropped by the drone. "Another five seconds and this thing would've pumped us with fifty thousand volts. Me and Kaylee'd be dancin' and boppin'."

"Can you deal with them, Wash?" Mal asked.

"I think so."

Jayne kicked the downed drone and returned to Kaylee. She nodded to him and brushed herself down.

"Back to *Serenity*?" Kaylee asked.

"I can take them," Wash said. "Confuse their onboard scanners and block any transmissions."

"But we might still run into them," Jayne said.

"I can keep track of you and them, and warn you if any are drawing too close."

Jayne hefted Boo. "Rather you guide me closer to them. I'd like me some drone potting."

"We've found something that looks interesting," Mal said. "We'll take a look-see, then back to the ship pronto. Jayne, Kaylee, you start heading back."

Jayne snorted.

"Alliance, Jayne," Kaylee said. "We already know this ship's got their interest, and now the drones might've sent signals."

"Which means it's got my interest too." He silenced his comm so that only Kaylee could hear. "I didn't come all this way to leave with nothin'."

8

It was not just another blast door. It was a whole structure, spanning the wide walkway they'd been navigating and stretching into the guts and bones of the old ship. New metalwork had been forced through old, leaving ragged, torn edges and junctions that had been clumsily welded back together. The new walls were solid and apparently without seams or joins. Upon discovering the blank wall facing them they had backtracked, heading left and right to get around it. Fifteen minutes' exploration had revealed the core of a new structure deep within the *Sun Tzu*, placed roughly at the ship's center of gravity as if to balance the intrusion of new into old.

"We can't come all this way and just leave this all sealed up," Zoë said.

"I concur."

"Even though it's pretty obvious that whatever the Alliance are hiding here, it's behind this bulkhead."

"It seems likely that's the case."

"We'd be stupid to mess with it."

"Stupid." Mal nodded. He stared. They both knew they could not leave this alone. He was a safe-breaker, and the structure before them looked like it was built to keep something safe.

"How long will it take?"

"Let's stop talking and find out."

The hidden structure was almost the size of *Serenity* and something about it chilled Mal to the core. But it also fascinated him, and when they found the doorway—so finely engineered that its edge was little more than a hairline crack within the sheer metal wall—he knew he had to get inside.

This was a vault. He could hardly imagine what treasures it had been built to accommodate.

He pulled a set of tools from his suit and set to work. Kaylee was great with tech and the moving, living mechanics of a ship, but Mal had broken into enough safes in his time to have a true feel for security mech and tech. He plugged in the small sensor and hung it in his ear, tapped on the metal to test if he could hear the subtle vibrations, then examined the edges of the door. He went from the floor upwards, across the top, down the other side, then back across the floor to his starting point. At first he saw nothing. On the second time around some of the light reflected beneath the door caught his eye, and on the third circuit he saw similar places on both long edges and along the top. It was a four-way locking system.

He used his finest blade, barely the width of a hair, slipping it into the door gap along the floor and manipulating it back and forth. At the same time he pressed a magnetic cutter against the joint, finger on the button, ready to send a burst that would disrupt any magnetic lock with a repolarizing surge.

It took longer than he'd hoped. Several times he had to tell Zoë to stop pacing because her footsteps caused vibrations that interfered with his efforts. When the fourth lock snicked open he exhaled, unaware he'd been breathing so lightly, and the door let out a gentle, deep thud.

"Opening time," he said, and he leaned against the door edge. It sank into the wall and slid back, floating almost silently into its recess.

"We need to reassess the quality of engineering on *Serenity*," Zoë said.

"I like a door I can hear opening."

They stood staring at the dark space beyond. Light from their suits penetrated a small distance before being swallowed by a haze, disturbed and drifting from the airflow caused by the opened door, moving like a living thing in pain. Mal breathed in and smelled something stale and old, like air that had been trapped for a long time. The floor just inside the door was speckled with dark patches of mold. He felt cool dampness against his skin.

"Well that's not at all disturbing," Zoë said.

"Reckon it's not been opened for some time," Mal said. "Got that feel about it."

"I agree. And it also has a feel like, 'Do not disturb.'"

"We've come this far," Mal said. He drew his sidearm, comforted by the heft of it in his hand, and stepped forward. Zoë was by his side, her own gun drawn. He was aware that to anyone inside the closed room, their suit lights would make them an easy target, framed against the doorway. "Let's move quick."

He moved into the new space and ducked to the left of the opened door, sweeping his head from side to side, trying to penetrate the haze. There was no echo, which led him to believe the space might be even larger than it felt.

"Wash, any sign of more drones?" Mal asked on an open channel.

"None moving," Wash said. "Still got tabs on the seventeen I spotted earlier. They're stationary and not very active. If they knew you were there I'd imagine they'd be on their way to turn you into mincemeat."

"Nice image," Mal said. "Thank you. Jayne, Kaylee, you headin' back toward *Serenity*?"

"Yep," Jayne said.

"Right. We've found a locked room that might just be the center of this ship. Investigating. More soon."

"Mal, I'm thinkin' we keep our voices and selves low," Zoë said. "The Alliance is all over the place, and I'm liking it less and less."

"Yeah, right. Me too." *And what danger am I keeping us in?* he thought. His responsibility for his crew sometimes weighed heavy, whether they knew it or not.

They'd have to get this done fast.

The room felt cool and damp even through their space suits, the hazy mist cold against his face. They'd already gone twenty steps from the door, and the open space seemed unbroken by walls or other interruptions. The floor was level and smooth, and when he glanced down he saw mold smeared beneath his boots. It was a slick green, something alive in this old dead place.

The further they went, the thinner the mist became, until they emerged at last from the cloud and cast their lights before and around them.

Mal gasped and heard Zoë do the same. It wasn't only the scale and design of the room that inspired their shock, but what sat at its center—a single suspension pod from Earth-That-Was, shimmering with countless diamonds of moisture, its contents hidden from view from where they stood. The space was a half-sphere, the walls sloping up behind and around them to form the curved ceiling, every wall and ceiling surface clear and smooth apart from the speckles of moisture. The haze hung low down and close to the walls, leaving the center of the large room mostly clear.

"What is this?" Zoë whispered.

"Something unusual," Mal said. "Maybe rich people had their own suspension room?"

"Even on a ship this big, that'd be pretty indulgent. And you're forgetting this place is retrofitted."

"Yeah. Right. Well, let's go see." They headed toward the strange pod. Mal had heard of such tech, and how the people from Earth-That-Was knew how to put people to sleep for long, long periods of time. Spooky. Unnatural. Compelling.

As they drew closer to the pod, dread grew deep in Mal's gut. "Zoë—"

"Look at this," Zoë said, stepping up onto the pedestal and sweeping her hand across the clear curved surface of the pod. "Oh, Mal, look at this." A tinkle of ice sounded a musical note through the room as shards slipped to the floor, and Zoë's gasp echoed.

"Zoë, this doesn't feel good."

"I don't know him," Zoë said, and she sounded confused. "I don't but... Mal, maybe you...?"

Mal stood on the pedestal beside Zoë and looked down at the sleeping man. For a moment he forgot the gun in his hand, his friend by his side, *Serenity* waiting for them not far away in the deep, cold silence of space. He forgot *everything*, and saw nothing but the man before him.

Peaceful in repose, wearing simple T-shirt and shorts, the strange tattoos on the man's arms and neck were stark and shocking. They looked military, but Mal only recognized one or two of them, and there were no regimental insignia. He was scarred across his throat and upper left arm with injuries that obviously continued beneath his T-shirt, and the ugly knotted tissue had healed badly, stitched and slotted on either side of the wound where medics had patched him up. The injury reminded Mal of the blast site on the main body of the *Sun Tzu*, and making such a comparison set that

127

deep star of dread in his chest spinning and burning.

"Who do you think he is?" Zoë asked, and Mal could find no reasonable answer. He spotted a slogan on the T-shirt, *Less is More*. It seemed so incongruous, a humorous statement in such a strange place.

"Someone we want nothing to do with," he said. He went to turn and jump from the dais, but then something caught his eye, a detail that merged with other stored information to make a connection that hung heavy in his mind. The man's face was cool and calm in repose, but there was something about his peaceful expression—confident and knowing, even while unconscious— that reminded him of River.

"River brought us here," Mal said, and he initiated an open channel on his comm. "Wash, what's River doing?"

"*Kuáng zhè de*, need you ask?"

"You saw that too?" Zoë asked Mal, and he nodded, and as she turned to jump from the raised area her empty holster banged against the pod.

Mal heard a soft, low whine, ending in an almost inaudible click.

A pause.

Then a series of lights flickered on around the room, a web of illumination stretching out from the central dais to the misty extremes of the curved ceiling and walls.

"I did nothing," Zoë said. "Wasn't me." They looked at the pod and saw what she had done. The touch-panel control pad was difficult to make out beneath the layer of thin frost, but the pulsing green light was obvious. It had not been there before.

"We need to leave," Mal said, and he glanced once more at the sleeping man. He was slight, with dark hair and delicate features. Wires were connected to his head and throat, and pipes and tubes snaked beneath his body and between his legs. One tube was inserted into a slit in the side of his chest, visible through a tear in his T-shirt.

Zoë grabbed his arm. "Mal!" She pointed. All around the room, a dozen small openings had appeared in the curved wall and dark, sinister-looking objects extruded. One of them turned back and forth with a soft grinding sound.

"What?" Mal asked.

"Still," she said. "Totally... still." Then she eased her gun from its holster and fired from the hip. She'd always been an ace shot, and her bullet struck the slowly turning object. It shattered, came apart, and scattered to the floor.

Around the room, several other weapons zeroed in on the falling mess and opened fire. Lasers lanced across the room, something hit the damaged weapon, others appearing to miss.

"Run, into the mist!" Zoë said, and Mal didn't think twice. They jumped from the raised dais and ran, and behind the slapping of feet against floor, Mal heard the gentle grinding of a dozen lasers tracking their movements and then opening fire.

Something snagged at his hair. Another shot passed through his suit beneath his arm. Then they were in the mist hanging around the edge of the circular room, and the weapons' targeting must have been confused.

Zoë grabbed his arm and tugged, and Mal knew not to question. There was no time. He followed her, and seconds after she pulled him through the open doorway it slid shut behind them, silent and swift. By the time he turned around to look at the smooth metal wall, the door's outline was almost invisible once more. Threads of mist faded away in the corridor's stark light. Beyond the wall, the distant rumble of working machinery sent a soft vibration in the air and through his feet.

"What just happened?" Mal asked.

"Nothing good," Zoë said.

"Who turned on the lights?" Jayne asked over an open comm,

129

and Mal realized he could see back along the corridor. A line of light panels glowed along both walls, giving a sense of perspective that was disorientating. The corridor was so long that lights met in the distance. It was almost more disturbing than when it had been swallowed in darkness.

"All over the ship?" Mal asked.

"It's gone from night to day where we are," Kaylee said.

"I thought you were heading back for *Serenity*?"

"Well…"

"Jayne?" Mal asked.

"Maybe we will now," Jayne said. "What's happened?"

"We found something—a man asleep in a pod. Not from back then, but someone the Alliance put here, I reckon, and with security systems to guard him. Seems like we woke up a sleeping ship."

"Er, guys," Wash said, "not sure what's going on down there, but it's not just the ship you've woken. Those drones appear uppity about something, and they're closing in on you."

"You said you could control them."

"I said I could track them and block any signals. There are no signals being sent, and I am tracking them. As they move toward you."

"Great," Mal said. He and Zoë shared a glance that he knew all too well. *We're outnumbered and in big trouble, but we've got each other's backs.* Their resolve and closeness had gotten them out of sharp scrapes before, both during the war and after. He only hoped it would work one more time. What Alliance sentry drones lacked in logic and intelligence they made up for in speed and firepower. Jayne must have been lucky before, possibly because the drone he'd taken down had been investigating what it thought was a malfunction, not an incursion.

Its seventeen comrades would not make the same mistake.

"Jayne, Kaylee, where are you exactly?"

"Still in the suspension hanger," Kaylee said.

"What?"

There was silence for a moment, then Kaylee said, "Jayne's looking for valuables."

"In the pods?" Mal asked, aghast.

"Well, not yet."

"Give me some credit!" Jayne said. "I ain't no grave robber."

"You'll be in a grave if you don't get back to the ship," Mal said. "Hustle. Wash, keep a channel open and see if you can get us around those nasties."

"I'll do my best. Head back the way you came, then pause at the first junction."

Hefting his gun, Mal led Zoë away from the sealed room.

"Hold there," Wash said. They paused by a corridor junction, breathing softly, crouched against either wall. Mal and Zoë moved and flowed as one. He was aware of her position, attitude, and readiness, and the same would go the other way. Jayne was an accomplished fighter and killer, but in a fight Mal would prefer Zoë by his side every time.

"Drone closing from your right," Wash said. "It's not slowing."

Mal pointed at Zoë, then at his head. Then he tapped his chest.

"Ten seconds away," Wash said.

Mal waved his hand with five fingers open, four, three, two…

On one, Zoë stood and turned the corner, and Mal stretched into the corridor on his knees. Their gunfire sounded like one shot. Zoë's took the drone in the head, and Mal's hit dead center in its metallic torso. As it jerked to a halt and turned in a slow circle, leaking sparks from its head and fluid from its chest, Zoë stepped forward and pumped two more rounds into it. With its control center destroyed, the wheeled drone trundled in a wide circle until it came to a stop against the wall.

"Okay, go the other way," Wash said.

"What's the lie of the land?" Mal asked.

"Three more incoming from the same direction," Wash said. "And five from the direction of the ship's bow. They're converging on where you saw the sleeping gentleman, not your position."

"They don't know we're here," Zoë said.

"That makes no sense," Mal said. "We've tripped the alarm; woken the ship."

"Better get a shift on," Wash said.

Mal and Zoë moved. One drone they could take easily, but three would be different. They hurried along long corridors, passing closed doors and a few that stood open, and with every step Mal felt more uneasy. It wasn't just that they had done something to wake the ship and its drone guardians; it was what they'd seen back there. One man, asleep in a lone suspension pod. A man who had not come here from Earth-That-Was. On a ship filled with dead people from centuries ago and countless trillions of miles away, piled in transport halls and left to wither and rot, it was this one man that the Alliance had seen fit to hide away and protect.

Something not quite right with that, he thought. *They're not* protecting *him. They're guarding him.* But he had to keep his wits about him now, and trying to work through the problem took too much headspace.

Ten minutes later Wash came on the comm again. "Two drones closing in on you from starboard," he said. "Maybe thirty seconds out."

"No warning, dear?" Zoë asked, exasperated.

"Sorry, I didn't see them until they moved, and there's something—"

"Not now," Mal said. He and Zoë assessed their situation.

They were at a wide vestibule where several corridors met. It had a high ceiling, a steady level of diffused light from panels around the walls, and a scatter of fixed seating set at jaunty angles. Maybe five centuries before this had been a relaxation area for the ship's crew.

"Chairs," Zoë said, and Mal nodded. As they darted for the chairs he heard the soft rustle of rubberized treads on metal… and then the sound stopped. *They heard us!* he thought, and glancing at Zoë he knew she'd heard the same thing. Kneeling behind a chair, he turned and raised his gun just as the first flash of laser fire sizzled across the backrest of his chair, singeing the hairs on the back of his hand. He fired three times and saw the drone spin on its hidden wheels, its weapon discharging harmlessly into the wall. Behind it the second drone opened fire, cutting its damaged companion in half and unleashing a storm of laser scatter into the room. Zoë cursed and rolled, coming up in a crouch with her gun hand extended. Mal ran to the left, drawing fire, and he saw the drone turn from the corner of his eye. He fired twice without looking, then leaped forward and slid across the floor, feeling the heat of laser contact tracking him and closing on his trailing feet. He heard two shots and a crackling sound, and the drone let out a long electrical cry, sparks jumping from its damaged head. Zoë stood and advanced, firing three more times and putting an end to their pursuer.

"You okay?" she called.

"Yeah. You?"

"Knee got a little cooked by melted plastic."

"Your knee got cooked?" Wash asked.

"I'm fine, baby."

"But cooked? Is it rare or well-done?"

"Just stings."

"Wash, any more of those things nearby?" Mal asked.

"I don't think so, but there is something a little more pressing. I've picked up a transmission from the *Sun Tzu*, it's not something I'm familiar with but—" Behind Wash, Mal heard another, softer voice. It was River. He couldn't tell what she was saying, but he sensed her excitement, and he'd not heard her saying that much in a long, long while.

"Wash?" Mal asked.

"Seems lock picking is another of her talents," Wash said.

"What's she saying?" Mal asked. The comm channel was open, and he sensed Jayne and Kaylee listening.

"River says the signal's out there and it's already been answered by an Alliance ship."

"*Gŏu shĭ!*" Mal said. "I thought you were blocking signals?"

"Thought so too. Nothing on scopes yet, sir, but I'm keeping a close watch." Wash's voice was quieter, and lacking any of the usual lightheartedness. This had gone from vaguely dangerous to deadly serious in the blink of an eye.

"Starting to feel like the time's come to get the hell outta here," Jayne said.

"If you'd done what I said…" Mal said, but he shook his head. "Wash, how much closer can you get *Serenity* to the ship? More time we can save, the better. Did she…?" He trailed off, staring into the distance.

"Mal?" Zoë asked.

"This isn't happening because of us," he said.

"What do you mean?" Zoë asked. "We've tripped an alarm and—"

"It's because of *him*," Mal said. "The drones don't even know we're here 'til we blast them. The defenses in that room were initiated to keep something in, not out. And the signal sent to the Alliance ship… I'd be willing to bet *Serenity* they're coming in because they think that gentleman back there, whoever he is, has woken up."

"Actually, Mal," Wash said, "I was just about to get to that. The room you left behind—" The comm went silent.

"Wash?" Zoë asked. "Wash! Anyone hear him?"

"Cut off," Kaylee said. "That ain't good."

"None of this is good," Mal said.

"Incoming!" Jayne shouted, and Mal heard shooting, and shouting, and the unmistakable ragged roar of laser fire. Then their comm link to Jayne and Kaylee also fell silent.

"Let's hustle," Zoë said, and they ran together, senses alert and alight, back the way they'd come.

9

River has never been this close to something so amazing.

"What are you doing?"

It's time for her to take control. Perhaps she has been in some sort of control since the first moment she saw the map, but now events are speeding up, and she can feel her future coming close.

Silas is awake! She can feel that, and she also senses his confusion and fear. He's been asleep for so long. She has to go and look after him. And in him, perhaps she can discover just what the Alliance had wanted with her.

"Get away from there, you ain't allowed—"

She only has to look at him. Wash, the pilot. He's a good man, she likes him, but he's also afraid, and she uses that to do and get what she wants. Simon is standing behind her in the doorway, and she senses his doubt. Mostly, though, he loves that she is this animated. He has rarely seen her so awake and alert, so in control of her own actions. She understands that for him this might even be something of a release. Responsibility is draining.

She loves Simon and will never let anything hurt him.

Wash tries to communicate with the captain and the others

down on the ship. He opens comms, but River passes her hand across the control panel, sensing which dials and switches do what, and when she finds comms she turns it off. Wash talks into space, then stops when he realizes what she has done.

She looks at him again. His fear is palpable, like a glowing aura. It pulses and changes color, and she stares at it in fascination.

"So pretty," she says, and even as she speaks the words she cannot really accept that they are true. Fear should never be pretty, especially when she causes it. "I'm sorry," she says, and his aura changes again, the colors not so vital and clear. His fear lessens. Perhaps he sees that she does not mean him harm, but she is still in his position at the ship's controls, and still in charge.

She has his gun. She cannot recall having taken it, but it sits in her belt in easy reach. Wash keeps looking at the weapon, but he understands the truth—that she can draw and use it before he even takes a breath.

She doesn't wish to use it on him, but he's realized that she will if she has to. That knowledge is deep within his eyes and speckled around him in a scattering of yellow thoughts.

"River, what are you doing?" Simon asks, and she glances back at him, smiling.

"Taking control," she says. "As much as I can and for as long as I can. Long enough to meet him, and then *he'll* take control, and together we'll be more than the sum of our parts. We'll be…" She smiles when the description comes to her. It's as if it has always been there, and now is the first time she has been able to understand its relevance. "We'll be two rivers flowing into one, faster and heavier, more powerful. And flowing both ways."

"Who is he?" Simon asks.

"You're my brother," River replies. "But he is my blood."

River takes control of the ship. She has never flown *Serenity* before, but a few seconds examining the consoles, running her hands back and forth across the grubby, messy surface of the panels and boards, and she understands all she needs to know. She probes inward, her consciousness flowing and seeping deep like water, penetrating and conducting back to her everything about the workings of the vessel. It's quite simple, really.

She slips into Wash's seat and senses him stepping forward again.

"No, Wash," she says, and in a blink she has the gun drawn and aimed back at him. Her finger strokes the trigger. She can't imagine shooting him, but there are many things she has done that she would never have imagined before. Not wanting to shoot him isn't the same as not needing to, and if he comes closer, tries to stop her, wrestles her aside, she *will* need to. "I don't want to shoot you."

"River, this is madness, you don't know what you're—" She switches her aim and Simon stops talking.

"I don't need to shoot you," she says. "*Either* of you. I need to... I want to..."

She flies the ship with her free hand. It takes only a tweak to take it closer to the *Sun Tzu*, and when she sees the place she is aiming for, she engages an automatic docking procedure that does most of the work. A thump, a judder, and then *Serenity* comes to rest.

"What have you done?" Wash asks. "We need to get away from here. Once the others get aboard we have to—"

"No," River says, and she spins the chair to face them both, her brother and Wash. She reaches back and turns the comms on again. She hears confused voices, and shouting, and the sounds of guns firing, but she knows this is just background noise to the future she has come here to find. "We need to stay. And I have to sing."

* * *

"What is that?" Kaylee asked.

"Sounds like… singing," Jayne said. "Spooky girl's singing. We're about to get frazzled, and she's singing a song. That's just shiny."

"I don't know the words, but it's kinda beautiful," Kaylee said. She frowned, unsure of whether that was an accurate assessment. Kaylee knew beautiful—colorful cloths and scarves in her cabin, like Inara uses in her shuttle; strings of pearly lights slung from the ceiling; a quiet moment in her hammock in *Serenity*'s engine room, swinging gently to the movement of the ship. That was beautiful.

This song was haunting.

Jayne was grasping a wound on his left arm and he wouldn't let her look at it. She smelled burnt clothing and singed hair, but he was still upright and functioning, so she thought it was pride more than anything that prevented him revealing his wound. He'd taken out the second drone, but the third evaded his first couple of shots, unleashing a hail of laser fire that cut across the room they'd entered and brought down a shower of smashed and broken shelving. One errant shot skimmed past Jayne when he'd stood and dispatched the drone.

Kaylee thought they'd been lucky. But now time was ticking, because the Alliance was on its way.

"It'll take them a while to get here," she said, more to comfort herself than Jayne. "They've gotta navigate through the planet's rings and approach the *Sun Tzu* carefully, like we did. And destroyers are much bigger than *Serenity*, more likely to get hit by a rock or chunk of ice. Yeah, plenty of time."

"Good," Jayne said. "Let's hustle."

"That needs cleaning and fixing."

"It'll give the Doc something to do when we're back on *Serenity*."

She was about to berate Jayne when Wash's voice came over the comm.

"Captain, and the rest of you. Change of plan. River's taken control of the ship, and she's docked it somewhere on the *Sun Tzu*."

"Somewhere, where?" Mal asked.

"If I knew that I'd tell you. She won't let me close to the controls."

"She's taken my boat?" he asked.

"Well, stop jerking about and take it back," Jayne said.

"I can't. She took my sidearm, and… well, you know."

Kaylee knew well enough. She'd seen River using a gun. She'd seen River fighting, flowing like sunlight. If Wash went up against her she could break his neck and gut him before he even saw her moving.

"This just gets better and better," Mal said. "Where are you now?"

"In your cabin, using your comm link."

"So is there any *good* news?"

"She's stopped singing," Wash said.

The silence was loaded. The *Sun Tzu* was holding its breath for whatever came next.

Wash climbed the ladder from Mal's cabin and paused with his head and shoulders at corridor floor level. Held his breath. Listened. He didn't like being away from the bridge. Apart from in his cabin with Zoë, the two of them nestled naked in each other's arms, that was the place he felt most at home. During jobs where they landed somewhere, ready to steal or haul or maybe track someone down, if the captain said, *Wash, you stay with* Serenity, that was when he was happiest.

He'd had a moment of happiness earlier, when the four of them left the ship for the *Sun Tzu*. Sure, he felt a frisson of interest in the old ship, but nothing like Kaylee or Jayne. *Stay with the ship, Wash.* That had been good enough for him. He was a flyer, not an explorer, and certainly not a fighter. For him the best view of anything, even amazing things like the *Sun Tzu*, was from the windows of *Serenity*'s flight deck.

River's strange song had ended. The ship hung in silence, apart from hums and grumbles that were so familiar that he barely heard them at all. The loudest silence he had ever heard was when the ship was landed and powered down, all systems offline. Hearing the ebb and flow of its engines, its heart, always gave him comfort.

He climbed from the cabin and headed up toward the bridge. As he approached he saw Simon at the top of the steps, sprawled on his back and with one hand overhanging the metal staircase.

"Simon!" He climbed quickly, then stepped over the motionless man and onto the bridge. It was deserted, and his empty flight seat beckoned. He checked Simon, found a pulse and gentle breathing and a bump behind his right ear, and crossed to the seat and sat down. He sighed. Then he scanned the controls, looking for any that River might have touched and left out of place.

There was plenty, but within seconds he had flipped switches and turned dials, and *Serenity* settled once again into his control.

He acknowledged what he had to do. In the silence, he had to find River. He could not just leave her loose on the ship, and even though he wasn't sure he could ever stop her doing whatever she wanted, it would be dangerous to just sit and wait.

"Where…" Simon asked, groaning behind him.

"Well, hello," Wash said. "Just a minute." He switched on comms. "Mal, everyone, it's me again, how are things going with you this good day?"

"Wash, what's going on?" Mal asked.

"She's gone from the bridge. Simon's got a knock to the head. I'll go looking soon, but meanwhile…" He scanned the scopes, figuring distances and speeds. "I'd say we have an hour until the Alliance ship reaches us."

"Can you identify it yet?"

"Definitely a destroyer. Probably sent to destroy."

"So where did she dock the ship?" Kaylee asked.

"That's the odd bit," Wash said. "It's pretty much where I was planning to take it, so you can get back on board quicker. Down in the blast hole in the *Sun Tzu*'s side."

"Safe?" Mal asked.

"Hmm."

"Wash?"

Wash sighed. "I couldn't have docked her better myself."

"Find River," Mal said. "Check the airlock and EVA hatches first."

"You think she's left *Serenity*?"

"Don't you?"

Wash looked back at Simon nursing the bump on his head and resting back against the bulkhead. He guessed she probably had. Why else would she dock the ship so close to the *Sun Tzu*?

"Yes, I think so," he said. "Which means she's now your problem, not mine."

"Don't sound so pleased," Jayne said.

"She's got my gun," Wash said, but Simon held up the weapon in his left hand. "Erm. She hasn't got my gun."

"Make your mind up, Wash," Mal said.

"Does she have a knife?" Jayne asked, and Wash couldn't make out whether he was joking.

"Drones?" Mal asked.

Wash looked on the scopes, scanned the ship, and tried to place where the rest of the crew were. He saw movement, but there was growing interference, and the readouts were hazy at best.

"Something's wrong with the scanners," he said. "You're on your own."

"Of course there is," Jayne said. "Of course we are."

"Keep comms open," Mal said. "We'll find her and come to you."

"You won't find her," Simon said, voice loaded with pain. "Not unless you find what she came here for."

"And what's that?" Mal said.

"Someone sleeping. She intends to wake him. She told me I'm her brother, but he's her blood."

Silence over the comm.

"Mal?" Wash asked.

"Yeah," Mal said. "I think I know where she's going. Fact is, her sleeper might already be awake. Next time I win a mysterious map and someone tries to kill me to get it back, tell me to throw the gorramn thing away and forget about it. This is getting complicated."

"We know there's something special about River," Mal said to Zoë. "And from the way the Alliance has gone to great efforts to hide him away here, there's something special about him too."

"You think they're alike?"

"I think River's brought us here for a reason. And she could read that damn map."

"If we find River and leave now, Mal, we'd have come all this way for nothing."

"You're starting to sound like Jayne."

"And if he said that, he'd be making a fair point. We need a score, and we've yet to scratch the surface of this ship."

"I think we have," Mal said. "Scratched the surface and gone in too deep."

Zoë tilted her head and he thought she was going to say something else. She pressed a finger to her lips. She'd always been more sensitive than him, her senses sharper. That had saved his life on more than one occasion. As her eyes went wide, he lifted his gun and stepped into a doorway, and Zoë did the same across the corridor.

He heard the sound then, a gentle *slap slap* that was unlike anything he'd heard from the drones. He signaled to Zoë, but she was already lowering her gun and stepping out into the corridor. Mal did the same.

River was running toward them. Ghostlike, clothes flowing around her, eyes wide and her smile wider, he wasn't sure he had ever seen her looking so happy, so carefree. So well.

"River," Zoë said, but the girl was not slowing down. *We need to grab her*, Mal thought, but he was unsettled, and he already knew that something far from normal was happening here. Something *River* was happening. He holstered his gun so that both hands were free, but River kept going, seeing them but seemingly smiling at something way, way beyond them. To his right Zoë was crouched with her arms out, ready to sweep River up and help her back to *Serenity*.

River had other ideas. She slipped to the edge of the corridor and fell sideways, running along the wall and then performing a full twist in the air above their heads, landing on her feet behind them, and sprinting away along the corridor. By the time Mal had processed what had happened and turned around she was out of sight around a corner, her bare footsteps soft echoes that faded to nothing.

"Tell me you saw that," he asked. "She just… that just happened?"

"She's certainly flexible, sir."

"Come on." Mal started after her. Zoë only paused for a moment before following, and Mal loved her for that. He knew what had flashed across her mind—*If she wants to be here so much, let her!*—but she knew what his response would be. River was part of their crew now, and they never left a crew member behind.

Their pursuit of River back through the heart of the *Sun Tzu* was mostly silent, but for a brief, metallic screech. They came across the source a couple of minutes after they heard it. The drone was across the floor, a shattered mess in puddles of hydraulic fluid, sheared bolts, and torn casing. There were no signs of its weapons having been discharged. River must have taken it out before it even knew she was there.

"We know where she's going," Zoë said.

"Sure we do," Mal said. "She's probably there already."

"And any defense mechanisms in the room? Booby traps? And that closed door?"

Mal shrugged. He had no answers, only more questions.

The ship loomed around them, heavy and old and mostly dead. Even though he'd not seen the vast hold full of suspension pods and shriveled corpses, he felt the dead close by, as if the echoes of their final breaths held weight and substance.

He didn't like this ship one bit.

But parts of the *Sun Tzu* were now alive. Lights glowed throughout the corridors, halls, and rooms they passed through, at a low level but still bright enough to see. The Alliance had brought the man here and instilled the vessel with some semblance of life, though it was a likeness Mal was unfamiliar with, and which troubled him deeply.

The man in the pod had not looked dead, yet his life had been a cold, remote thing.

"We're getting close," Zoë said, and Mal recognized the area they were passing through. They rounded a junction, and at the end of the long corridor they saw River. She was standing motionless before the hidden doorway into the strange new room, arms held away from her sides, head tilted as if listening. She must have heard as they moved closer, but she was not listening for them.

"River," Mal said. "What's happening?"

"He's very close," she said. "He heard my song. He... I don't know why he didn't answer, but he heard, singing in the dark, one voice becoming two. He sang with me, even though it wasn't an answer." She turned and looked at them, and the smile he'd seen had fallen away. "Why won't he answer me?"

"If you're talking about the guy in there, it's because he's in suspension," Zoë said.

"Asleep?"

"Very asleep."

"Oh, no," the girl said, and the smile came again. "I don't think he's ever been truly sleeping." She took one step forward and put her hands flat against the metal. Mal could see the door outline, and something about it was different from before. It was lighter, more obvious, as if a bright light was shining through from inside.

"We're just here to get salvage and get out," Mal said. "Whoever he is, he's Alliance business."

"Me too," River said, tapping a finger against her temple without turning around. "I'm all twisted and turned, and maybe he'll straighten me out. Maybe *I'll* straighten *him*."

"Who is he?" Zoë asked.

"His name was Silas, once," River said. "But names are very private things. They're windows onto the soul, doorways inside, and maybe he changed his name long ago. But he *will* want to tell me."

She ran her hands around the door, concentrating, her head dipped and hair hanging either side of her face. Mal watched, nervous and alert for the sound of any more drones approaching. He trusted Wash to tell him if he saw any more on his scopes, but for now he wanted to keep quiet. Afraid, he was also fascinated. Something about River—and about the man they'd seen asleep in the room beyond the door—was bringing life to this long-dead ship.

With a gentle click the door opened and slid into the wall, as it had before. A waft of mist flowed out around River, lessening her for a moment, making her seem almost translucent, as if she were not quite a part of this world. Mal sometimes thought that was the case. She was a seer for sure, and she had a deep wisdom implanted in her that she was only occasionally able to tap. Never at ease with who she was and what had been done to her, she flew with them on *Serenity*, but most of the time appeared to be traveling on her own.

The mist had mostly faded, and as River went to take a step into the room, Mal grabbed her arm.

"It's dangerous!" he said.

"Not when you're with me," River said, and she pulled away from him and walked into the room.

Mal and Zoë closed in behind her and stared inside.

On the dais in the middle of the room, the suspension pod's lid was fractured and cast aside. The man inside was sitting up, staring straight ahead with his arms by his sides. His breath condensed in the air around him, very slow and measured. His face bore no expression, though his eyes were open. His hands were not visible. Tubes and wires were still connected to his head, throat, and chest, and Mal wondered how long someone so deeply asleep might take to wake.

"Beautiful," River said as she walked toward him, and before Mal or Zoë could react she was across the room and standing at the base of the pedestal. She stared up at the man.

He did not appear to notice their presence. Slowly, he lifted his hands and started drawing wires and tubes from his body, barely flinching as they emerged from veins in his arms and slits in his sides. He unclicked several interfaces from ports in his head, where angry red flesh had grown around the attachments. Spurts of a clear, viscous fluid accompanied each disconnection. When the final wire was pulled from his throat he stood upright in his pod, swaying slightly, kicking aside networks of cables and clear tubes, and stretched his arms toward the ceiling. Like a dead man finding life again, he groaned, twisted, going up on tiptoes, and with each twist and turn Mal heard his bones clicking and popping. Light glimmered from the knotted muscles on his bare arms and legs. He looked like a wild animal, preening, readying itself to pounce. Then he stood motionless, staring forward and still apparently unaware of them standing there watching him. Unaware, or uncaring.

So strong after so long, Mal thought, but then the man's calm, measured poise faltered. His hands began to shake, and then the shiver traveled up his arms to his shoulders, torso, and head. He went to crouch and slipped, falling onto his side on the pod's open lid, sliding to the raised dais, and dropping to the floor. He hit with a hard thud, landing on his shoulder and hip. He remained curled into a fetal position, hands clasped before his face, eyes wide and staring.

River went to him and knelt by his side. Mal rested his hand on his gun.

"I sang to you," she said. "Did you hear?"

The man did not answer. He was looking into some distance none of them could see, perhaps still immersed in whatever dreams had haunted him during his deep, deep sleep. What were the Alliance doing with a man like this in this out-of-the-way place? Why had they gone to such great lengths to transport and keep him here?

What might happen now that he was awake?

Mal's hand remained on his gun, ready to draw it at a moment's notice. He saw that Zoë was equally prepared. If this man was anything like River, his reactions upon waking from suspension might be unpredictable at best.

The sides of his head were shaved, and Mal could make out a series of regular holes stretching from behind his ears and down toward his shoulder blades. There were similar wounds in his throat and at his temples.

"That from the suspension pod?" Zoë asked.

"I'd say not," Mal said.

"They look red-raw."

"This is something else. Suspension pod, for sure, but more than that. He was being contained."

"He isn't anymore."

The man didn't react to their voices, not even River's. She spoke soft words that Mal couldn't quite hear, and the man only shivered as if cold, his stare never breaking. Whatever he was looking at, Mal hoped he never clapped eyes on it himself.

"Wash?" Mal asked. "Status on that destroyer."

"Closing, but cautiously. Whatever you're doing, I'd suggest stopping and getting back to *Serenity*. We're docked quite nicely, and I've powered down all but vital circuits so that we're running silent, so their sensors shouldn't pick us up. But they'll see us as soon as they're close enough."

"Stand by." He looked at Zoë, frowning.

"We don't have long," she said. "River?"

River did not turn or reply.

"River, we have to leave. He can come—"

"Whoa, now!" Mal said.

Zoë raised her hands, silently asking him what else they could do.

"We're already carrying two fugitives from the Alliance," he said.

"So what's one more?" Zoë asked.

"One more we know absolutely nothing about," he said. "I'm not about to take a stranger onto my ship." *Especially not more than a stranger*, he thought. *No way. No how.*

"Si..." the man said. He had trouble speaking. His throat convulsed, as if he was trying to force something out, and his head nodded against the floor. "Si... Silas. I am Silas." His eyes were still wide and afraid, but Mal saw something—a brief glimpse to the left and right, a rapid flutter as if taking in his surroundings and assessing them all—that gave him pause.

"You really are," River said. "I'd hoped, I wondered if you were real. My name is River. I sang you awake. Did you hear me? I sang my song, and I think it was your song too."

Silas fixed her with his gaze and slowly sat up, resting back against the pedestal. He glanced at Mal and Zoë over River's shoulder, then stared at her again. His eyes were glassy, unfocused, rolling.

"River?" he asked.

"That's me. That's my name… Silas." She smiled and nodded, as if tasting the name afresh. "Silas." She reached out and ran her fingers down one side of his neck, fingertips running over the raised, swollen wounds where wires or tubes had been inserted. "I know this." She touched her own neck where the pale shadows of old scars marred her skin. "You're just like me. I heard about you, back at the Academy. You were a story. A myth. A *legend*. The first one they made like us. The one where everything went wrong."

"Everything went right," Silas said. "I'm awake. Awake and alive."

"Yes, both of us," River said.

"Or maybe I'm still dreaming." Silas went to stand, pushing himself up against the pedestal. "I've been here, asleep, for so many years. Or decades. Or longer. Maybe I'm still here."

From somewhere deep and distant Mal felt a thud that traveled up through his feet. Another, and another, and then from nearby a gentle stutter of machinery starting up. Zoë looked panicked, and Mal worried for a moment that the room's defenses were initiating themselves once again. But this was something different.

"Kaylee?" Mal said. "You been playing with something you shouldn't have?"

"Not me," she said.

"Any idea what we're feeling?"

"Could be local life support," she said. "Could be the ship's engines firing up. It's so vast it's difficult to tell without going there."

"We're not going there," Mal said. "We're leaving. Us and one more passenger."

"One more?" Jayne asked.

"Oh, you'll like this one, Jayne," Zoë said.

"So alive," Silas said again, and as he turned in a slow circle lights burst into life around the room, high up on the curved ceiling and low down closer to the floor. He started shaking again, and his smile transitioned into fear once more. He held out his arms and River hugged him close.

"*He's* doing that!" Zoë said. "All those wires and pipes are gone, but he's still linked to the ship somehow."

Mal couldn't disagree. As Silas turned, so the tech around the room turned on, as if urged alive by his glance. *Somethin' to do with his waking*, Mal thought. *Maybe even somethin' defensive.*

"He looks terrified," Zoë said.

"I think he's bluffing," Mal said, and when Zoë glanced at him, confused, he shrugged. "I play cards. I know the tells."

"He's just confused," River said.

"How did you find me?" Silas asked, and before Mal could urge otherwise, River replied.

"We followed a map."

Silas smiled weakly. "The map." He frowned and slumped against her.

"I'll help you. I'll sing you back to health."

"Singing or not, we have to do it on the move," Mal said. "The Alliance are close."

River seemed to understand the urgency at last. She held Silas's hand and urged him away from the dais and the suspension pod that had been his home for an unknown amount of time. He was hesitant at first, but after taking an initial faltering step he took another, then another. He wore only the plain shorts and T-shirt, and his bare feet crunched onto debris on the floor. He gave no sign of noticing. When after a few steps he paused and swayed, River held him up beneath the arms.

When Mal caught Silas's eye, he saw something there that reminded him of River. A hint of confusion, but deeper down a knowledge and wisdom that made all around them seem like children.

He didn't like any of this one bit.

The pair reached the edge of the room and the open doors, and it took all of Mal's self-control not to flinch back. Silas smelled cool and stale and he projected a strength, a power, that belied his weakened appearance.

As they left the room and headed back toward *Serenity*, Zoë took point and Mal brought up the rear, with River supporting a weak Silas between them. With everything getting so mixed up and troubled, he tried to put his finger on just what had changed, and what was disturbing him so much. It took until they reached the small rest room where he and Zoë had taken on the two drones before he realized.

The ship was no longer dead. Silas had woken, and the *Sun Tzu* had woken with him.

Mal couldn't help thinking that neither had ever been meant to happen.

10

We are woken by someone pressing the buzzer on the door comm. That is unusual. It wakes us before our normal time, and we sit up and look around, confused and groggy from our disrupted rest. Our room's dimensions seem slightly altered, the colors and shapes out of sync with reality. We feel sleep flittering away from our senses as reality settles around us, and we fold back the blankets and stand on the cold floor.

The buzzer sounds again. One of us shouts a response and goes to the door. Whoever is sounding the buzzer would never enter without our permission, and we keep our door carefully closed and triple-locked from the inside. It's not possible to sense nervousness through the impersonal electronic buzz, but still it is there, as if the sound is a troubled exhalation or the meaningless rattle of unspoken, unwished-for words.

We open the door. There is an ensign standing there, a small man in Alliance uniform. He takes a step back when the door opens, even though he has seen and served us many times before. His name is Stannard.

We do not like being awoken before our usual time. It disrupts rhythm, and rhythm runs our lives. We wake, we eat, we wait, we sleep, and so it has been for many years. Sometimes we have tasks that disrupt us from the ordinary, and for a while we breathe different air, or experience different locations. But we are not wired to be concerned with boredom. Our main reason for being always persists—to be here, ready, in case the unthinkable happens.

The waiting is sometimes tiresome, but far better than the alternative.

Stannard looks more nervous than he should, we think, and even as his eyes flicker down to our blue-gloved hands and up again to our faces, we see that it is more than our presence disturbing him. Stannard has come to tell us some troubling news.

"Has he risen?" we ask. It is the first thing we think about. *Always* the first.

"No," Stannard says, frowning. "At least, we don't think so."

"Think? It's we who are here to do the thinking. You and your like do the doing. Why have you woken us?"

"The ship has come online. A signal has been sent. A security breach, but that doesn't mean—"

"Of all the things it could be, he is the most likely," we say. We take a deep breath, our first beyond the knowledge that something terrible might have happened. "Haven't we told you that before?"

"No... no you haven't." Stannard is sweating. Thin, slight, he is wiry and strong, but in front of us he is like a child.

"We shouldn't need to," we say. "The ship holds him. Whatever goes wrong with the ship is because of him. Any other possibility is meaningless."

"There's no indication—"

"You did well to wake us," we say. "We'll need to open up our lab. You can take us there. Wait, while we dress."

The ensign waits just outside the open door. He averts his eyes, but we see him glancing once or twice, catching glimpses that he might carry away with him to tell his crewmates, or his family back home, or perhaps his grandchildren if he lives long enough to sire them. We are similar, but not identical, in thought as well as appearance. One of us is taller and has reddish hair, the other strong limbs and green eyes. Head down, still he looks up and sees us both. We don't mind.

He might be awake, we think, and a frisson of fear passes through us. It's a strange experience, and difficult to recognize. We were not involved in his creation, because it was before our existence, but we were tasked with his incarceration. Too precious to destroy, too dangerous to hold close, the old ship from generations past was deemed the perfect place in which to hide him far away from the Core using ancient suspension devices superior to our own. The ship was made to look derelict. We hoped he would be safe.

The first of his kind, he has never been bettered. But out of sight does not mean out of mind, and the Academy has spent years attempting to create his like again, with little immediate success.

A small part of us feels a shimmer of excitement at the chance to see him once more. But mostly all we feel is fear. We have always been prepared, and now we must ensure that Silas is put back down.

Dressed and ready, we reach beneath our cots and bring out two heavy steel cases. Usually we would carry one each and make our own way to the laboratory, but this morning is different.

"Enter," we say. Stannard steps inside and we give him one of the cases to carry.

"But…" he says.

"One of us will carry the second case. You lead the way."

As we follow Stannard through the corridors and up and down staircases toward the lab near the destroyer's engine rooms, we fill the time ensuring that everything is happening as intended.

Yes, we're scanning for strange signals.

No, there's no sign of other ships having approached the planet.

Yes, we're activating remote scanners in the rings to search for movement other than the Sun Tzu.

"We are closing in on the ship?"

"Of course."

"All weapon systems are online and fully functional?"

"Yes."

"Good."

"You think we might need them?" Stannard asks.

We do not answer. Not because we don't know, but because we do.

We reach our lab and Stannard waits while we open the door. We come here every day, but this feels different. The lab smells older, more stale, as the door opens, and the lighting seems more subdued. We are concerned with how fear is coloring and tainting our senses.

We do not reveal that fear on the outside. That would be unprofessional and counterproductive.

Once we are inside he follows and deposits the case on one of two large tables. The rest of the lab is clear and clean, surfaces bare and polished, cupboards closed and locked with biomechanical security. There are screens on two walls displaying nothing, and a series of colored markers hang unused next to whiteboards.

Everything we need is in the two cases.

We each stand at a table and place our blue-clad hands on the cases' shiny exteriors. We notice that Stannard is still inside the lab. He's retreated to the door but is still watching us, eyes wider than usual, his stance a little more confident. He's been inside before, but he has never carried one of our cases, and has never been so close to either of us.

Maybe he thinks he's becoming something like a friend.

"You can go," we say, and we stare at him until he backs through the doorway and it whispers shut behind him.

We turn our attention to the cases, open them, and only then do we look at each other, and only then do we allow the inner fear we have been feeling to manifest.

"We can hold him down," we say, as if to convince ourselves.

"Yes, if he's risen, we can hold him down."

We set to work.

Later, the door chimes and Stannard's voice brings news that changes everything.

"We've found evidence of another ship docked against the *Sun Tzu*. We're still too far away to get any accurate readings, and the rings are disturbing our sensors, but there's definitely something there of a different construction and origin."

"Hurry," we say. "We need to get there quicker."

"The commander says to tell you we're going as fast as we can," Stannard says. "The rings around the planet make anything but a slow approach dangerous."

"Dangerous?" we ask. "You have no idea what that means. Hurry. *Hurry!*"

One of us emits a shuddering sigh of fear. We don't know which one.

"Really, Jayne?"

"What?"

"*Really?*"

Kaylee was relieved that Jayne hadn't stooped to robbing the corpses in the suspension halls. She didn't think he was that low, but he'd worried her for a while when he'd gone looking. Some Earth-That-Was jewelry was in circulation throughout the 'verse, handed down from generation to generation and usually held as precious and private, and she knew that many of these items were worth a small fortune. She was thankful that she hadn't seen any gleaming or glittering on any of the withered bodies in those failed pods. If she had, and Jayne had seen it too, she suspected they might still be in that great hold.

It meant that they'd left all their precious metals and stones somewhere secure when they were being prepared for their long sleep and journey. Jayne would obviously realize that, but the ship was so huge it might take weeks or months of searching to discover where these stores might be. They didn't have weeks or months. From the sound of growing panic they'd heard in Mal's voice, could be they only had minutes.

Jayne, ever resourceful, had still found something worth dragging back to *Serenity*.

"Clothes? Books? Tins of food?" Jayne carried a backpack over each shoulder, still keeping his hands free so that he could reach for his guns. Though he was strong, she could see how the bags were weighing him down. She found it difficult to understand his priorities.

"People love Earth-That-Was clothes," he said. "Got a few items myself, over the years. And these tins of food are antiques."

"They all look the same. You don't even know what's in 'em!"

"Five-hundred-year-old food, Kaylee. No one's gonna eat that. They just like having the tins." He frowned, shrugged. "Mayhap the mystery of it keeps them intrigued."

"That's pretty deep for you, Jayne."

"I am deep."

"Just don't let it slow us down." She turned and led the way, ignoring the sarcastic expression she'd seen forming on Jayne's face. She knew what he'd been about to say. *So go on ahead and look after yourself*, or words to that effect. It was the last thing she wanted to do, but the first thing she would do if Jayne tried anything stupid. There were a thousand places where he could stop to top up his haul, and she had to make sure they moved quickly and safely.

Yet five minutes later, it was not Jayne that brought them to a halt.

"I'm sure this is the way we came," Kaylee said, pointing at the closed doors.

"I'm pretty sure too." He placed his backpacks gently on the floor and drew his gun, turning his back to the blast doors closed across the corridor in case it was the sign of an ambush. By whom or what Kaylee didn't know, but she was glad to see Jayne still prioritizing their safety above the relics.

"Whatever's happened to initiate these systems on the *Sun Tzu* must've caused some of these old doors to close, but…" She moved closer and examined the door control panel. It looked odd, protruding from the wall, and she realized it was not as old as she'd expected. In fact, like those new doors around the ship's damaged area, she recognized many of the components. "Oh, shiny! This is Alliance stuff too."

"How is that shiny?" Jayne asked.

"Because it means I know how to bypass it." Kaylee took out her small tool pouch and set to work. "The old tech we've seen is weird, all those wires and junctions, and squiggly bits I don't understand. Weird, but fascinating. But this…" The components and controls were familiar, and in moments the old doors squealed open into ungreased recesses and let them pass.

"New tech on an old ship," Jayne said. "What's the point in that?"

"Retrofitting," Kaylee said. "The Alliance taking advantage of the old structures to make use of the ship for—"

"You all got your ears on?" Mal said through their comms, interrupting her.

"Here, Mal," Kaylee said as she worked, and Wash also confirmed that he was listening.

"We found someone," Mal said. "Someone alive. Reckon he's the reason this ship's here. Says his name's Silas, and he an' River…"

Jayne and Kaylee stared at each other. "He and River what?" Jayne prompted.

"It's almost like they know each other," Zoë said, quietly. "From what she was sayin' to him, they're from the same place."

"Everyone back to *Serenity*," Mal said. "Alliance is closing in, so let's keep quiet 'til we're on board and away from here."

Kaylee and Jayne moved on and encountered several more closed doors blocking the corridors, all of which Kaylee managed to open in moments. If it had been the old, original tech controlling the doors she didn't think she'd have been able to resolve them so quickly, although she'd have relished the opportunity to try. To have her hands on components that her ancestors might have assembled made her feel as if she occupied the same space as a ghost from the past. She wanted to touch more of the ancient tech, hold it in her hands, feel the weight, the surfaces still greasy after all these centuries.

There was no time.

She felt the greatest thing she had ever found slowly slipping away, and as they moved she did her best to take everything in. Some of the lighting panels were open, diffusion covers gone, modern glow-elements exposed and fitted into fixtures half a millennium old. She paused at one rattling air duct and shone her suit torch through the grille to see a new fan spinning on an old spindle. At one corridor junction a duct cover lay on the floor and a mass of wires spewed out like spilled guts. Fixed within their snipped and stripped mass were three modern joint boxes, multi-gauge devices that used a basic form of AI to track and connect relevant wires and conduits as and when they were activated. The meeting of new and old fascinated her; the knowledge required to do this was staggering. They might be Alliance, but the people who'd done this had amazing minds.

With the ship humming and vibrating, and a low level of lighting shining throughout the corridors and rooms, halls and stairwells, Kaylee saw plenty of places where this new tech had supplanted or replaced old. Jayne probably didn't notice, and she thought most of the crew wouldn't either. This was her treasure trove, and she was leaving it all behind.

But she already felt close to this ship. Doors opened for her, and her understanding of the new Alliance tech merged and melded with very old Earth-That-Was engineering gave her the sense that the ship was growing to welcome her. It was a strange feeling, and nothing even approaching the sense of rapport she had with her dear, battered Firefly, but it gave her some sense of comfort.

"The Alliance destroyer's skimming the rings," Wash said over the comm.

"I thought you'd shut down all non-essentials," Mal said, meaning scopes and scanners as well as most other systems on board *Serenity*.

"I did," Wash said. "My eyes are still working."

"You've got visuals?" Jayne asked.

"Either that or panoramic three-dimensional daydreams."

"Get ready," Mal said. "As soon as we're with you, we're leaving. Let's just hope the Alliance is more concerned with the *Sun Tzu* than with us."

"You know what the Alliance is concerned with," Zoë said. Her disembodied voice sounded loaded with meaning. *That man they've found*, Kaylee thought. Part of her wished she could see him, meet him. A bigger part hoped she never would. There was something spooky about a man sleeping on a ship of the dead, then waking when they arrived. As if he'd been waiting for them all along.

"Yes, but they won't know we've taken him onto *Serenity*."

"Wait, you're seriously bringin' him?" Jayne asked.

"No time for this," Mal said. "How close are you?"

"Pretty close," Kaylee replied. "Are you getting through corridor doors okay?"

"Silas is opening them," Mal said.

"Silas," Kaylee said. It had a strange, mythic ring to it. No one said any more, and the name hung over the open comms like an electronic echo. For a few seconds she heard it everywhere—in the whisper of an opening door, the vibrations beneath her feet, and the more distant rumbles of machines working in places she would never see. There was no telling what these rumbling machines were doing, nor whose calling had brought them to life.

Silas... Silas... Silas...

Mal moved from foot to foot and wished he had Kaylee with him. The four of them should have stuck together when they'd boarded, but he wasn't a man who dwelled on regrets too much. If he did he'd have been crippled by them.

"Having trouble?" he asked.

"Leave him," River said. "He's been through so much." She held Silas up with her left arm around his back, and touched the scars on her neck with her right hand as she said this.

Silas was slumped against a bulkhead, and the doors before them remained stubbornly closed even though he'd passed his hand across the surface sensors several times. This action had opened three previous sets of doors, but not this one.

Mal went to work on the door. As he crouched to the panel, Silas stood upright. From weak and slumped to strong and tall, he resembled a broken thing rejointed, a dead thing given life once more. He shrugged River's arm from around him, shoved Mal aside, and hovered his hand over the door control.

Mal staggered, then rested his hand on his gun. But something made him keep it holstered. Instinct, an urge to survive, he wasn't sure what.

"Back away!" he said to Zoë. She moved away from Silas, and River had fallen motionless, as if waiting for whatever might happen next.

Silas pressed his hand flat against the control panel. Sparks sizzled and flew. Mal froze, unsure what was happening and wondering why the door was not sliding or squealing open like the others. It was only as he realized that this was something different—this was not simply Silas opening another door—that he took a step toward him.

With a loud thud that pulsed into his ears and thumped up from the metal floor, everything went dark. The lights glowing from behind missing diffusion panels snicked off, leaving a brief, temporary glow from their elements that faded within seconds. Their suit lights also blinked off, and Mal felt the main power source in his suit fall silent and empty. It was a strange sensation, like having something living and huddled up against him die. He crouched ready to defend himself. He held a hand in front of his face and could not see even a shadowy outline.

Someone shouted. He thought it was River, but it might have been Zoë. She'd been down on the floor so close to Silas when the lights went out.

"Zoë!" Mal called.

"I'm here." In the pitch blackness, she sounded very far away.

"The door?" he asked.

"Open."

"River."

"Here…" River's voice seemed to fill the entire corridor. "…and gone. I'm here, and he has gone." She started singing a mournful song in a language Mal did not know and that he suspected was no real language at all, but rather an ebb and flow of textured sounds.

Behind her voice was silence. The background hum of the ship, and the vibrations he'd felt through his feet, had ceased, returning the *Sun Tzu* once again to a dead, cold place. Mal heard his own panicked breathing and that of Zoë and River, and in the distance a couple of soft, rhythmic slaps that might have been Silas's bare feet on metal. Other than that, silence.

"What's he done?" Mal asked.

"He's gone," River said again.

"I know he's gone!" Mal snapped, and he closed his eyes—though that made not even a slight difference to what he could and could not see—and breathed deeply a few times, trying to center himself, find a balance, and see away the panic.

"Mal," Zoë said, "your suit lights out too?"

"Dead as this ship."

"So how are we going to move?"

"I'm thinking on it." In truth he hadn't been—he'd been wondering why Silas had done this, who he was, and how much more dangerous than River he might be. He'd suspected that the man had been shamming when he acted weak and disorientated, and this seemed to confirm that. He'd thought he'd heard Silas moving into the distance, perhaps because the Alliance were closing, but what if he was still there? What if he remained close to them, very close, leaning in toward Mal so that soon he would be able to smell his breath, feel his long damp hair against his cheek?

Maybe Silas could see in the dark. That could be why he had done this, to give himself an advantage.

Mal drew his gun.

"Mal?" Zoë asked. She knew the sound of steel against leather.

"Just bein' cautious," he said.

"But he's just like me," River said. "He won't hurt you."

"That don't comfort me none," Mal said. It was strange talking in such total darkness, as if mind and body were disassociated. His voice floated free, and the link between mind and mouth—a link he had been informed many times was tenuous at best—felt less certain than ever.

"Wash?" Mal said, but as he'd suspected there was no reply. Upon waking Silas had somehow started some of the ship's systems, and he'd been able to open the corridor doors with a simple touch of his hand. He seemed to have a close affinity with the ship that had been his prison, and an ability to turn its resurrected systems to his own advantage. Now, he'd shut those networks down again, along with all other power sources. Mal's suit systems ran comms as well as lights, and both were out of order. The ability to do that, the power it might take, was staggering and terrifying.

"River, can you guide us back to *Serenity*?" Zoë asked.

"I can follow Silas."

"Is he going to *Serenity*?" Mal asked, a cool, solid knot of fear settling in his gut. *If he gets to the ship and takes it and leaves us here...*

"Not just yet," River said. "I don't think... not just yet. Maybe later."

She sounded uncertain, almost dreamy. "River, if he's just like you, maybe you know what he's doin'. Does he mean us harm?"

"Take my hand," River said, and that was no real answer. Mal felt cool fingertips stroke his cheek. He flinched, shocked, and his finger tightened on the trigger. He stepped back away from her touch, feeling a moment of deep desperation. How the hell were they going to move anywhere like this? The thought of being led through this dead old ship while holding on to River's hand chilled him to the core. Putting his trust in her was something he could not do, because he rarely put his full trust in anyone. Even his crew. Even Zoë.

"Take mine," Zoë said to the girl, and it was as if she was reading Mal's mind. He let out a silent sigh of relief as he felt Zoë also hold on to his hand. He knew her touch, and recognized the warmth transmitted between them.

They started moving, and Mal had to fight the urge to stay still, crouch down, and hold his gun ready to lift and fire at the first sound. Deep animal instinct told him they shouldn't be trying to walk through these spaces that were darker than the Black. Yet not only did they move, but quickly. He thought about how River knew the way to go, and how to steer them safely, and he didn't like it one little bit. He was very aware that she was special— nothing like him, or the rest of the crew, or even her brilliant, cold brother Simon. Now if what she said was right, it seemed that she and Silas had a lot in common. Thinking that she was something more than them just spooked the hell out of him.

Something thudded through his feet. At first he thought it was the impact of Zoë's or River's steps just ahead of him, a vibration transmitted through the solid metal floor. Then they paused and the feeling came in again, part sensation, part sound. It was a hesitant clicking, like a motor starting, jamming, and stopping again. A light rattling noise carried on the air, and then further along the corridor a low light flashed several times—on and off, on and off.

"What's happening?" Zoë asked.

"Dunno. Let's keep our wits about us," Mal said. Comms

crackled, and disembodied voices croaked and whispered. He couldn't tell who they were, or even if they were someone he knew. Mal was a rational man, but in this deep darkness on an ancient ship of the dead and gone, he couldn't help thinking of ghosts.

With a final heavy thud the lights came on again, and though the illumination levels were the same as before they seemed blinding, surging on and flooding the corridors and walkways with bright, unfiltered light. Their suit power was reinstated like a mother's warm embrace.

Mal swore and covered his eyes, then squinted and turned in a circle, gun aimed out ahead of him. There was just the three of them, and then empty corridors ahead and back the way they'd come. Silas truly had gone.

The bulkheads and floor shook with a heavy, short shiver, and then the hum and vibration of distant machinery settled down once again.

"So is that him too?" Mal asked, and his answer was a panicked voice breaking in over the comms.

"—close, and they've seen *Serenity*, there's a shuttle closing. It'll take a minute for *Serenity*'s systems to wind up again, and even if I did take off I'd lay good money on them blowing me to pieces in seconds. And I'd win the bet. And I wouldn't be here to collect."

"Wash, we've been offline for a good while."

"Tell me something I don't know."

"How close is the destroyer?"

"Close enough for me to count its guns. The answer being very close. And lots."

"Lots?"

"Of guns."

"Sit tight," Mal said. He looked at Zoë, desperate and wide-eyed, but she had nothing to offer him. *This is all on me*, he thought.

"Wash, you can't let them take my ship."

"My thought exactly," Wash said, "for about three seconds. But I can't fight them off because, well, I have no weapons, and an Alliance destroyer has approximately three thousand ways to blow me to atoms. And I can't outrun them, probably not in a straight race, and definitely not starting from a powered-down standstill."

"Maybe you should try to out-talk them," Jayne said over the comm. "You're fair good at that."

"Oh, right," Wash said, and he sounded distracted.

"No wise-ass comeback?" Jayne asked.

"Jayne, shut up," Mal said. "Wash? What's got your attention now?"

"Something that should soon get yours," Wash said. "There are at least five shuttles heading down toward the *Sun Tzu*. Five that I can see, anyway."

"Is now the time to ask how many soldiers those shuttles can carry?" Kaylee asked.

"Pack 'em in and forty to a boat," Mal said. "I reckon they're coming for him, not for us." He gauged how River looked at him. He was anticipating sadness, fear, and perhaps sorrow for the confused, dangerous Silas. What he actually saw was a smile.

"What's he doing?" Mal asked her.

"Being Silas," River said. "Being amazing."

"So we sneak back to the ship and hope they'll ignore it when we take off," Jayne said. "Sounds like a crappy plan."

"Didn't seem to bother you none with those bags over your shoulders," Kaylee said.

"Enough!" Mal said. "We're still in control here. Wash, keep comms open as long as you can. If they follow standard operating procedure, they'll block comms while they're boarding *Serenity*. But do what you can to stall them, and make sure Simon's hidden away."

"What about you?" Wash asked.

"We'll have to make it back to the ship as best we can. What comes after, we'll know once we get there." He closed comms for a moment and looked at River. "You said you and he are alike?"

"They made him and hid him away," she said. "Then they made me."

"Then you better start tellin' us what you think can be done."

11

Wash didn't like the feeling of *Serenity* sitting dead beneath him. The ship was a living, breathing thing, and he was used to her grumbles and hums, shakes and shivers. He sometimes viewed her as a big, dumb animal, strong and capable in her own right, but requiring him to edge and ease her where they wanted to go. He wasn't her master so much as her handler, and the sense of her lying dormant and motionless against the hull of the *Sun Tzu* was disturbing. He almost felt a form of grief. *Not dead, just dreaming*, he thought as he rushed back along the forward hallway, passing the crew quarters and heading into the dining area and galley.

"Doc?" he called. No answer. "Doc, you need to hide!" Wash stood there for a moment listening to the unusual silence around him. *Serenity* was rarely this quiet.

"Doc!" Wash wanted Simon to answer if only to break the silence, but the truth was already hitting home. Not only had River escaped the ship, the Doc had gone after her. It hardly came as a surprise.

He ran through the galley to the aft hallway, then down the gangways to the infirmary. The stillness and silence persisted. He checked storage cupboards and the passenger dorms, then climbed up to the catwalk and checked the door indicators on the port and starboard shuttle docks. Closed and locked up, as they had remained since Inara's departure.

"Doc!" he shouted one more time. If he was still on board there'd be no reason not to answer, so Wash ran back to the bridge, assuming he was alone.

He checked the proximity scanners and saw that the combat shuttle was so close he could almost reach out and touch it. He moved in front of the control console and craned his neck to look from the window, just as the shuttle passed overhead and turned neatly to face *Serenity*, almost nose to nose.

Difference was, the nose of the Alliance shuttle was spiky with guns.

Heart thumping, Wash backed up to the console, touched a control, and isolated a comm direct to Mal.

"Mal, Simon's also left the ship."

"Understood."

"And I'm face to face with our friends."

"Good luck, Wash. When we reach you—" The signal burst apart with a loud, squealing crunch. Wash winced and circled back around the console, dropping into his chair and covering his ears. He knew what had happened—the Alliance had taken over the ship's comm systems—and he also knew what he was about to hear.

"Hands away from the ship's controls! All members of your crew should disarm and prepare to be boarded. Change airlocks over to manual, or we will blow them from outside and you'll risk catastrophic decompression."

Wash could even see the Alliance soldier doing the talking. He was sitting in the shuttle's second mate's seat, a big, imposing figure who'd likely remain seated while directing his troops to do the dirty, dangerous work. He was probably ugly too.

He knew he didn't have very long. He swayed a little in his chair, rolled his eyes up—feigning faintness in case they were using a magno-scanner and could see him better than he could see them—and dropped to the floor behind the console.

"Attention! Remain in sight! Prepare to be boarded!"

Wash crept his hand up onto the console and, without looking, switched the external airlocks in the main door and above and behind the observation window over to manual. At least then the Alliance had the option of entering without using explosives, though from previous experience he knew this didn't necessarily guarantee that they would.

He wished Zoë were here. She was good with a gun or knife, or with her fists if it came to that. Most of all, he wanted to hug her to him, feel her warmth, know that whatever happened the two of them were in this together, and to the end. One of his greatest fears was that one of them would die without the other by their side. It was a dangerous 'verse, and their choice of employment filtered even more danger into their path and through their days and nights. If that was their fate, he selfishly hoped he'd go first. He couldn't imagine living without her.

"Remain in sight!" the voice said again.

Wash could already hear the heaving, clomping impacts of magnetic boots across the ship's exterior hull, and soon the soldiers would be activating the airlocks and entering *Serenity*. If they came in through the EVA hatch above the observation lounge, he'd have a minute at most. If they decided to blast the cargo doors for the sake of speed, and forego the comfort of an airlock, he'd die in seconds from the intense cold, or his blood would freeze in his veins, or perhaps his heart would explode from the sudden change in pressure. If he wasn't thrown around the bridge and battered to death. Damn, he loved space. So many interesting ways to die.

What would Zoë do? he wondered, and it was as if she answered immediately. He didn't actually hear her voice, yet her sweet and confident tones galvanized him into action. Crawling out of the bridge and through the open doors, he went down the stairs into the hallway headfirst, then stood and ran back toward the engine room. He passed quickly through the dining area, expecting to hear the hiss of an opening airlock at any moment, then slid down the ladder that led to the main reactor room.

This was Kaylee's territory, a functional space with splashes of color where she hung her light lanterns and scarves, and the hammock where she sometimes slept when the ship needed attention, as if she were nursing a sickly child through the night. Kaylee's stamp was everywhere here, but Wash knew his way around the accelerator core well enough to be able to remove a vital settlement node. He snapped up a multi-tool from one of Kaylee's tool rolls and unscrewed and unbolted the node, careful not to nudge any of the delicate wire sensors inside. It was the size of his fist, and the reactor would not work without it.

Wash hid the node beneath a floor panel. He stood back and looked at the panel from several angles, making sure he could place where he'd hidden it.

"Gotta remember this, Hoban Washburne," he muttered, and then he sensed rather than saw movement in the doorway behind him.

"Keep nice and still," the voice said, "and I won't have to blow your back out through your chest."

Wash dropped the small multi-tool and raised his hands.

"What're you doing back here?"

"Accelerator coolant leak," Wash said. "Had to bypass the compression coil and check the grav dampener isn't, er… check the filaments were in line and the catalyzer wasn't spilling too much dense fluid otherwise—"

"Shut up and turn around! Nice and gentle. I don't like space walks, my ass is itching and I can't reach it in this suit, and all that makes my trigger finger twitchy."

Keeping his hands high, Wash turned around to face the Alliance trooper. He was a short, angry-looking sergeant, and behind him was a female private who also had her gun leveled at Wash.

"Where are the crew?" she asked.

"Not here."

"We can see they're not here!"

"Over there." Wash nodded to his right. "On the ship."

The sergeant glanced to his left, but the private took another step into the engine room and shouted, "Hands high!"

Wash stretched higher, breathing deeply.

"Don't try to distract us!"

"I wasn't," he said. "Look, I'm just the pilot."

"Then what're you doing back here?" the sergeant asked.

"I told you, coolant leak." He saw the sergeant glance to one side, and heard the faint chatter of radio comms in his earpiece.

"Back to the bridge," the sergeant said. "Private Harksen is right behind you. Any tricks, any movements, any surprises from out of the shadows, and you'll be blasted. Got that?"

"No tricks, no surprises," Wash said, but as they left the engine room he thought, *I hope Simon really has left the ship.*

There were several other Alliance soldiers on board. They'd entered through the airlock above and behind the galley area, and they stalked *Serenity* in pairs. Wash knew it would take them hours to search the entire ship thoroughly. Anything that occupied them and kept their weapons not pointing at him was a good thing.

Once back on the bridge, Private Harksen nudged him into his pilot's seat. She scanned the panels, then threw the switch that disabled ship-to-ship comms. They'd already be blocking them, as well as the crew's suit-to-suit communications, so she was just making sure. "Keep your hands away from the controls," she said.

"Naturally." Wash folded his hands in his lap. He was nervous but not scared. They'd been boarded by Alliance before and survived to tell the tale.

Yet something about this felt different.

The sergeant stood back through the doors at the head of the stairway, communicating with others on *Serenity* as they conducted their search. Wash found it odd that they'd not asked him for whatever they were looking for, but maybe they were just ensuring that the ship really was clear of other crew.

"So you fixed the problem?" Private Harksen asked. She was standing behind the captain's chair, gun still pointing at Wash's chest.

"You mean the…"

"In the engine room. The problem. Fixed?"

"Fixed," Wash said.

"So this bird's ready to fly?"

"Ready."

Private Harksen nodded, glancing left and right. She was nervous. That's what was different about this, Wash realized. She and her sergeant were bullish and aggressive as Alliance soldiers always were, but something else was settled behind their eyes. Nervousness.

Wash eyed the access hatch to the escape pod above the bridge. If things went south with these grunts on board, it would take him too long to get there. He'd be humped.

"We good in here?" the sergeant said as he entered the bridge, and Wash expected the private to be evasive, keeping their conversation to herself.

"Ship's ready to fly, and he's the pilot," Harksen said, pointing at Wash with her gun.

"Good. Stay here, stay ready. He doesn't move to eat, sleep, or piss, and neither do you. Understand?"

"Affirmative, sir."

"Good. And don't kill him unless you absolutely have to."

With the man who must be Silas so close to them, Kaylee couldn't even bring herself to speak. Jayne had heard too, but he was more cocky and brash than her, and far more likely to give them away. So she grasped his arm and pulled him down beside her. She switched off her comm and indicated that he should do the same, eyed the bags over his shoulders, wondering how many ways they could make a noise—bash against the bulkhead, contents clanging together, thumping on the floor if he dropped them. She breathed through her mouth because it sounded quieter.

Why am I so terrified to give myself away? she wondered, confused at why they'd both felt the compulsion to hide. Silas had not done Mal and the others any harm when he outed the power and fled, but then they had River with them. And when Kaylee stole another glance into the large open space, she realized why she was so afraid. His name was Silas, Mal had said, and he might have been asleep for a long time, though not as long as the rest of this ship. The Alliance had placed him all the way out here, away from everyone and everything, too precious to destroy, too dangerous to keep awake.

Now he slept no more.

Silas remained standing in the center of the large space. It was a vestibule of some sort, with a high domed ceiling and at least six corridors converging from different directions. They hadn't come this way, and Kaylee had been about to berate Jayne for his navigational skills when she'd heard fast footsteps approaching. The acoustics of the domed room made it difficult to tell which direction they were coming from, so Kaylee had led them to the edge where the curved wall met the floor.

Silas was short, lean, dressed in simple T-shirt and shorts. His skin was glimmering with moisture or some kind of gel, and she saw scars and marks on his neck and throat. Something about his bearing also seemed familiar, and it didn't take her long to recognize why—so much about him reminded her of River.

She and Jayne were hunkered down behind a chest-high pedestal, which might once have been some sort of reception desk, or perhaps even a bar. There were piles of papers stacked in a recess beneath the desk, and maybe they contained the names of the crew, even pictures. Though in danger she was curious, but now was not the time to look. Kaylee pressed her fingers to her lips, and Jayne nodded. Did he look afraid? She wasn't sure she'd ever seen him looking *truly* afraid, or if he ever could be. He rested his hand on his gun, but he knew not to draw it from its holster.

A deathly silence filled the space. Even though the ship's power had come on again, sending a rumbling whisper through the air, that somehow went to make the quiet even deeper, a solid thing hanging heavy around them.

Silas breathed in deeply, then exhaled with a heavy sigh.

He can smell me, Kaylee thought. *He'll know where we are, he'll come to us and—*

Jayne touched her arm and caught her attention. He cupped his ear and she did the same.

Someone, or something, was approaching.

Kaylee leaned to the side and peeked around the edge of the pedestal again. Silas seemed distracted, his head tilted to one side as if listening. As before, it was difficult for her to tell which direction the growing sound came from, but her imagination caught on fire, and she saw tunnels filled with crawling, scrabbling shapes, cadavers trailing pipes and tubes, still seeking their final destinations even though they had arrived in the 'verse long, long ago. She imagined their mouths drooping open in silent screams, and their long, cracked fingernails scratching along cold metal walls.

Her breathing came faster, and she blinked quickly to banish the image. When she opened them again she saw Alliance soldiers pouring out from one corridor into the open space.

They spread either side of the corridor entrance, and several of them crouched down and leveled their weapons at Silas. Others continued around the room's perimeter, half-encircling him. They were still wearing their full space suits and helmets, and they were all heavily armed.

Kaylee caught Jayne's eye, and he raised his eyebrows and hunkered down some more. She did the same. She could hear the crackling whispers of Alliance comms, a soup of voices from which she could discern no sense.

She shrugged at Jayne. *What do we do?*

He shrugged back. Touched his gun. Nodded up and away from them both. *There's going to be shooting.*

And then we can run, Kaylee thought, but she had no idea which direction to take. If she'd been the praying kind, she might have asked for salvation. Shepherd Book would have known the correct words, and the right way to say them.

"I've been asleep for so long that the whole universe is my dream," a voice said. Kaylee peered around the pedestal, looking past a pair of soldiers at Silas, still standing in the center of the room.

"You're completely surrounded in this room," one of the Alliance troopers said. "And beyond, you're also surrounded in this ship. And even if you escaped the ship, you'd be blasted into the Black."

"I know the Black so well," Silas said. His voice was deeper than Kaylee had imagined looking at him, edged with an age and wisdom that belied his physical appearance. "I was born into the light, but you took me away and cast me down into the darkness."

"I… have orders to ensure your safe recovery." The soldier in command no longer sounded so confident. Still crouched down low, Kaylee looked around the wide space at the soldiers around the room's edges. They were standing or crouched, and all of them were ready to fire. They were shifting from foot to foot, aiming their weapons but twitchy. She couldn't tell who was doing the talking, because they all looked the same in their space suits and helmets. She could not see their faces. She was glad.

A hand closed around her arm and pulled her back behind cover. She felt Jayne's breath on her ear, then heard his voice, soft and urgent.

"We gotta keep low and quiet," he said. "We gotta have no one knowing we're here. Especially *him*." She heard the fear in his voice, and her question was answered.

Yes, Jayne could be afraid.

"I am the only reality," Silas said. "My dreams are the only real place. Tell me, what does it feel like to be imaginary?"

The room fell silent as the question hung on the air.

"What does it feel like?" Silas asked again after a long pause.

"Er…" the commanding soldier said. He had nothing.

Kaylee's breath caught in her throat and she thought, *That was the end of something and the start of something new.*

After a shuffle of rapid movement, and the first gunshot, the screaming began.

Bullets whipped the wall above their heads, and Kaylee leaned against the back of the pedestal, hands pressed over her ears. The shock of the sudden violence, the noise, grasped a cool fist around her heart. Jayne leaned beside her, gun in his hand, eyes wide but aware. Shards and shrapnel rained down on her, and she heard more shouts and screams, more gunfire, the stomping of feet, the terrible crunching of bone audible even above the shooting, and a heavy wet thump as something landed close to them.

She made a mistake and looked. The soldier was still blinking, even though her helmet had been torn from her head, and that head wrenched from her neck. Her body lay further away, still connected by stretched skin, stringy ligaments, and a widening pool of blood.

"Oh—" Kaylee gasped, before Jayne tugged her toward him so she could no longer see.

"We gotta go," he said, and she knew he was right.

"He did that?" she asked.

"Looks that way. We've gotta *go*!"

Kaylee nodded. If they waited until this was over, maybe all they'd be was the final two victims. They had to leave now, while everyone else was dying.

A long, high scream rose up, echoing from the walls alongside the gunfire. It was cut off in mid-flow, but the shooting continued.

Crouching, gun in his right hand, Jayne counted down with the fingers on his left.

Three…

Two…

One…

They stood and ran, and for those few seconds Kaylee looked around the room at the chaos, the carnage, and more bloodshed than she had ever witnessed. Shock thumped at her, a heavy heat in her chest and gut, but she kept running, unable to unsee. She could smell and taste blood on the air. The mist of terror before her eyes was red.

It's like that time when River shot those men, she thought, because the speed and brutality of this felt the same.

Bodies of Alliance soldiers lay scattered around the room, some of them in pieces, steaming in pools of blood and sliding down the walls. Space suits were ripped and torn, helmets crushed. A couple still writhed and crawled, calling and reaching for help that would never come. Walls were torn and speckled with bullet holes, and here and there flames licked where incendiary rounds had been used. The few soldiers remaining alive were retreating up corridors, their continuing gunfire flashing and silhouetting them against their surroundings.

Silas was a flickering vision dashing back and forth across the room. He splashed through spilled blood and spread delicate footprints across the floor, sprang from walls, ducked into and out of corridor entrances, and wherever he paused for more than a heartbeat he left a dead or dying soldier behind. Kaylee heard bones breaking and crunching, but there seemed to be no pattern to how he killed. She saw him dispatch one man with a chop to the throat from behind, a knee in the back, and then a rapid movement that snapped his spine. Graceful, deadly, terrifying. He moved on to a woman carrying a heavy machine gun, seemingly dodging bullets as he danced and jumped from floor to wall and down again, knocking the weapon from her hand and catching it up as it bounced from the floor, turning it around and pressing the hot barrel to her face—

Kaylee managed to turn away just as the machine gun sang its deadly song.

She followed Jayne into an arched doorway and ran into him as he skidded to a halt. Looking past him she saw two soldiers trying to drag a third behind them, leaving a trail of blood from the injured man's shattered legs. He was groaning in pain, helmet knocked aside and face covered in blood, but when he saw them he gave one sharp shout and brought his gun up to bear.

Jayne shot him between the eyes. The armor-piercing round slammed his head back, and the two soldiers hauling him heard the shot even above the cacophony from behind them, felt the change of weight in their companion, and turned around. They would not hesitate, Kaylee knew. There would be no discussion, no conversing with them. Everything that moved and did not wear an Alliance uniform was an enemy.

Jayne shot them both in the throat above their armored suits. One fell onto her back, dropping her weapon and clasping both hands to the wound. The other staggered back but raised his gun, pulling his trigger as it came up and stitching a line of bullets across the floor toward them. Jayne shot him once more in the head, then he dispatched the other soldier with a similar shot.

Kaylee could hardly breathe through the shock. The deafening gunfire continued behind them, the domed room and corridors catching the echoes and bouncing them up and down, back and forth, until it sounded like one continuous, apocalyptic roar. Jayne's shots had hardly added to the noise, but Kaylee couldn't help thinking, *What if Silas heard?*

She shoved Jayne in the back, said, "We have to run!"

12

River has never felt so conflicted. She hates Silas for that, but in a way she loves him too. How can she not love someone whose dreadful trauma has made him her brother? Looking at him is like looking in a mirror and seeing her own eyes. They were created by the same forces, and her fervent hope was that Silas would be able to give her answers—why was she created? What did they do to her at the Academy? What is her purpose?

And yet she feels loyalty to her blood-brother and friends.

Simon is always there for her. Even now she has a feeling that he is on board the *Sun Tzu*, and if that's true then he has come solely to find her. Though he gives everything, he asks for nothing back.

The crew, too. They've become like an extended family to her, each in different ways. Acceptance has not been easy for them, and she can hardly blame them for that. Sometimes she finds it difficult to accept herself. What she has become—what she has been *turned into*—is something that is difficult to inhabit alongside her usual self. She knows so much more. She sees so much more. When necessary, she flows and moves with the grace of light, almost without the encumbrance of flesh and bone. All these experiences are strange, and here she hopes, with Silas, to find a way to accept and process them. To embrace them.

"Wait," Mal said. "Heads up. Hear that?"

Zoë listened.

"Kaylee?" Mal asked. "Jayne?" There was no answer. Their comms were down, and Wash had also gone offline. The Alliance must have blocked all communications that were not their own.

"*Hún dàn* Alliance," Mal said. "We're cut off. And can't you hear that gorramn noise?"

Zoë listened again, frowning.

"It's singing," River said. "Music flowing, and dancing, like ballet."

"Maybe you hear that, but I hear shooting."

"I might hear it too," Zoë said.

"So the Alliance are on board," Mal said. "They have *Serenity*, and now they've come for your friend."

"He wouldn't harm them unless they make him," River said, frowning.

"Intimidated the hell outta me," Mal said. "So what's his story? You brought us here to find him."

"The map brought you here." Sometimes when she looked like that, Mal saw so much more in her young woman's eyes. So much wisdom.

"You said he was just like you."

"He was the first of us, many years before," River said, and her eyes went distant, almost dreamy. "Those who made me, and others like me, thought they'd failed with Silas. We heard about him, stories whispered among test subjects, rumors passed in secret. And we realized that they hadn't failed at all. What they thought of as a mistake created something amazing. They were so scared of what they made that..." She paused and seemed to return to the moment.

"That they shut him away out here," Mal said.

"I never dared dream I might find him," River said. "I've come to help him, and ask him questions."

"About what?"

"About me," River said.

"Whatever's happening here is beyond us now," Mal said. "You might've come seekin' answers, and we came looking for valuables, but now we gotta concentrate on escaping with our lives."

"I vote we go away from the sounds of shooting and killing," Zoë said.

"*Serenity*'s that way."

"Then we go around."

"If they're threatening him, he'll be done by the time we get there," River said. "It's not a battle we're listening to."

"Then what is it?" Mal asked.

"It's just him moving on, and someone's in his way."

"Let's hope that someone isn't Jayne," Zoë said.

"Even Jayne ain't that stupid." Mal believed it, yet he couldn't shake the idea of Jayne standing up to Silas. Pride might make him do that. And stupidity. Jayne surely had enough of the latter to fill up three people, and then some.

"They're on their own just like we are," Zoë said. "Jayne and Kaylee'll head back to the ship."

"If it's even still there when we arrive."

"It'll be there," Zoë said. "Wash will make sure of that. And besides, it can't not be there."

"Why?"

"Because if it's gone, we're humped."

"I can get us to *Serenity*," River said.

"Maybe we're needing to find our own way," Mal said. He couldn't trust her, not normally, and certainly not now, when everything was far from normal.

River closed her eyes and pressed her hand to the bulkhead.

"I said, we'll find our own way."

"Mal, could be the girl—"

"Could be the girl can lead us right into that." He pointed along the corridor in the general direction of the echoing gunshots. At that moment, they ceased. The silence that replaced them was heavy. Mal heard his own breathing, and he rested his hand on the gun at his belt. "We move slow and careful. Keep our ears wide, and our eyes wider."

"And hope he doesn't turn out the lights again," Zoë said. "Ever felt you're being toyed with?"

"Too many gorramn times."

"Now that is a really, really big destroyer," Wash said. "I bet one of those makes a real mess when it explodes, eh?"

"Shut up," Private Harksen said.

"Or what? You can't kill me unless you absolutely have to."

"The sergeant said nothing about severe injury."

Wash nodded and sat back in his seat. Harksen definitely did look like she could hurt him, that was for sure. He wasn't someone averse to fighting if the need arose, and he'd been in enough scrapes in his time to claim a certain talent for the gun. However, Wash had always been more inclined to talk his way out of trouble. Zoë was usually there if more than words were needed. In Harksen, he saw that same simmering danger that was ever-present in Zoë.

He had to be careful. Truth was, he often talked so much that he just put himself deeper in trouble, rather than climbing out. Yet the captain definitely needed to know what was happening. Trouble was, Wash had no idea how to go about telling him without Private Harksen stopping him in his tracks.

Nestled down in the damaged crater on the surface of the *Sun Tzu*, his view over the ragged rim and out into deep space was now obscured by an Alliance destroyer. Smaller than the city-sized cruisers, still the destroyers were huge vessels, easily fifty times the size of *Serenity*, bristling with weapons, sensor arrays, and docking arms and bays containing combat shuttles and the smaller short-range enforcement vessels that did most of their dirty work in-system or in atmospheres. It looked mean and eager to cause injury to whoever might meet it face to face.

Next to the old Generation ship from Earth-That-Was, the destroyer looked like a child's toy.

Wash froze and caught his breath. The idea of toys gave him an idea. It was foolish, and stupid, but it was a passive attempt to communicate with Mal and the rest of the crew.

"Hey, do you like dinosaurs, by any chance?"

Harksen eyed him up and down, her weapon never wavering. It had been pointing at his seat since the sergeant left her on guard, and Wash read her as an efficient, well-trained soldier. A grunt, if he had to choose a term. But a good one.

"Huh?" Still the gun didn't waver, but she was unsettled now, and unsure what he was doing. He guessed that Private Harksen was more used to being shouted or shot at.

"Beasties from Earth-That-Was. I've got these little fellas. I've never really named them." He reached for the model dinosaurs he kept on his flight console. "I've had them here a while. They keep me company. This is a triceratops, I think, or a T. rex. And maybe this one is a stegosaurus. Or it could be they're the other way around?" He held one dinosaur in each hand, moving them back and forth, playfully butting their plastic heads as if they were having a fight.

As he lifted one model up and swished it through the air, he knocked the comm switch with the other, thinking, *I just hope they've canceled the blocking signal.*

"So do Alliance soldiers always carry guns like yours?" he asked. He hadn't been able to turn off the speakers, so if the comm channels had been opened successfully, these were the first words the crew would hear, and they'd hopefully be canny enough not to reply. *Just listen,* he thought. *And Jayne, if you can keep your mouth shut for just a short time, maybe this'll work.*

Private Harksen didn't even glance down at her gun. She didn't take her eyes off Wash and what he was doing, and while he didn't think she was suspicious of the dinosaur models, his actions had made her even more alert and on edge. He'd witnessed itchy trigger fingers before, and he didn't like provoking an itch, not one bit. He had to make this quick.

"Okay, don't want to answer that one. Can you tell me why that big destroyer is so close to the *Sun Tzu*, then? And down toward the stern too. Eh, what do we think about that, dinosaurs? And how come your sergeant only left you and a couple of others on board *Serenity*? Although you're the only one needed to guard me, I'll admit to that, I'm not happy being on the end of your gun."

A noise sounded over the speaker. It was a loud roar, but then it broke into a rattle of gunfire, a shout, running feet.

"Zoë?" Wash blurted out.

"What the hell—?"

He glanced back just in time to receive the butt of Harksen's gun on his nose. He fell back, gasping as the pain spread across his face and down his neck, and blood from his pulped nose flowed down over his open mouth.

Harksen turned off the comm again and spun Wash's chair

around, turning him away from the console. Wash could hardly see. His eyes watered, and the pain roared through his skull, hot and overwhelming. He wasn't a man who dealt well with pain, and that had been even more the case since Niska had taken and tortured him.

"I told you I was allowed to hurt you," Private Harksen said. "Next time it won't be so gentle."

Next time, Wash thought. *Damn, there better not be a next time.*

Despite the agony in his face, from what little he'd heard before Harksen knocked off the comms, it sounded like the others were in far more trouble than him.

Their suit comms crackled back to life as soon as the Alliance had completed boarding *Serenity*. And, Mal guessed, had landed on the *Sun Tzu*. It was their standard procedure, but it didn't comfort him one little bit.

Especially the first sounds that came through their earpieces.

"You heard that, Mal."

"I heard Wash filling us in on what's going on."

"And then he was hit."

"Hit, not shot." Zoë frowned at him. "Zoë, Wash has been hit before, and he was already ugly. He'll be fine."

"He better be," Zoë said. "I'd be lost without him. You know that, sir."

"I know that."

"Something's coming," River said, and those simple words uttered in her gentle, matter-of-fact voice sent a chill down Mal's spine. He didn't chill easy.

"*What's* coming?" he asked.

River frowned, listening, then crouched and pressed her hand against the floor. They were in another corridor, one that looked like any others they'd been in. Closed doors lined both walls, with thirty feet between each doorway. Mal wondered what was behind each door, and the mystery had been nipping at his heels as they ran. He was so frustrated that they didn't have time to explore further. It wasn't all about the loot anymore—not so much, anyway—but the knowledge as well.

"Oh…" River said, and then she started shaking. "Oh no, oh… two by two, hands of blue…"

"River?" Zoë asked. She knelt next to the girl and held her, perceiving instantly when she needed comfort. It was another reason Mal trusted and relied on Zoë so much.

"They're coming this way," River whispered, almost too quiet to hear.

"Those blue-handed guys?" Mal muttered. He'd heard of those blue-handed freaks from Ariel, and just how many Alliance personnel they'd brutally killed just to try and get to River. Zoë glanced at him, then behind him, and he turned to the nearest closed door in the corridor wall. He tried the opening pad and nothing happened, the workings were clogged with dust. He pulled his tools and got to work, but River's soft, desperate whimper and Zoë's calming tones put him on edge, and he dropped one of the implements. He moved quickly so that it bounced from his foot and didn't make too much noise.

"She's withdrawn," Zoë said. "Mal, she's somewhere else. I haven't seen her like this in ages."

"She's terrified," Mal said. He picked up his tools and set to work again, concentrating, breathing long and slow, trying to apply himself to *this* door and *this* lock and nothing else. No long, twisting corridor; no unseen battle in the distance; no trouble on *Serenity*, Alliance boarding; no vast, hulking ship that might very well become a drifting sarcophagus for them all.

No Hands of Blue. He felt sick even thinking of them, knowing what they were and what they could do.

With a click the locking mechanism shifted and the opening pad glowed red beneath the dust. Mal tapped it and the door ground open. He winced at the noise it made, then ushered River through. Zoë had to help her, and he saw with alarm that the girl was staring vacantly into the distance, unmoving.

Mal entered the room and hit the panel to close the door. It jammed halfway.

Zoë stared at him, wide-eyed.

River moaned again and broke from Zoë, retreating to the farthest extreme of the small room, curling into a ball in the corner. It was a sleeping quarters, with a bunk bed against each wall and a couple of easy chairs and table in the center. It had been vacated, with little left behind. Mal was glad. The last thing he needed now was a shriveled corpse in pajamas.

He tried the door again. Motors whined and ground. The leading edge shuddered and moved, but stuck again a hand's width from closing.

River's eyes were wide and staring at the door. The room's low-level lighting was on, and Mal tapped at the control and turned it off, plunging them into darkness. The only light in the quarters now was that filtering in from outside, a tall narrow band slanting in through the stuck door like a reaching arm.

Mal heard footsteps. He drew his gun, ready to shoot at a moment's notice. His heart was hammering, despite his attempts to calm himself. Zoë was pressed against one of the bunks away from the band of light, gun in hand, and River was barely a shadow in the corner of the room. There was one set of footsteps, but it carried a faint, confusing echo. *Two as one*, he thought, and then shadows flitted by the door and passed beyond. They were heading the same way as Mal and the others, toward the violence rather than away, and as they passed along the corridor he moved to the door and peered through the opening. He saw them from behind, moving from light to shadow, two tall, identically dressed women in dark clothing with hair tied up in buns, and hands clad in blue. They each carried something bulky in their right hand. They did not pause, but Mal still held his breath as they disappeared out of sight. He glanced back and forth from the corridor to River, watching for any sign of relaxation in her that might mean the blue-gloved pair had moved on.

Zoë caught his attention and raised her eyebrows. Mal indicated that they'd passed, and Zoë tapped her ear and leaned toward the doors. Mal nodded and listened. They were out of sight, but that didn't mean they were out of earshot, and perhaps they had sensed River and were even now creeping back along the corridor pressed tight to the wall, lurking closer.

There was no movement or sound outside, and when he glanced back at River she was slowly uncurling from the ball she'd hugged herself into. She crawled to the doorway and crouched below Mal, sniffing at the light slanting in.

"Gone away," River whispered, and she looked up at Mal. He saw the terror nestled in her eyes, and even knowing a little about what those blue-gloved freaks were capable of, he realized how brave she was being. He nodded and smiled.

"We've got you," he said.

"But who's got you?" she asked. She pulled herself to her feet. "They weren't looking for me. I don't think they know I'm here. It's him they want."

"That's a good thing for us," Mal said.

"But not for him."

"He's out of our control," Mal said.

"So would I be if it weren't for Simon. If it weren't for…" She glanced at Mal and he knew who she meant. Him, and the rest of the crew.

"He was in the Academy with you?" Mal asked.

"Long before me," River said. "He was their first. Their experiment. There was talk of a failure, but…" She shivered. "We knew of him as a legend, like a god. Or a devil."

"They're goin' the way we need to go," Mal said.

"Which means we change direction," Zoë said. "Right, sir?"

Mal thought about this for a while, and he felt a sense of restrained panic settling around him, the sort that always hovered but only really possessed him when he felt control slipping away.

"River," he said. She looked at him, frowned. "River?" He was really asking her now, and he saw a flicker of something other than fear in her eyes. It might have been gratitude, but he thought it was more likely pride.

"I want to help him," she said. "None of this is his fault. It's *their* fault. But we can't mix with the Hands of Blue," she said. "They have weapons that'll make your brains boil and eyes bleed from your skulls."

"Remind me to invite them next time we have a dinner party," Mal said. "Okay, so we find another way back to *Serenity*. Hopefully they'll be kept occupied with whatever that shootin' and screamin' was all about."

"Not Jayne and Kaylee," Zoë said, and it was a hope more than a statement. If she'd been of a godly bent, it would have been a prayer.

"Hopefully not. Back the way we came, then we'll jig along another corridor. Let's move."

* * *

We walk toward the firestorm, and we are pleased that the distraction is going so well. While Silas is slaughtering the soldiers, we are able to get closer, closer. There was the chance that a force of troopers would be able to take him down, but that chance was remote. It was always going to be us in the end.

The soldiers are bait.

As we near the site of battle, the shooting ends. We pause, silent and ready, and one of us looks at the schematics of the ship contained in our hand-held scanners. Heat traces are clear, but the activated systems on board are interfering with the readings. Thermal blooms grow and fade again, and in places whole areas of the ship are alight on the screen. We will have to rely on other means of detection.

"He'll still be close," one of us says.

"We should hurry."

"But with care."

We move forward, passing through areas of the old ship where we walked one time before, long ago, when we first imprisoned Silas here. He is our creation, but we realized quickly that he was far too dangerous to keep awake, and yet too remarkable to destroy. Out here, far from the Core, held in the grasp of one of the ancient yet advanced Earth-That-Was suspension devices, we always hoped that he would be safe. Between then and now little has changed, and we have always hoped that we would never be here again. He's not like the others. He was the first.

And he is far, far worse. We hoped that the soldiers would keep him occupied for longer, but there are plenty more on the way. We move quickly, cautiously, but by the time we reach the site of action we sense that he is long gone. All he has left behind is the evidence of his abilities.

The dead are everywhere. Even those shot cleanly through the heart have been torn and mutilated. He always did like the blood. He was made that way, and we respect that, because there's something almost experimental about his actions, a clean appreciation of his talents that he wishes to explore and reveal. We sometimes feel the same urge to explore, though he is more... human than us. A curious difference.

He is gone, but we can follow. We have the equipment required to put him back down, if we can get close enough. For that, we have to retain the element of surprise. And for that, we have to achieve our aims as quickly as possible.

13

Simon wondered if he'd been foolish coming onto the *Sun Tzu* on his own to look for his sister, but it wasn't the first stupid thing he'd done for her, and he was sure it wouldn't be the last. He'd given up one life for River, and started another, and over the time he'd spent on *Serenity* he was sort of getting used to it. He'd seen a huge difference in River lately, especially since he'd managed to get some idea of what they'd done to her mind. From that he'd been able to formulate a medicine and treatment plan, and slowly but surely he could sense an improvement in her well-being. Though his life had changed he was still a doctor, although for a much smaller circle of patients than he'd ever intended, and there were other plus points too. Kaylee, for one.

Coming here had changed everything. He'd always known that there were others like River—he'd seen them at the Academy when he rescued her, and sometimes in her darkest moments she remembered them, calling them her shadows or ghosts—but he had hoped never to meet one. The more River's rehabilitation and acceptance progressed, the worse he knew the implications would be should she encounter another experimental subject of

Dr. Mathias and the Alliance.

He'd sneaked off *Serenity* and onto the *Sun Tzu*, worried with every second that passed that Wash would spot his movement and do something to stop him. Neither of them was a fighter, yet both of them would if they had to. But Wash had not seen him leaving, and now Simon felt like he'd stepped back in time. This old, almost legendary ship was a wonder, an echo that hung heavy and still around him. The ghosts of humanity's past whispered with every step he took, and he was in equal parts fascinated and daunted. But it was the ghosts of the present that drove him forward.

From what he'd heard on the comms, Silas sounded confused and dangerous. River had told him the story of Silas, the legend, and now it seemed that the myth was based on fact. Silas and River were alike and had been formed in the same place. Simon was terrified that if Silas and River met, she would regress back to the scared, vulnerable teenager she'd been when he had first rescued her.

He would do everything he could to ensure that encounter didn't happen.

Having slipped from *Serenity* and onto this vast, ancient ship, the sense of staggering space and size was humbling. He hurried through endless corridors and hallways, through control rooms and communal spaces, passing countless closed doors that might have held back scenes and stories from half a millennium before. He also passed a few open doors, and he could not shake the sense of curiosity and awe that urged him to push through and take a look beyond. In one room there were several racks of shelving, and on every shelf were several hundred pairs of new sports shoes, petrified now and covered in dust. There was a mass of different colors, styles, and sizes, but all of them appeared new and unworn. He found the scene subtly disturbing, not because they had never been used—although that was haunting enough—but because they had been manufactured, stacked, and stored with a sense of optimism for the future. Many of those transported via the *Sun Tzu* must have migrated into the 'verse and helped establish humanity as it was today. There was a good chance that he was descended from someone who had traveled on this ship. But none of these shoes had found their purpose.

A sense of purpose was important to Simon. For a long time River, his *méi méi*, had been his reason for living, and her safety and well-being would remain his prime *raison d'etre* for as long as he lived. But life also needed an aim, if not a final destination. Those shoes had sat there for five hundred years, and might remain so for five hundred more. They had become pointless.

He shook his head. Perhaps it was the sheer size of this vessel, and the impossible task he'd set himself, that had made him maudlin. How would he find his sister in a ship that was more than a mile long? How many rooms did it contain, how many miles of corridor?

How many dangers?

Simon paused, head tilted. He thought he'd heard a noise, but it was probably just a stutter from old equipment cycling up for the first time in an age. The diffused light from ceiling panels seemed to warm his skin. He knew it was a psychological effect. The air inside the *Sun Tzu* was below freezing, and he already felt ice forming on his eyelashes and stubble. He'd heard Mal and the others on the comms stating that life-support systems had been kick-started when Silas had woken, but it would take some time to warm the whole ship. The dead had no need of such basic comforts.

As he continued, he heard the sound again. It was an echo, fading around him as if a last distant breath. Even so far away, he recognized the sound of gunfire.

The Alliance are on board already! Before he'd left the bridge he'd seen the trace of an approaching Alliance destroyer on the scopes, and then he'd heard Wash telling Mal and the others that combat shuttles were incoming. He hadn't been keeping a good track of time, but it seemed that the Alliance had a sense of urgency about what was happening on board the *Sun Tzu*.

Of course they did. They knew about Silas because they had made him what he was, long before they had done the same to River. They had placed him here, out of the way and safe in some form of suspension device. The tales River had once told him said that he had been a much earlier experiment, something imperfect, a trial subject when River had been more refined, benefiting from the mistakes they had made when they had been messing with Silas's brain. But it seemed those mistakes had made Silas more deadly than even the Alliance could ever have dreamed.

He headed toward the sound, and it grew louder the further he went. Echoes overlaid echoes, a constant low-level grumble that carried the promise of terrible things. He hoped River wasn't involved. He also hoped the crew weren't entangled in the violence, but he felt a sinking dread, and a certainty that they must be. He started to run, not knowing what to do when he got there, only knowing that he had to find River.

He hurried across a suspended walkway, sprinted along a wide, low corridor, and around the next corner he saw two tall women emerge from a wide, arched opening. He was far too late to hide from them.

They looked right at him. Simon cried out in shock, stumbled, and went sprawling, hands out to take most of the impact, and he slid to a stop.

No no no! he thought, but he was not imagining this, and it was no nightmare. He wished it was. The pair of these monsters who had almost captured them on Ariel were a trillion miles away, and he'd hoped they were the only ones. His hope withered and died as he saw the two women, and his heart stuttered, and he thought the shock and fear would be enough to do him in. He wanted to stand, turn, and run.

One of the figures raised her blue-gloved hand toward him, holding a thin, narrow implement.

Simon felt the first terrible probing in his ears and eyes. A pressure on his ear drums, a constriction at his throat, and then his eyeballs felt bloated and throbbing, like the worst hangover he'd ever had, growing harder, hotter, swelling within their sockets and threatening to burst.

"I can..." he croaked, and he clawed at his throat because the words would not come.

The second figure stepped forward. In one hand she carried a metal and glass object, but her other hand was free. She reached for him as if to stroke a fallen pet, but she never quite touched him. He saw nothing in her eyes. No expression at all. On his hands and knees, level with her legs, he saw spatters of blood on her shoes and trousers.

His head pulsed and pounded, and he felt the first warm, wet dribble of blood from his right ear.

I can't leave River like this! he thought, and then his last chance at survival screamed at him, a terrible risk and yet the only way he might yet make it through to help her, save her. Because though she was powerful, he was the steady rock around which she lived her life. He pinned his sister to the world, and if he died here and now she would be set free to drift and be caught up in the storms that existence continued to throw at them all. If they knew who he was, and that River was there, perhaps they could combine forces to bring Silas under the Alliance twins' control.

"I know... River... Tam," he said.

The first figure lowered her hand, and as soon as the object pointed away from him at the floor he felt a lifting of the pressure inside. It brought such a rush of relief that he fell onto his stomach and cried out, tears and blood spattering the floor before his face.

"What about River Tam?" one of the twins asked.

"I'm her brother," Simon said. "She's here. Together… we can help you put… put Silas down."

"We've already put him down, long ago," they said. "He just needs… reminding."

"He will listen to River."

He saw a shadow of expression on their faces for the first time. Their surprise gave him a brief pang of satisfaction, but he could never, ever forget who these people were—if they were even people at all, and he'd always had his doubts—and what he was dealing with. They were surprised at what he knew about Silas, and that River was here, and most of all at his offer of help.

Their faces quickly became blank again, implacable, cold. The Hands of Blue would never betray any sense of weakness.

"Talk," they said.

When Kaylee and Jayne reached a series of viewing platforms and bubbles along the side of the *Sun Tzu*, she hoped the vast sense of scale, and of being lost deep within the belly of a giant beast, would fade away. It did not. If anything, seeing out into deep space while also aware of the huge, dead ship they were currently lost and trapped within gave her an even greater sense of hopelessness. Yet it was beautiful too, and it meant that they were hopefully one step closer to escape.

I'm in a mausoleum, she thought, and then she saw the hulking mass of the Alliance destroyer and gasped out loud. Jayne's reaction was similar. The viewing port was high and long, the platform they'd emerged onto set with dozens of low-back reclining chairs for people to sit in and gaze upon the wonders of deep space. Every chair was empty. They were the only two here, but they did not feel alone.

The destroyer was settled against the *Sun Tzu* further toward its stern, a forbidding gray mass that blocked out her view of the stars in that direction. Even though it was still dwarfed by the *Sun Tzu*, it still seemed to lure her closer with its terrible gravity. She was looking at its tail end, its drive a low, glowing yellow in repose, its hull busy with gun emplacements and docking arms for combat shuttles and attack ships. Most of these docking arms were empty after releasing their shuttles to ferry troops across the small distance to the *Sun Tzu*.

She had already witnessed what had become of some of those troops. She felt almost sad for them.

"Will you look at that," Jayne said.

"Not a pretty picture."

"Huh?"

Kaylee glanced to Jayne and saw that he wasn't looking out at the Alliance ship at all. His attention had been grabbed by something inside the viewing area, past the recliners and set against the far wall. She followed his gaze.

"Jayne, I can't believe you."

"But we're here now, so why not?"

"Why not? Because you can hardly carry what you've already collected, especially in these bulky gorramn suits. Because we have to escape, survive, and get back to the ship to help Wash. And because that man Silas is far from human, and I think he's more dangerous to us than all the soldiers and spaceships the Alliance can throw at us."

"I agree," Jayne said. "But he ain't here. And if we're nowhere near where he is, I'm free to indulge my natural desire to ensure this trip isn't the total hump-up it's quickly becoming."

"Unbelievable."

"Believe it." Jayne stalked away toward the drinks station, and by the time Kaylee had joined him he'd already selected several bottles and placed them on the bar. She picked up one and shook it.

"It's open."

"So?"

"So… it's been open for half a millennium. You think what's left in here will be good?"

Jayne snatched the bottle from her and twisted off the lid. He examined the label, raised his eyebrows, nodded in admiration, and took a swig.

Kaylee had time to step back and to the side before Jayne spat the drink out in a fine spray. He wiped his mouth and looked at the bottle again, as if the label were to blame for the foul taste rather than his own stupidity.

"Even the sealed ones might be ruined," Kaylee said.

"I thought wine was supposed to mature with age."

"Like you?"

Jayne looked hurt. Kaylee smiled and shook her head, amazed that she was able to find humor in such a dire circumstance.

"These two are wine," she said, tapping the tall, slender bottle. "This is brandy. This is whiskey, and by the looks of it…" She leaned forward to examine the label.

"Scotch," he said. "Single malt. Saw a bottle of that go for a thousand credits once. Guy who bought it said he'd never open it. You ask me, he was a *fèi fèi de pi yǎn*."

Jayne took up the bottle, tested the lid, then opened it with a hard twist. He sniffed the open neck, took a swig, smacked his lips, and sighed.

"But it's worth a fortune!" Kaylee said.

"This ship's still full of stuff, and I need a drink." As he offered the bottle to Kaylee he looked past her and up toward the overhead viewing window.

Kaylee took a sip of the Scotch. When she swallowed it burned all the way down, and settling in her stomach it spread a heat through her core. She took a larger swallow and closed her eyes, and the combination of sensory inputs—taste, scent, touch—inspired a clear memory of a time not so long ago when the crew were all together. They were seated around the galley table, Jayne and Book chatting and laughing, Simon and River quiet and watchful, Inara and the captain pointedly ignoring each other after some argument or other. Kaylee had looked around the table and realized that these were her people and her family, and the power of that memory almost brought a tear to her eye.

"You know we gotta go out there," Jayne said. She opened her eyes again and he nodded past her at the window. "Find an openin' if we can. Or if we can't, you'll have to close some blast doors, seal off an area, and I've got stuff in my kit that'll blast one of those windows out. Maybe we do it here." He looked around the large area.

"Any decompression will attract the Alliance," Kaylee said.

Jayne nodded as he continued to examine bottles from behind the bar. Any that were open he set aside, and most of the full bottles joined them. When he had six or seven placed on the bar before him, he turned to Kaylee.

"The Alliance are comin' in," he said. "What we saw back there, that was just the beginning, and Wash is gonna need us. You know he ain't a fighter." He looked contemplative. "Might talk the Alliance troopers on board *Serenity* to death, I suppose."

"I ain't a fighter, neither."

"I can take care of that."

"Are you really gonna—?"

Jayne held up his hand and tilted his head. Kaylee listened too, and she heard the sound of distant voices, low and secretive. Accompanying them were the echoes of footfalls on metal.

Jayne made an obscene gesture and she knew immediately what he meant: *Alliance.*

He grabbed the bottles he'd chosen and put them carefully into a stuffed backpack, slung it over his shoulder, then picked up his second pack. He pulled his gun and tried to shoulder the pack, but Kaylee grabbed it from him. She didn't want the encumbrance, but she'd much rather have Jayne with a free gun hand.

He pointed toward a darkened doorway at the far end of the viewing area.

"So we're not gonna blast the window?" she whispered, leaning in close.

"Not unless we have to. If they're gettin' in somewhere close, maybe we can get out the same way."

Jayne approached the door and found it nonfunctional. He raised an eyebrow at Kaylee and she was already there, digging out her tool pack and getting to work. Though lacking in modern refinements, there was a comforting honesty in the tangle of colored electrics, distribution boards, and mechanical switches. Unlike some modern laser-based controls, these structural components would take a lot longer than a few hundred years to degrade and fall apart. They also took longer for her to pick.

After a couple of minutes the door whispered open and Kaylee eased back, allowing Jayne to slip through first. The next area was similar to the one they had just left, with several large viewing domes in the ceiling shedding starlight over the scene, a score of comfortable chairs scattered around the edges, and large, low tables at the room's center. The walls were lined with books, floor to ceiling, almost all the way around. There must have been thousands of them.

"I've never seen so many books!" Kaylee said, keeping her voice low. She could still hear voices and movement from beyond the room, carried through to them via strange acoustics. Maybe the large areas of glass caught and directed any sound.

Jayne rubbed his fingers together and shrugged.

"Probably priceless," she said, and she saw his eyes light up. She hadn't meant it that way, but she couldn't be bothered telling him. Way across at the other end of the room was an open doorway, and beyond they saw a wide metal stairwell. A flash of movement made Kaylee catch her breath. She dropped, Jayne already on the floor beside her, and they both became motionless. She looked left and right without moving her head. There was nowhere to go, nowhere to hide, not without risking being seen. They watched a line of Alliance soldiers passing by the open doorway, heading down the staircase beyond with soft, dull footsteps.

If one of them turned and looked into the room, they couldn't help but see Jayne and Kaylee crouching down.

None of them did.

They're not looking for us, Kaylee thought. *They're not interested in the ship or what it carries, cos they already know all about it. They're only interested in him.*

After the last soldier passed they waited for a while, listening to the soft echoes retreating.

"Might sound foolish, but could be we're safer out there than here in the ship," Jayne said. "Come on." As they crossed the remainder of the library Kaylee glanced around at the books, fascinated and excited for differing reasons. Quite a few of the tomes had fallen from the shelves and lay on the bare floor like tumbled leaves, and some were open, exposing pages that might never be read again. Kaylee wondered what treasures they contained—accounts of times and places on Earth-That-Was, pictures, names and faces of people long-since gone and from a history that informed everything and everywhere humanity was today. This was a treasure trove of knowledge, and she wished

Inara or Book were here to see it.

Jayne saw the books as money, and he picked up a few and tried to read their spines before placing them quietly back on the floor, unsure what might make them valuable. And with his loaded backpacks, Jayne could carry no more.

He moved to the open doorway, looked down, and pressed his finger to his lips. Kaylee looked up, not down, and she could already see a hopeful sign. Just four flights and two landings above them, a heavy set of blast doors stood open. She could make out a blinking green light beside them, as if they had recently been activated.

They ducked back through the doorway.

She stood on tiptoes and whispered into Jayne's ear. "Airlock. We must be right under the destroyer's stern here."

"Could be they've set up an umbilicus to cross."

"Doubt it," Kaylee said. "Those soldiers are suited 'n' booted for a space walk. I'd lay a bet that we'll be able to get out and walk along the *Sun Tzu*'s hull."

"With that big ugly destroyer hanging above us."

"Either that, or we try to get past 'em." She nodded at the doorway leading to the stairwell.

"Only four flights of stairs," Jayne said.

"Only four."

They stood in the open doorway again, readying themselves, breathing deeply. Then with a quick glance below—she could see some movement, but they must have been several flights down— Kaylee led them out and up the first fifteen steps, working hard to move smoothly in the awkward space suits.

They made two flights and were turning on the large landing when Jayne banged his backpack on the handrail. Glass shattered. Priceless whiskey first dripped from the torn bag, then flowed, falling through holes in the sheet metal flooring and dripping down the stairwell.

"What was that?" a voice said from down below.

"Volk? McMahon?" Another voice.

"No, sir, they've gone on ahead. There was no one coming after us."

"Stand down, drop weapons, on your knees!" the first voice shouted.

Jayne and Kaylee froze, staring at each other, and she thought, *I can't blame him for that, not his fault, but what a* hún dàn*!*

"Go!" he said, and they started sprinting up the stairs. It was a rash move, Kaylee thought, because neither of them knew what waited for them at the top. If it was simply a closed and locked door into an airlock, they'd have no time to open it before the soldiers down below reached them. And if the troopers knew some of what awaited them in the *Sun Tzu*, they might be more likely to—

The noise was deafening. She'd been shot at before, but never like this, never as if the whole world was exploding around her, the smell of violence gagging, and she could see bullets and metal fragments spinning and ricocheting from the open treads and landings. At first she thought the stairwell walls were flashing dozens of small lights, then she realized that bullets and shards were scarring the walls with countless metal wounds.

Jayne leaned over the banister and fired Boo several times.

"Jayne!" Kaylee shouted, grabbing his belt and hauling him back. She didn't know whether him leaning out into the fusillade was stupid or brave, or perhaps both, but he fell back toward her easier than she'd expected, pressing his arm against his chest and holding the gun there. She saw the bloom of blood on his shoulder, and he swayed into her.

She slapped him across the face. Not hard, but hard enough. It must have been the shock that focused his mind. He nodded and they started up the stairs again, and she could feel scores of bullets impacting the underside of the treads, hear them whipping past her as they found a way through. It wouldn't take long until she caught a bullet too. She already knew what it was like being shot. She'd only survived last time because of Simon. This time she'd be on her own, bleeding along with Jayne onto the cold metal decking of a spaceship filled with the dead.

Someone down below shouted and she wondered what was to come. The shooting faded as quickly as it had begun, and she expected an explosive round to slam into the landing they found themselves on.

At least we'll die quickly, she thought, and the shout from down below was cut off, only to rise again in a high, shrill scream.

The shooting started again, but this time none of it was directed at them. There were a few random shots to begin with, increasing into a constant roar and rattle of gunfire. Looking through the holed metal landing Kaylee could make out shapes shifting just a few floors below. They were shooting away from the stairwell at something along one of the adjoining corridors or rooms, and some of the figures were still, silent, and bleeding their last.

"It must be Silas," Jayne said. "He's bringin' the fight to them. I'm warmin' up to him."

An explosion rocked the staircase, sending a wave of heat up into their faces. Shrapnel zinged and whistled from metal. Someone screamed. Voices were confused, shouting and crying, calling and pleading.

"Let's make the most of this!" she said, and they hurried up the rest of the stairs to the airlock doors. Jayne held his injured arm awkwardly, but he still looked strong and determined. He'd moved his gun from his right hand to his left. He could shoot with both.

The door was closed, though the green light beside it glowed to show it was in operation. Kaylee accessed the controls and checked the status. If the troopers had just entered, the space should still be pressurized. But it could be there were still other soldiers waiting outside to make their entry, and if so the airlock would be slowly venting once again.

"We're good," she said. "But the Alliance'll probably register the airlock being used."

"I'm pretty certain they know we're here," Jayne said through gritted teeth. The shock of his wound was giving way to pain, and too much blood was seeping out. They should be pausing to dress the wound, not running and struggling.

How far to Serenity? Kaylee wondered. *And what happens when we get there?*

"So what do we do about that big bullet-shaped hole in your space suit?"

He looked at her for a long, silent couple of seconds. "Huh. Not to mention my arm."

"In the airlock," she said. "Let's get safely out of sight. I've got an idea."

"You do?"

"Sorta." Kaylee palmed the door control and the airlock doors slid open to welcome them inside. Jayne leaned against the wall, breathing hard. The possibility of him passing out was not a good one. Outside the ship she'd be able to grab him and pull him along with her easily enough, but she was relying on him once they boarded *Serenity*. If there was gunwork to be done, she'd need him awake.

She opened the backpack she was carrying, pulled out the three bottles he'd stuffed in there, then tugged out a couple of the clothing items too. She flicked open a knife she carried on her belt and cut off the arm from an extravagant silk shirt.

"Really?" he said, but she didn't respond. She had no idea how long they had until the Alliance soldiers came after them. She had a feeling they were still otherwise engaged.

"Trust me," she said. She opened her utility belt and took out a small tube with a nozzle at one end.

"What's that?"

"Readyfix. Used to seal holes quickly."

"Holes in a person?"

"No."

"Wait a minute—"

"Hey, I'll never tie a tourniquet tight enough to seal the hole. Once we're outside, the cold'll get in an' freeze your arm, or your suit'll decompress and you'll die slow an' horrible."

Jayne stared at her for two seconds before saying, "So shut up and do it."

"Arm up," she said. She saw how much it hurt, but Jayne did as he was told. She tied the sleeve above the wound and the tear in his space suit, passing it under his armpit and tying it as tight as she could over the top of his shoulder. He groaned, but the sleeve would act as a tourniquet while she did the next bit.

She had no idea if the Readyfix contained chemicals that would kill him anyway.

Pressing his arm across his chest, she stuck the nozzle into the hole in his suit and activated the tube. It hissed and squirted, the thick fluid quickly expanding inside and outside the suit, bubbling, then growing solid after brief exposure to the cold air. He groaned, squeezed his lips together in pain.

Kaylee withdrew the spent tube and dropped it.

"You good, Jayne?"

"I'm good."

"Sure?"

"I got no choice."

Kaylee packed the backpack and slung it over her shoulder.

"Hey," Jayne said. "Thanks, Kaylee."

She nodded. From Jayne, that was a lot.

"You're not going to pass out on me?" she asked.

"Flesh wound. I've had worse."

They slipped on their helmets, sealed their suits, connected a tether between their belts, and Kaylee shouldered both backpacks. Beyond the airlock doors and beneath them, the shooting and dying continued.

14

The instant between not knowing him and knowing him—being adrift, and then finding herself in his mind and dancing alongside him—was one of the most terrifying moments of River's life. Though she is with Mal and Zoë she finds herself in freefall, spiraling away from the world and everything she knows as if pulled. Some trailing part of her has been caught in the great, turning engines that power things, and she is helpless as she's dragged toward those grinding gears and chomping wheels that hide in unseen realms. She is beneath everything, in places where human perception does not function and no human is meant to be. Breathless, hopeless, she opens her mouth in a silent cry…

And then she is with Silas, and everything between then and now was merely a held breath.

She can see and feel where he is, and she knows that if she shouts and he shouts at the same time they will not hear each other. But in other ways they are closer than two people can ever be.

She always wondered if finding him would be like this. Some of the others at the Academy were close to her, but never in this way. Never so close that she felt like she could touch them. She'd always known that Silas might be different—they all had, when they talked of him in hushed tones, sharing and perpetuating his myth—and now she felt the whole truth opening up inside and around her.

Silas is distracted and does not notice her. Not yet. But he soon will, because he and she are so similar that it's like staring back at herself.

She sees from his eyes, smells with his nose, feels impacts and breaking bones through his fingertips, and she hears the screams of dying men and women that sound like the most wonderful concerto. He sweeps and dances among them, ducking bullets, twisting this way and that to avoid clumsy guns being fired at him. He grabs one man by his dangling space-suit helmet and lifts him, swinging him around in a graceful arc to slam against a stairway banister. The man cries out and Silas swings him again, a broken rag doll now, legs and arms splintered and trailing as his torso erupts beneath a hail of bullets. Blood and insides spatter the treads, and Silas and River take a moment to admire the beautiful patterns the blood makes against ancient metal.

In this moment she thinks he senses her at last, but there is no time to reflect.

He falls to his knees as bullets strike the wall above his head. He rolls forward several times, then leaps up and pushes away from the wall with both feet, landing on a staircase and bouncing up it toward the three soldiers firing at him. Their aim tracks his progress but never quite meets it. He dispatches the first with a straight-fingered stab to the throat, the second with a hard punch that bursts her heart in her chest, and the third he flips over the handrailing, watching as he spins and falls several floors in a parody of flight. Silas's senses are slowed so much that the man's fall takes some time, and he imagines him evolving on the way down, growing wings and taking flight.

Silas has evolved, never quite asleep when he should have been, becoming much more than he was when they put him down. River understands some of that.

The man strikes the bottom of the stairwell and breaks.

Silas moves, dodges, and kills, a balletic dance of grace and power that she watches through his eyes and experiences through his other senses. Through him she is also dancing, flowing with each movement and drifting back and forth among the death and chaos of that battle, untouched by any of it.

She remembers the pain she felt at the Academy, and the subjects who came and went, killed by things the scientists there did to them. She remembers the fear.

She blinks. *Wrong.*

More death. More art in a spatter of blood, poetry in a final breath.

This is wrong. She is seeing people being killed, broken, ripped apart, and in fact there is nothing graceful about their deaths, nothing to celebrate in the way their insides are spilled and their memories and histories snuffed out.

River, she hears, and he is trying to speak to her even as he continues killing.

She pulls back.

River!

As she pulls away from Silas, he tries to grab on. It is a terrifying sensation, attempting to remain herself while someone else is trying to make her theirs. She has spent years finding herself again—with the help of Simon and her friends in *Serenity*'s crew—and Silas is trying to change all that. She can understand his fascination, because that fascination goes both ways. She knows him and he knows her, because they were made by the same people in the same place. Yet the mistakes they made with him, their first experiment—the reason they hid him out here, away from civilization where he cannot do any harm—they tried to refine with River.

They made many other mistakes, she thinks, and she knows the truth of that because she is in his mind and behind his eyes. *They thought he was asleep, but in fact he remained partly conscious for all that time. Improving. Growing. Evolving.*

And in his mind, he was no mistake at all.

"River!" This time it is not his voice.

Snapping back from Silas she actually hears a tearing sound, as if a physical link between the two of them has been broken. And she feels his rage as she withdraws. He liked having her there, seeing what he was doing. He liked showing off.

Now he knows her, he'll want her with him again.

"River," Mal says kneeling by her side. Zoë is standing behind him looking fierce and angry. "You went away for a while, there."

"He's not what I hoped he'd be," she says.

"Who?"

"Silas. I thought in finding him I might find more about myself, but if that's him… if that's *me*… I'm not sure I want it." She looks up at Mal. "He's killing them."

Mal freezes. "Killing who? *Who*, River?"

"Dozens of them have come for him, maybe more, and he's killing them all."

"May be a distraction," Zoë says.

"Yeah, for the blue-handed freaks," Mal says. "We don't want to be anywhere near him when—"

"I can't be near him at all," River says, and she stands, pushing away Mal. Fear has taken root in her heart. It's a sensation she has known before, but never like this. Never so rich. "We need to go. I should never have come. He's not what I hoped, he wants me, and with me he'll be even more powerful than he is now. Even more powerful than…"

"Than?" Zoë asks.

"Than anything."

They made him walk in front of them. Simon didn't know where he was going, but the twins seemed to think he was heading in the right direction, because they followed silently behind him. As he walked through the metal guts of the *Sun Tzu*, up stairs, along passageways, and through large open spaces, he had time to consider what he had done. By offering up River he had put her at dreadful risk, and he knew just how deadly the blue-handed twins could be.

Once they have Silas and River they'll kill everyone else, he thought, and he had no doubt that was true. He had seen the blood on their shoes and legs. He was expendable to them. Everyone was.

The idea of ceasing to be had never troubled him too much, though the nature and method of going from something to nothing did. The pressure in his head, his pulsing eyeballs and bloodied ears and the sense that he was sinking into water, deeper and deeper until his organs were set to burst and his head to implode… that had been an awful feeling. Being dead, though, would mean that he had abandoned River to all the awfulness the 'verse was still striving to throw at her. She had already been a victim of that, much more so than most people ever were, and his reason for staying alive was to help her. He would be with her forever, and there was no sadness or reluctance in that thought.

He would do everything he could to remain alive, because if he died River would be on her own.

All he had to do now was to ensure the Alliance did not get hold of her.

He felt their strange, deadly weapon primed behind him. His

FIREFLY

head ached and his eyes throbbed, and the slick probings of dark fingers winnowed through his brain. If he made a break for it he'd be dead within ten steps.

Simon had no choice but to lead them onward. There was no escaping them now, until the time came when they encountered Silas, or River, or both of them together. Then he would have to take action that might save her life, and end his.

Kaylee could never get used to that moment when she moved from inside to outside.

Inside a ship, *Serenity* or otherwise, she was protected by hull and inner structures, cradled within the web of mechanics and systems designed to protect a human's frail body against the harsh rigors and dangers of the Black. Limits were applied, spatial horizons made sense of. Inside a ship, she felt safe.

Outside, her own true nature was brought home to her by the sheer incomprehensible vastness of space.

As she and Jayne drifted from the airlock she gasped, misting the visor of her helmet for a heartbeat before its life-support systems cleared her screen again, allowing her to peer into the depths she would never know. However long she flew, however fast, she could never reach the stars she was looking at. Indeed, many of them were no longer there. She was looking deep into the past, seeing a history when she never existed, and anyone or anything close to those distant stars looking in her direction would see her only when she was long, long gone.

"Smashed another gorramn bottle getting out," Jayne said. "Hope it's not the good stuff."

He moved to check, groaned in pain, and Kaylee gasped as the action caused them to start drifting apart. She fired her suit's retros and he did the same, leveling them up and turning them so that they could drop down, magnetic boots attaching to the *Sun Tzu*'s hull. The mental shock of space walking affected her deeply, but on a more practical, physical level it also took her a minute or two to adjust.

"Let's keep it slow and easy," Jayne said. "We gotta... wow."

Kaylee had already seen. Directly outside the airlock their view straight ahead was into deep space, but once they'd righted themselves and clamped onto the hull, the Alliance destroyer loomed above and ahead, floating a short distance from the *Sun Tzu* toward the stern. In that direction also lay the damaged part of the old ship, where *Serenity* was now docked. Their route home lay between the *Sun Tzu* and the destroyer, a gap that from this distance looked almost too narrow to walk between. Kaylee guessed it was actually a hundred feet or more, but the ships hid a heavy shadow between them.

"There," Kaylee said, pointing to their left. In the opposite direction to *Serenity*, an Alliance combat shuttle was docked against the larger ship, magnetic stays extended. An airlock hatch was open on its side. It seemed lifeless, but the cockpit windows were dark and impossible to see through from this angle, reflecting only a speckle of stars.

Jayne heaved his gun up and aimed.

"Jayne," Kaylee said. "I think we're good. Surely they'd have hailed us by now?"

"Or blown us into dust." There were weapons arrays on the shuttle's front and top, small caliber but more than effective at this range. None of the guns tracked them. Nothing on the shuttle moved.

"Those troopers we saw were just one shuttle load," Kaylee said.

"Wash said he saw a load of shuttles parting from the destroyer. There must be hundreds of troops on board the *Sun Tzu* right now. Just waitin' to find Silas so he can kill them too."

"We could take it," Kaylee said. Distances were difficult to make out in space, but she reckoned it was a good few hundred steps beneath the destroyer's hulk until they reached *Serenity*. The shuttle would get them there in seconds. "And those Alliance aboard *Serenity* would see a friendly ship approaching."

"Better chance of taking them if they see nothing approaching at all," Jayne said. "Besides…" He nodded up at the destroyer.

"Yeah," Kaylee said. "Guess they'd notice one of their shuttles being stole. I just ain't too keen on walkin' under that thing."

"Me neither, but it is what it is."

They set off, making slow but steady progress. They soon passed into the shadow of the destroyer, and though having its mass floating above them was disconcerting, it blocked most of the view of deep space. Kaylee did not feel settled or at all calmed. Her senses told her that the two large vessels should crash together at any moment, yet she knew that without outside influence, they might drift in this manner for years.

Jayne walked to her left, his bad arm still held across his chest, the two backpacks now weightless and floating behind him. Fluid leaked from one of them, beading and drifting along with him. In his good hand he held his gun. Kaylee almost laughed every time she saw it, because against the might of the Alliance vessel it was nothing.

"How's the arm?" she asked.

"That gunk is holding. If it don't, my eyeballs'll explode and my blood'll boil," he said. "Tell me if you see that happening."

Halfway beneath the destroyer, just when Kaylee thought she could make out the edges of the damaged area on the *Sun Tzu*'s hull far ahead, something urged her to turn around. Perhaps she saw a shadow cast and moving somewhere ahead of her, or a reflection flickering in her visor. She planted her foot and pivoted, and Jayne copied her action.

The shuttle close to the airlock they had exited was moving. It lifted away from the *Sun Tzu*, magnetic stays retracted, and its nose rose slowly, so slowly, to point at the destroyer's stern.

"Survivor?" Jayne asked.

"I don't reckon so," Kaylee said. "The airlock door is still open."

"Now why would someone fly a spaceship without closing…" He drifted off, because then they both knew. They were a long way off, but not too far to see the figure push away from the shuttle and land on the *Sun Tzu* close to the airlock they'd exited less than fifteen minutes before. The figure grasped one of the handles around the airlock and pulled itself inside. Kaylee wasn't sure, but she thought she saw the doors slide shut once more.

"They were wearing an Alliance space suit," Jayne said.

"Yeah, he was," Kaylee said, because they both knew who they had been watching.

If they had any doubts at all, what happened next convinced them.

Moments after the figure disappeared back into the *Sun Tzu*, the shuttle's drive fired and it powered up and away from the old ship, accelerating into the side bulkhead housing one of the destroyer's three main, massive boosters. The initial explosion was small, a bulb of fire within the shuttle that bloomed and split its hull as it grew, blasting pieces of the wrecked ship out and down to ricochet against the *Sun Tzu*. The secondary explosion, within the booster of the destroyer itself, was much larger. Flame coiled and boiled, metal split and twisted, and the whole ship above them vibrated. The silent destruction was almost surreal, but the results were terrifying. A haze of flame spread toward Kaylee and Jayne, wreckage spinning and firing in all directions as several parts of the giant booster broke away.

They turned and ran as fast as they could, ensuring that at

least one of their magnetic boots retained contact with the ship at all times. Moving in space was a skill that took practice, and Kaylee had always been terrified of being set adrift like that bounty hunter Early who'd come after River, spinning and turning helplessly until her suit's life support ran out and she suffocated, then still moving, tumbling through the 'verse forever until someone found her in a thousand years or a million, or until the end of time. If she lost her footing now—or if part of the wreckage smashed into the *Sun Tzu* by her feet, or struck her in the back and knocked her away from the ship—her nightmare might well become real.

Jayne was close beside her still holding his gun, and he reached for her with his wounded hand, not trusting the delicate tether that kept them connected. If one of them went, they'd both go. There was camaraderie in that, but also survival instinct and logic. Two of them sent spinning might be able to help each other.

More light flared behind them from another silent explosion, casting their own frantic, dancing shadows ahead, dark limbs flailing and waving as if they had already been cast adrift. The damaged area of the ancient ship was visible ahead of them now, and somewhere below that ragged rim was, hopefully, home.

As the destroyer above them began a slow and terrible spin up and away from the *Sun Tzu*, Kaylee could only hope that *Serenity* was still there.

Why can nothing ever be simple? Mal thought as a low rattling sound grew into something louder, more insistent, and more deadly. At first he'd thought it was small-arms fire sounding in from a distance. Now he was sure it was something much worse. *Why, when we're almost home safe and dry, is there always something that arises to ensure that we're well and truly humped?*

"That's coming from outside," Zoë said.

"I was thinkin' the same," Mal said. He glanced at River but she gave him nothing, just that expression that might have been fear, or might have been dawning delight.

The cacophony increased, and it was a deeper sound than gunfire, transmitted through the ship and into the soles of his feet, his chest, his bones. At first it sounded like something tapping on the ship's hull, then drumming, then hammering, with no rhythm other than one of destruction and chaos.

"Something exploded," Zoë said.

"You're sure?"

"Something outside has come apart and is hitting the ship."

"Maybe we're drifting into the planet's rings?" Mal asked. If the *Sun Tzu* had been moved somehow and nudged into the rings—by Silas, perhaps, or some deeper programming meant to kick in should he awake—they'd be battered and broken into pieces in minutes.

"Don't think so," she said. "I've heard something like this before."

"And what happened?"

"I didn't die."

"Evidently."

"That's the best that can be said."

"We're almost home," River said. "We need to hurry. I've seen him, and now I think… I think he's seen me."

"Seen?"

River was close to tears. "I wish I couldn't see. I've done things, bad things, but nothing as bad as he's doing right now." She went away a little, eyes losing focus, mouth dropping open. "Right, right now."

Beneath the impact sounds from outside came the rattle of

more gunfire. It was distant, and behind them, and it ended quickly.

"He's closer," River said. "I can't lose him. I can't *loosen* him!"

"It's okay, River," Zoë said, and she grabbed her hand and squeezed.

They ran, Zoë leading the way, Mal bringing up the rear. River was between them, and he watched for any sign that she was going to veer off, stumble, or fall beneath the weight of fear so obviously building around her. He'd warmed to her over the time she'd been on board, but he had never grown to trust her.

He expected River to fail him now.

"He's closer," River said.

"Shut up and run."

"Much closer. He's dancing through more soldiers. He'll kill you both… he'll kill the whole crew without even thinking about it."

"How do you know?" Zoë asked.

"I would if I were him."

"River, save your breath for—" Mal snapped, but she cut him off.

"He's calling me his little sister."

They reached one of the retrofitted blast doors. It was closed, and Mal couldn't tell if it was one they had passed through before. He set to work on the lock with Zoë standing guard, facing back the way they'd come with her gun drawn.

Sweating in the cumbersome suit, he worked at the controls, thought he had it, and heard and felt a heavy thud as the door double-locked. He swore under his breath and tried again, disabling the lock, hearing the mechanism slide open, and then Zoë said his name. He knew her voice and tone. This was serious.

Dropping his tools, Mal drew his gun as he turned, finger closing around the trigger and exerting half of its firing pressure.

Two Alliance troopers had turned a corner in the corridor and were running for them, flexible helmets off and slung on their backs. Zoë crouched into a shooting stance, and Mal aimed, but then he saw terror on their faces. Their eyes were wide, arms swinging by their sides. Their weapon straps were slung over their shoulders, the guns swinging loose, and if they didn't slow or stop they'd be on Mal, Zoë, and River in moments.

Mal and Zoë swapped a nervous glance. Neither of them wanted to shoot, but they both would if they had to.

They didn't. A brief cough of gunfire rang out and the two troopers dropped, sliding into each other. One of them twitched. The other lay still, dead.

Let it be Jayne, Mal hoped, but it was not Jayne who stood at the end of the corridor. It was Silas. He seemed taller than before, wider, altogether larger, as if in the hour since surfacing he had become more solid in the world, finding his place and inhabiting it with confidence and certainty. He held an Alliance gun in one hand and wore an Alliance military space suit. As he and Mal locked eyes he cast the weapon aside and ran at them.

Zoë's aim never faltered.

"No!" River said, and she touched Zoë's arm, preventing her from firing.

Even skidding to a stop before them Silas was graceful and lithe. His eyes were more alive than they'd been before, more self-aware, though Mal still saw a distant madness in them. Blood spattered his clothing and face. His hands and arms were red and sticky almost up to the elbows.

"You're me," Silas said, staring at River. He looked her up and down, all his attention focused on her. "I mean, you're *like* me."

Mal still gripped his gun but kept it down by his side. He'd heard the shouting and screaming, seen the bodies. He didn't know how Silas would kill him if he lifted his gun, he only knew that he would. He considered dropping the weapon, but that would feel too much like surrender. At least like this he was ready.

He glanced sidelong at Zoë without turning his head. He saw the tension in her, the caution, the readiness. She was thinking the same.

River stood before Silas, tall and still. She had taken two steps and was now in front of Mal and Zoë, facing the man so that Mal couldn't make out her expression. Even if he could it might not tell him much, yet he was sure that she was protecting them both. He wanted to whisper her name, remind her that she was a valuable member of their crew. He really believed that.

"I thought I sensed you earlier," Silas said. "I wasn't sure. I thought maybe you were a dream. I'm still having dreams."

He looked at Mal when he said this, and the weight of his gaze was a shock. His expression was open and honest, eyes deep and striking, and Mal experienced a dizziness that he couldn't quite explain. He didn't feel belittled or challenged, but he did sense that he locked eyes with someone who wasn't quite human.

"Not a dream," he whispered, and every muscle in his body tensed.

Silas's presence, his aura, seemed to reduce them. When he moved—when his expression changed, hardening from open and loose to determined, even furious—Mal's stomach dropped and a dull, cool thud beat through his torso. He'd felt terror like this before.

To his right, Zoë had felt it too. She dropped to one knee and went to raise her gun, and Silas's attention flipped to her. As he moved forward he looked from Zoë to Mal and back again, and Mal knew with sickening certainty what he was thinking.

Which one of us is he going to kill first?

He was sizing them up, assessing which of these two people posed the more immediate threat, and his mind must have been moving a hundred times faster than a normal person's.

As Mal raised his own gun, hoping against hope that at least one of them might get in a lucky shot, River spoke.

"Brother," she said, and Silas froze by her side, one step away and three steps from Zoë.

"Zoë, hold," Mal whispered. He and Zoë fell motionless.

Silas turned so that he and River were face to face. He reached out and lifted her hair, examining the marks and scars on her neck, running his fingers across the back of her neck and scalp. As he did so, River did the same to him.

"I always knew I was not alone," Silas said. "They'd never have made only me. I was the first, but they made others too."

"Yes," River said. "Many others, but none as... primal as you. I sensed you the moment we arrived here and it was like looking in a mirror."

"I made sure you'd come and find me," Silas said. "They drugged me and beat me and brought me here. Before they put me down I created a map, a lure, and made sure one of their greedy soldiers took it. And then I waited. Asleep, frozen in time while the map went out into the 'verse. I hoped it would find someone who could read their way here. I never imagined it might find someone like me. Someone like *you*." He frowned as he glanced at Zoë and Mal, as if only just remembering they were still there.

"They brought me," River said. "They're my friends. My crew." Mal bristled a little at her expression of ownership, but he bit his tongue. She was doing her best to save them. Pride had let his tongue get away from him on more than one occasion; this was a moment when shutting the hell up would serve him best.

"You've no need of them anymore," Silas said. "You're with me now. Now you've woken me, I'm going to leave this place, and you'll come with me. Out there together we can be whatever we want to be."

River frowned. "They're my friends. They came with me to rescue you," she said.

"*We* woke you," Mal said. "Brought you up from your nightmares."

"She woke me," Silas said, nodding at River.

"Still, you need us if you want to get out of here."

"We're special," Silas said to River. He seemed confused now, perhaps angry. "We don't need them with us anymore. We have everything we need here."

"Come with us," River said.

"What?" Mal couldn't hold back his surprise. "No. No way, not on my ship, haven't you seen—?"

"Your ship?" Silas asked. "You're part of my sister's crew, isn't that the case?"

"Mal," Zoë cautioned, because she knew without looking what Mal's reaction would be. A situation as delicate as this, and as loaded, could escalate in a heartbeat.

Mal saw the moment when Silas made his terrible decision. *We won't all survive this*, Mal thought, and the knowledge was a sick knot in his gut, because Silas was the deadliest thing he had ever seen, and he would have marked Zoë as his first victim. Mal started squeezing his gun's trigger as he brought it up, falling back, hoping against hope that he would be faster than Silas.

Everything about the strange man changed in an instant. He fell to his knees and clapped his hands to his head, moaning as a stream of blood erupted from his left nostril. No longer threatening, he now presented a wretched figure.

Mal's fall ended and his gun fired, and it was only at the last moment that he shifted his aim to the side, the bullet flicking at Silas's loose sleeve and ricocheting along the corridor.

He almost shot one of the three people standing there.

"Oh, no," River moaned, and though she did not bleed or grasp her head, she went to her knees beside Silas.

Mal hadn't believed that their situation could get any more precarious.

He should have known from prior history that it could *always* get worse.

15

Not knowing what had happened to Zoë and the others hurt Wash almost as much as his smashed and bloodied nose. Feeling the shudder, seeing the flash, and hearing the impact of something heavy against the ship's hull started the clock ticking toward the potential of more pain than he had ever known.

"What was that?" Private Harksen asked. She remained at a distance from him, gun aimed at his chest, but she skirted around toward the captain's chair so that she could see through the window. The far edge of the crater in the *Sun Tzu*'s surface glowed and faded again, illuminated by something originating above and behind them. "Sun emerging from behind the rings?"

"Explosion," Wash said.

"What?"

"You're an Alliance soldier," Wash said. "Haven't you ever seen things explode in space?"

"No."

"I have." He reached for his control panel and she tensed, her gun steady on him. "Scanners," he said. "You want to see what's happening?"

Before he could activate the rear scanners the opposite edge of the crater lit up again, a flickering illumination that probed deep into the wrecked depths of the damaged zone, sending shadows jigging and twisting.

Wash didn't like this one bit. *Wherever you are, Zoë, get your ass here now!*

Harksen edged closer to the windows so that she could see out. Wash eyed the comms switch again, but his nose was still smarting from the impact of the gun stock, and the scanners and scope controls were on a different board. He turned them on, adjusted a few dials, peered at the screens.

"Uh," he said. He wished he could think of something else, something pithy or useful, but everything on the sensors looked so humped that he could only make that one noise.

"What?" Harksen snapped.

"Not good," Wash said. "Observation lounge. Come on, keep your gun pointed at me if it makes you feel in control, but we need eyes on what's happening."

"Why?" she asked, and something about her reaction was off. *She's already said she was expecting something to happen,* he thought. He stood from his chair and headed down the steps to the gangway. He moved slowly so the private didn't think he was trying anything tricksy. Entering the dining area and observation lounge, he saw two more troopers sitting in their comfy chairs eating food he and the crew should have been eating later that day.

"Hey!" he said. "That's my dinner."

"I'll shoot you," one of the troopers said. "What's up?" he asked Harksen.

"Going to find out," she said.

"What's up is, there's a major light glare from somewhere behind us," Wash said. "Sensors show a spike in radiation and a heat bloom, and all of that points to us being humped. While you're sitting in our seats eating our food—"

The two troopers threw down the remains of their stolen food and stood.

"We need to take off," one of them said.

"Now!" the other agreed, approaching Wash with a threatening air.

"Not until we know what's happening," Wash said. "We take off blind, we might fly into an explosion flare, hit debris, or flip the ship into an unseen gorramn wreck." All that was true, but in reality he had no intention of even attempting to fire up the grav drive until Zoë and the others were back on board, gun to his head or not. Wash didn't consider himself a brave man, but he was loyal, and to him that was far more important.

"Go," Harksen said. "See."

Wash climbed onto the chairs in the observation lounge, grabbed some of the window struts, and hauled himself up so that his head was up in the dome. He looked toward the rear of *Serenity*, past her stern and the torn structure she was parked against... and his mouth fell open.

"Oh, *gǒu shǐ*," he said.

"What is it?" Harksen called up to him.

"Your destroyer's broken."

Several hundred feet toward the *Sun Tzu*'s bow, the Alliance destroyer's stern was slowly lifting away from the larger ship, while its mass was moving forward directly toward the crater where *Serenity* now sat. The movement was slow but definite, and fire pulsed and writhed around the stern as it came. Debris from the explosion was still spreading, speckling the space around the three ships in a fiery starscape, bouncing from the surface of the *Sun Tzu* and rolling outward in a destructive wave. He saw several fist-sized clumps of twisted metal strike *Serenity* and bounce away. One slid against the observation dome and set a light scratch into the reinforced glass curve.

"Come down here," Harksen said. "We're going!"

"Are you all just privates?" Wash asked. He realized it was needless provocation, but he needed a few seconds more. He thought he'd seen something.

Or someone.

As Harksen grabbed for his feet and tugged him down, he looked from the dome one last time. The view was quite sickeningly awesome, a graceful, ongoing scene of destruction that might well end in all three ships being smashed apart, or knocked from stable orbit and sent spinning into the unnamed planet, or skimming the planet's rings until that circling plane of ice, stone, and metal debris tore them to pieces.

And in all that chaos, two figures were moving closer along the *Sun Tzu*. Barely visible, caught beneath the daunting shadow of the burning, turning Alliance ship, Wash was sure they were wearing *Serenity* space suits.

He hoped one of them was Zoë.

Another tug brought him crashing down onto the soft seating. The breath was knocked from him, and he rolled onto his side and sat upright to find three guns pointing at his face.

"If you shoot me, who flies the ship?" he asked.

"Me," Harksen said. "But I'd rather you do it, since heaps of junk like this Firefly aren't so familiar to me."

Wash paused only a second to see whether she was joking. It seemed she was not. He stood and headed back for the bridge, Harksen following on behind. As he went, he heard Harksen and the other two troopers whispering behind him.

"We can't just go."

"What do you suggest?"

"What about the others?"

"They're down on the ship, there's no way we can—"

"We could transmit extraction points, swing around to a couple of the airlocks."

"Every second we stay here is a risk."

Wash climbed the stairs to the bridge, and only Harksen came with him.

"Fly us out of here," she said. She followed him to his seat and rested her gun on its back, not touching his skin but close enough for him to smell the oil on its barrel. He wondered how many times she'd fired it in anger, and realized that it didn't matter.

Beyond the window, the ragged slopes of the crater's opposite wall were now flicking and blinking with flares from the destruction above and behind them. The destroyer was shifting and spinning, and Wash didn't know how long it would be before its bow struck the *Sun Tzu*, or the conflagration in its stern spread and the whole ship exploded. If that happened they could all wave everyone and everything they knew and loved goodbye.

"Do it," Harksen said.

"My friends are on that ship," Wash said, thinking of the absent crew, and the two figures he'd seen running along the *Sun Tzu* toward the crater and *Serenity*. *How long do they need?* he wondered. *Maybe they're here already.*

"So are mine," Harksen said. "Sacrificing ourselves won't help them one bit. I'll count down from three."

"No need to count," Wash said. He ran through primaries, preparing the ship for ignition and takeoff, and he went through the whole procedure trying not to focus on that fact that none of it was going to work.

Time. He had to buy them time.

He settled back in his seat and hit the grav-drive initiator… and nothing happened.

"What?" Wash said, holding up both hands. "What?"

"Don't mess with me." Harksen leaned forward on the gun, shoving it so that it pressed against his skull just behind his ear.

"I'm not messing with—"

"Out of the seat."

Wash caught his breath. Had he pushed her too far? If she was simply getting him to move so she could shoot him without making a mess over the controls, now was the time he had to fight back. He tensed, and the gun pressed in even harder.

"Easy," Harksen said. "Nice and slow."

He stood and moved away from the seat.

"Rogers!" Harksen called, and one of the other troopers clambered up the steps and appeared in the doorway. "Watch him."

"What're you doing?" Rogers asked.

She glared at Wash.

"Fix it!"

"But I don't know—"

"I'm losing my patience," she said. "And we're—"

Something hit the ship so hard that it shuddered, and the view outside changed a few degrees as *Serenity* was shifted aside. A torn, jagged piece of metal spun away ahead of them, crossing the crater until it struck the far wall. As it did so, a shadow fell across their whole view.

"We're running out of time," Harksen said.

We all are, Wash thought. "I don't know what's wrong with the ship. But I can probably figure it out."

"Then get figuring."

* * *

With silent destruction filling the void around her, all Kaylee could hear was her own panicked breathing.

The Alliance destroyer was describing a slow spin above and behind them, its smashed and flaming stern lifting from the force of the explosions, debris scattered, fire bursting from the damaged hull before being extinguished in the nothingness of space.

Jayne nudged her arm and pointed down at where *Serenity* was docked against the near slope of the crater, nestled among wrecked and ruined superstructure. He signaled that they needed to jump down onto the ship's back, and Kaylee knew his plan. They'd check through the observation dome to see if the coast was clear, then enter through the nearby airlock and retake the ship.

Simple. Sure. A plan completely lacking in risk or danger.

She indicated that Jayne could go first.

They edged along a ledge of broken structure, then pushed themselves off toward *Serenity*'s back. As they drifted, Kaylee caught her breath.

Oh my poor girl! The ship had sustained damage. It appeared cosmetic, but there was always the risk that a surface scratch or dent might hide a deeper, more damaging trauma. Kaylee should really run a complete hull pressure and stability check before the ship took off, but that was not going to happen. Once they had the ship back in their control, once they'd rescued the rest of their crew, they were going to run.

Jayne landed just before Kaylee, and he reached back to slow her descent, fearing that the impact of their boots on the hull might alert the Alliance troopers who'd been left to guard the ship.

The idea that they'd already murdered Wash was a thought Kaylee could not allow to take root.

"It's all gonna be shiny," she whispered, words that only she could hear in a 'verse that didn't care.

They went to their hands and knees and slid toward the observation dome. Peeking inside, they looked down at the comfortable seating below. There was no one in sight. Kaylee climbed up onto the structure covering the gravity rotor housing, preparing to access the emergency EVA hatch just forward of it. Once inside they'd still be hidden from anyone on board the ship, until they exited into the dining room.

She glanced at Jayne before accessing the controls beside the hatch. They both knew that the action would illuminate a light on Wash's control panel, but unless anyone knew what they were looking for it would be just another light.

Wash would notice, if he was still alive.

She was inside in moments, Jayne dropping down beside her, and it took a few more seconds to reseal the hatch and ensure air pressure levels were matched and safe. Jayne had already taken off his helmet, and she followed suit.

"So what's the plan?" Kaylee asked.

"Drop down into the gangway, go to the bridge, shoot anyone that ain't Wash." Jayne shrugged. "Maybe shoot him too."

"He might already have ensured no one can take off. I showed him how."

"Okay, good. Here." He handed her a knife, keeping hold of his sidearm. "You know how to use that?"

Kaylee glanced at the knife in her hand, blinking rapidly. "I'd rather not."

Jayne listened briefly at the ladder leading down into the gangway, then climbed down. Kaylee tucked the knife into her belt and went after him.

She glanced back toward the stern and engine room, eager to go that way but aware that rescuing Wash was the priority.

"Bridge," Jayne whispered. "We'll move slow and quiet. We got the advantage here."

They passed through the dining area and moved along the forward hallway, passing the closed access ladders to the crew quarters, and as they approached the steps up to the bridge, two sets of legs were coming down.

Jayne crouched, gun raised, and Kaylee went down beside him.

The Alliance troopers came into view, neither of them looking along the gangway. They were talking in low voices, guns slung over their shoulders, and though Kaylee saw concern in their expressions, neither of them seemed troubled by anything on board the ship.

Jayne stood, and the movement caught their attention.

"Hold," he said quietly. They wouldn't have left Wash up there on his own, and Kaylee tried looking past them to see what was going on.

The engines whirred, coughed, stuttered to a halt. Something felt and sounded wrong. The core was wound up and spinning, ready to unleash its tremendous power and blast them out and away from the *Sun Tzu*, but it wasn't working properly. She tilted her head, listening, feeling.

Wash did something to stop it working, she thought, but that didn't feel quite right. The core was functioning, but whatever he'd done made it feel strange.

"We can't take off," she said softly. Jayne heard but didn't acknowledge. He had bigger problems.

"Guns down," he whispered. The troopers had frozen, both with hands halfway to the weapons slung on straps over their shoulders. Jayne had the draw on them, and he'd drop them both within a second if they made a move.

"Do as he says." She drew her knife and stepped forward, making sure she kept to one side and out of his field of fire.

"Anything?" she heard someone ask. The trooper's comms

crackled, and they glanced at each other.

Kaylee shook her head. The air was heavy, charged, like a storm moments before thunder cracked it apart.

"Guns… down," she whispered, and she was almost pleading.

"I said…" A face appeared at the top of the stairs as a woman crouched to look back and down into the gangway. Her eyes opened comically wide.

The troopers both went for their guns.

Jayne dropped them, the two gunshots so close that they sounded like one. Kaylee flinched back, then took a step forward as the woman crouched in the bridge doorway raised her own gun.

Jayne fired several times, his shots ricocheting from the top step and lower doorframe.

Kaylee was committed to going forward, knife raised, but she already knew that she'd never reach the trooper before being cut down.

Jayne's next shot also missed, the angle all wrong. His bullet nicked the woman's left boot as her own weapon leveled toward Kaylee's face.

A shadow moved behind her and the woman tipped forward, finger squeezing on the trigger. Gunfire sprayed against the opposite wall as she fell, tumbling down the steps and rolling twice before landing on the two fallen soldiers.

Kaylee took two steps forward, ready to kick her gun away, but the soldier had gone for a pistol hidden in her belt. In one fluid motion she rolled onto her side and pulled the weapon, aiming it at Kaylee.

The knife thudded into the side of her neck with a sickening sound, knocking her head to one side. Kaylee dropped and rolled, but the woman was dead before her hand loosened and dropped the gun.

"Good job I always carry two knives," Jayne said, holding up his gun. "Outta rounds."

Kaylee pressed her eyes closed and took in a few deep breaths.

"You okay?" Jayne asked. He squatted beside her, and when she saw what he was doing she coughed to cover the sound of the knife being tugged from the woman's flesh.

"Yeah. Fine."

"About time," Wash said from the top of the steps.

"You're welcome," Jayne said.

"You're injured."

"I've been shot before, it's only—"

"Wash, what's wrong with her?" Kaylee asked.

Wash knew exactly what she meant. "I removed one of the settlement nodes."

"Figured. Okay, I've got it." She stood, stepping over the three dead soldiers and handing Jayne his knife.

"She weren't going to shoot me," Kaylee said.

"Not now, she ain't."

She pursed her lips. "Thanks," she said. "Wash, gimme sixty seconds, then take off." Kaylee ran back along the gangway. It was only as she reached the dining area that Wash called after her.

"I hid it under the floor panel, third left from the core's front mounting."

Kaylee nodded. "Sixty seconds, then get the old girl in the air."

She ran through the aft hallway to the engine room, snatching up a tool roll as she entered, retrieved the part from where Wash had hidden it, and got to work. She smiled as she did so. She was home, and despite everything that had happened and was still happening, in this place she always felt safe.

She'd finished reattaching the settlement node within forty-four seconds.

16

*W*e have him!
　　We must be careful.

Of course, of course, but we have him, and everything we planned has worked.

A hundred dead troopers might not be so pleased.

They're soldiers. They're supposed to die. And if he'd escaped this ship, the death toll might have been far, far higher. Imagine him reaching some of the Outer Rim planets.

Imagine him reaching the Core.

We feel a chill at the very idea. Silas is fury, Silas is hate, and we have a very good concept of what he might do to exact his vengeance on those who made him like he is.

He should be grateful.

It's not our place to question. We have our own reasons for gratitude, and deeper down, perhaps our own reasons for hate. Our greatest drive, though, is duty.

And that we will perform to the end of our selves, and beyond.

We close on the subject, and for a few moments he is all we can see. He requires our complete attention, because the immobilizer device one of us holds is only on a short charge. Its power output is massive—enough to disrupt his abilities and control his unnatural talents—and so it cannot last for long.

Silas is shivering, sweating, yet even so he somehow manages to lift his head to stare at us.

We feel that stare, and its promise of pain.

We are experienced in pain. We increase the immobilizer output and bestow some more upon him. He screams. We open the smaller case we have brought with us and attach the necessary cords and connections to the ports on his neck and the back of his skull. He writhes. We move back and prepare for control, as he starts crying tears of blood.

We take a breath, exchange a glance, and switch the immobilizer to the control nexus.

Silas stops shivering and screaming, and settles down onto his hands and knees. Blood spatters the deck.

"Stand," one of us says, and he stands.

"Follow," one of us says, and he follows us back toward the place where he has slept for so long. Back toward containment, and control, and safety for them and everyone else in the 'verse.

Those who have died to allow his capture will be called heroes.

"I'm going to crush you both," he says, and we turn a dial on the control nexus that freezes his voice. He can think in threats, but we have no wish to hear them.

Now that we have him under control, we realize that the other people who were there have gone. One of them was River Tam, another fugitive from the Academy. She fled with the others, leaving the man she must have known—and who perhaps she somehow came here to find—to his fate. We cannot blame her. We cannot blame any of them, and her temporary absence does not matter. We'll return to capture her soon, and anyone between us and her will be destroyed.

For now, we have Silas. The rest can wait.

"What the hell were they doing to him, Mal?" Zoë asked.

"Torture. Tranquilizer. Gorramn mind control. I don't know."

"You can control a mind like that?"

"No," River said. "Not control. Only confuse. And his confusion… will not last. We have to run as fast as we've ever run before, because next time he won't talk. He'll kill you all to get to me."

Something in her had changed. Mal sensed that, saw it in her face. Where before Silas had filled her with wonder, now there existed dread. Dread, and fear.

They fled that corridor as fast as they could go. Mal led the way, Simon and River behind him, Zoë bringing up the rear. He didn't like that—if someone or something caught up to them and picked off a straggler, he wanted it to be… He didn't want it to be Zoë—but their panicked flight steered itself. He tried to keep close to the crater, heading around the damage, taking staircases and ducking along dark corridors where condensation dripped from the ceilings now that life support had been kick-started throughout the ship.

This amazing ship that he wished they'd never found. That gorramn map he'd pored over for hours had been made by Silas, with the explicit intention of bringing people here to effect his escape. That gave Mal the creeps.

"Great," Mal said. "He'll kill us all. Why can't I pick a crew with normal quirks? Smelly feet, bad eating habits, a few casual sexual perversions. How come I pick one with a mind altered by the Alliance and a monster for a brother?"

"My sister is no monster," Simon said.

"Never said she was, Doc. And why the hell didn't you stay on the ship like I ordered?"

"We *have* a normal crew," Zoë said. "Smelly feet, bad eating habits, sex perversions."

"Jayne," River said, and she laughed, so unexpectedly that it made the others laugh too. Mal heard a low hysteria in the sound, but it still felt good.

They are hurting me, but I'm allowing it. They are drawing me after them, but it won't be for long, because they have no idea what I've become. They *think* they know me, and in allowing them to think that I'm encouraging them to lower their guard. If they had any real comprehension of how dangerous I was, they would kill me here and now.

They could do that. They would do that, if they knew, if they knew, if they knew. I will not let them know.

So I allow them to draw and drag me on, freezing my voice and controlling my limbs, as I gather myself and prepare to fight back. I'll only do so when I'm ready—soon, very soon.

I will not underestimate them as they have underestimated me. I understand my limits.

I'm still in exactly the place I've always wanted to be... or will be there again soon. I feel distance growing between River and me, and the hurt that courses within me cannot be denied. It hurts more than their meager controlling mechanisms, mechanical things plugged into me and through me. Physical things can have cause and effect, as I'm feeling right now, but they are so... basic.

I was basic once, like them. A physical thing. Then they took me and experimented upon me, and made me superior. They think they know me, because they know what they made of River.

If only they knew what I have become, left here alone to grow and evolve. And what River will become, given my guidance, and given time.

I shrug, and one of the wires slips from its port in my spine. The Hands of Blue do not notice. They are too confident in their ability to hold me like this.

She's further away again, taken by those people who claim she is part of their group. Perhaps she even believes that, but the truth is that she belongs here with me. We have grown and evolved apart, and once drawn together our evolution will know no bounds.

We will be unstoppable.

I twist and another wire drops away, sparking against my skin. I cough to cover the sound. They don't notice.

River, I say silently in my mind, and I can feel her hearing, and I open my senses to absorb her reply. There is none. It must be them, blocking my senses with their cruel, pathetic machines. It can't be that she isn't replying to me.

How could she want something *other* than me?

I say her name again, and this time I sense something in return. It's not what I want, or hope for.

It's fear.

Don't be afraid of me! I think, and a shred of anger bleeds into the thought, radiating out toward River. She hears, feels, and her fear grows. Rage boils inside me.

I rip away from their control, and I surge.

We have him, and we are too knowledgeable about his potential to let our guard slip. We understand what he can do. We know every detail from those who helped create him.

We move quickly back toward the containment facility. We

understand that the ship is in turmoil, but once Silas is put down again we will be able to settle the chaos, ease the trauma of the past few hours. It might take a nudge from the *Sun Tzu*'s ancient retros, a subtle tweak in its orbit to remove it from the danger posed by the disintegrating destroyer. We can do that. Together, we can do anything.

We look at each other and allow a smile, because our work here—to recapture him, put him back down, because the Alliance can never let go of something so powerful—is almost done. Afterwards we can decide whether to stay or, perhaps, find a way to leave.

Something changes.

We pause, frowning, and ahead of us the restrained form of Silas also pauses. We are close to a wide curving stairwell, the landing leading further along the ship, ornate stairs heading down toward one of the entertainment theaters built for the ancient crew. There are old images on the walls, people who died centuries ago dressed in strange clothes and made-up to imitate some creatures we know and some we do not.

Trying to analyze the change, we consult our instruments. One of us sees that several wires and contacts have fallen from the ports along Silas's neck and up into his hairline, and—

"They wouldn't simply come loose," one of us says.

"We know that," the other says.

Silas is already standing, but between one moment and the next he seems to grow, his slight form filling the hallway, his presence drawing the eyes of people in those faded long-ago posters, as if they are staring into the future and seeing something unbelievable. Something dreadful. He is like a nuclear core filled with such terrible, pent potential.

We try to boost the restraining signal, but he is ripping away the rest of the wires, turning, lashing out with one hand, and he catches one of us across the face, tearing skin and laying bare the pale flesh beneath. A rich red blood flows and spatters across the walls. Silas grins.

One of us cries out in pain, and the other exerts all the power she has through the weapon we always carry, directing a crippling signal directly into his brain. His left eye floods red as capillaries burst, but his grin only grows wider. It's as if pain is power to him. It is sustenance.

He lashes out again, grabbing one of us and lifting, smashing us against the stair railing, inner structures breaking and outer skin rupturing and spewing life-fluids, and then he heaves and shoves and one of us falls away from the other.

We have never been so far apart. As one falls down through the stairwell and smashes to pieces far below, the other cries out.

We... I... run.

Such loss of identity is shattering. I am cast adrift. Half of my heart has been pulped, and its rapid beating is only half as strong as it has ever been before. I am made dizzy by the chaotic blood supply pumping through my veins. My mind is split in two, and though I quest, search, probe for the other part of me, there is nothing there.

We are dead. I am all that is left.

I run, and if Silas pursues me I neither hear nor sense him. I am powerless, weaponless. We should never have tried to contain him, whatever our desires, or our instructions from the Alliance's upper echelons. He is far too strong. If I had a superstitious cell in my body I would know him as a god. Or a monster.

There is only one thing left to do. I cannot survive like this, I *will* not, but I might stretch myself to completing the task we should have embarked on the moment we knew of his rising.

Destroy the *Sun Tzu*.

Destroy Silas.

* * *

I'll never stop loving my sister, Simon thought, but he was more afraid of her than he had ever been before. Previously his fear had been rooted in doubts about what the Academy had been trying to do to her. Altered, damaged, their experiments and treatments had scrambled her brain, and sometimes he wasn't sure she could tell the difference between fact and reality, or even past, present, or future. She was adrift in her own mind, and since the moment he'd thrown away his own future to rescue her he'd done everything he could to be her lifeboat.

Now, in Silas, he saw what they had been trying to do. Perhaps if he'd left River with them for long enough they would have made her into a killing machine like him, brutal and cunning, vicious and merciless. Maybe she was already partway there. Kaylee had witnessed some of her skills with a gun, and she was stronger than any of them, more agile and silent. The Alliance had been recreating and remolding her for war, and though every part of him wanted to ease and soothe her into a life of peace, he now wondered whether that would ever be possible.

"I'll look after you," he said, and River glanced at him. "I'll *always* look after you."

"I know," River said. The certainty in her voice might have brought a tear to his eye, if they weren't in such a dire predicament.

He was glad that she knew that.

"I'll look after you too," she whispered as she leaned in close. "All of you."

Mal had never been so pleased to hear Wash talking in his ear.

"All things considered, Captain, I think next time you win a map and suggest we all follow it in the vain hope that there might be a mountain of loot or something intangible yet valuable at its end, you can go hump yourself."

"Agreed," Zoë said. Mal glanced at her, eyebrow raised.

"I feel I'm voted down on this," he said.

"Considering everything that's happening, yes," Wash said.

"So what's happening?" Mal asked. He was with Zoë, River, and Simon, the four of them working their way around the artificially damaged and rebuilt areas of the *Sun Tzu* to a place where Wash could hopefully retrieve them. But in Wash's voice he sensed an urgency he didn't like.

"Nothing good," Jayne said. "I got shot." There was the sound of shuffling feet and Jayne's voice raised in protest, and then Kaylee came on the line.

"That destroyer's humped, and it's breaking up," she said. "It's in a tumble and it's already struck the *Sun Tzu*. Wash has had to take off and we're circling around the old ship's far side."

"We felt the impact," Mal said.

"It's knocked the *Sun Tzu* into a decaying orbit."

"How long 'til we crash into the planet?"

"Long enough. Head down through the ship away from the crater. We're almost there, and once we identify an airlock or access hatch on the outside, we'll direct you there."

"Got that," Mal said. "How bad is Jayne?"

"Flesh wound."

"It hurts!" Jayne protested.

"Suck it up," Mal said. "Keep all comms open."

"You okay, honey?" Zoë asked.

"I'm good," Wash said. "Jayne and Kaylee saved my butt."

"And such a cute butt it is."

"Eww," Kaylee said. "Wash, can you just fly this ship?"

"Keep us informed on progress," Mal said.

"What happened to…?" Kaylee asked.

"Gone," River said. "They took him away. They want to take me away too."

"They won't get a chance," Simon said.

"Right," Mal said. "No chance." He urged them to move, worrying about the blue-handed pursuers and their intentions, worried about Silas and how secure he might be with them, stressing about the *Sun Tzu* and what might happen to them before they had a chance to be taken off by *Serenity*. Worrying about pretty much everything, in fact. It seemed this mission was going as well as any mission they had ever embarked upon.

Mal kept his lock-picking kit to hand, and they soon came to another set of retrofitted blast doors. This time he was more careful, and instead of double-locking the doors they drifted open less than thirty seconds after he'd started work on them. He was getting better. The crew moved through and he went to follow, then he thought again. Thirty seconds to open, the same to close, and maybe that would be time well spent.

Whether or not the Alliance succeeded in putting Silas back down, someone would soon be coming after River. He wasn't sure who he feared the most, but the blast doors might hold them up for a while.

"Go," he said, waving them on. Simon and River went ahead, while Zoë hung back waiting for Mal. "Zoë, go! Stay with them. Wait for me at the next staircase, then we're heading down."

The ship shook. This was not a gentle vibration but a sudden, shattering jerk, knocking them all to the floor and reverberating between walls, floors, and ceilings, like the loudest clap of thunder caught forever within these narrow spaces. Mal sprawled and slid into the half-open doors, impacting against his side and bruising his ribs. Winded, he rolled into a sitting position. A queasiness settled in his stomach and he recognized it as motion sickness.

"We're in a spin," Zoë said. She stood and staggered against a wall.

"Wash?" Mal asked.

"Yeah, hi, well, that's not too good, the destroyer's knocked a hole in the *Sun Tzu* and—"

Mal felt rather than heard the decompression beginning. It was a strange tension in the metal beneath him, like a coiled spring filled with a dreadful potential.

"Zoë, run!" he shouted. He snatched up his tools and got to work. The first set of doors swung shut just as a roaring sound began and the atmosphere started flowing, then *screaming* past him, sucked back through the door opening toward whatever new wound the stricken Alliance destroyer had poked into this doomed old ship. The doors sealed and groaned beneath the plummeting pressures beyond, and as he stood and worked on the secondary blast doors, he glanced through the viewing portal and saw movement.

Silas was there. Further along the corridor beyond the doors, battling the hurricane of air carrying debris being sucked past him, he clung on to door openings and hauled himself along the corridor's wall against the flow. He gripped doorframes, handles, and controls panels, then grasped on to service piping and duct routes cast into the walls. He pulled, dragged, crawled toward them, and even when several items of chunky furniture were sucked from a room and smashed into his shoulder and head, he did not let go.

His eyes were squinted against the storm, but focused on Mal.

"Mal, what is it?" Zoë asked. The air on their side of the door still seemed to stir, as if agitated by what was happening beyond.

"We need to go," he said. The blast doors slid shut, cutting off the view beyond, and he engaged the double-lock. He turned around.

"Him?" Zoë asked when she saw his face.

"We need to go," Mal said again. "I don't think there's any fighting him, Zoë. There's only running."

Without saying another word, the two of them ran after Simon and River.

17

Wash couldn't breathe through his nose. It was probably broken. He didn't mind that—it had been broken before—but it was a strange point of focus for him, considering the utter chaos he was trying to fly *Serenity* through, the chance of matching the *Sun Tzu*'s crazy spin that was quickly turning into a plummet, and the possibility of ever being able to station *Serenity* close enough to the ship for Mal and the others to make it across. The likelihood of any one of those things happening was low. The chance of all three working out was astronomical.

Leaving behind the crater and the doomed destroyer had not removed them from any danger, because debris was sweeping along the length of the *Sun Tzu*, most of it small, some of it larger and more treacherous. He dodged the shards he saw, heard others impacting against the hull. Combined velocity was low so damage was hopefully negligible, but he still winced at each thud or scrape.

It stings. And I can smell my own blood. That's weird. The *Sun Tzu* itself was also moving, knocked from geostationary orbit into a slow, uneven descent toward the planet. He had to match that movement, and it took delicate touches, almost caresses, on the ship's controls to do so.

"Your nose is bleeding again," Jayne said, and he went to perch on Wash's control console.

"I know it's bleeding again!" Wash shouted. "It's gorramn broken, and gushing gorramn blood down my best gorramn shirt, now get your ass off my spaceship control console, sit in the captain's chair, and make yourself gorramn useful!"

Jayne skipped across to the captain's chair and sat down, too shocked at Wash's outburst to respond.

"The handle on your left, the gray one with the leather picked off from its lower edge by Mal's nervous little fingers, you see it?"

"Got it."

"Okay... Jayne... you need a steady hand here. Your one good hand's steady, right?"

Jayne held up his free hand. It had blood on it. "Steady as a rock."

"I need to concentrate on yaw and drift, and I'll need you to edge that forward, just *edge* it, when I say."

"Retro?" Jayne asked.

"Right. It'll slow us. But just a touch, Jayne."

"Just a gentle touch," Jayne said. "I'll pretend I'm touching a woman's—"

"Just wait for my word," Wash said. "Kaylee?"

"Here."

"Hold on to something."

"That's comforting."

"Just in case," Wash said.

"Just in case what?" Jayne asked.

"Just in case I get this wrong and we crash into the *Sun Tzu* in a blazing exploding mess."

Wash took a deep breath and readied his hands over the controls.

"Mal," he said, "I'm bringing *Serenity* in close to make a sweep along the ship's hull. I think sensors'll pick out an airlock, but—"

"Send me coordinates, then get there," Mal said. "The hull's breached, and Silas is onto us."

"Okay," Wash said. "That's more pressure. Good. My nose hurts, but pain doesn't matter because you forget it, given time."

"Your nose?" Zoë asked. "Is your nose damaged?"

"*I* was shot!" Jayne said.

"Don't worry, baby. My nose is fine. Just be ready."

The worst thing about the *Sun Tzu*'s movement was its unpredictability. Back around the other side, the destroyer must have impacted it again, turning its movement into a slow spin and twist too complex to match by eye. Wash needed the ship's computers to plot a burn, but there was no time.

And his nose was bleeding again.

He grabbed the ship's controls, took in a deep breath through his mouth, and dipped *Serenity* down toward the larger, older ship. He eased them closer, drifting, floating, and just as it looked as though they were going to strike its surface he whispered, "Jayne."

Jayne teased the retros and they fired, so quickly and softly that there was no real trace or feel of them on the flight deck.

It worked. The movement of the *Sun Tzu* settled in their vision as *Serenity* matched its spin, and Wash allowed himself a brief, deep sigh.

"Mal, we're close, and there's an airlock…"

Kaylee was already on the scopes, scanning the ship's surface and picking out what must have been an access point.

"Transmitting coordinates," Kaylee said.

"Got 'em," Mal replied. He sounded like he was running.

"Mal, something's smashing through—" Zoë said.

"We're minutes away," Mal said.

"We'll be there," Wash said.

"Be ready to blast away on my order," Mal said, and Wash frowned. Jayne looked over at him, and Kaylee froze with her hand on the console.

"Mal, once you're on board we'll—"

"If I tell you to go, you go, whether we're on board or not," Mal said.

"No," Wash said.

"Yes!" Zoë said. "He's coming, and if he gets us, that doesn't mean you all have to die too."

There was silence on the flight deck. Wash held their position, then drifted them along the ship toward the airlock they'd found.

"Just get here," he said. "We're ready."

"And we're a minute away," Zoë said, the words a promise.

Jayne stood. "You need me here, Wash?"

"No, we're good."

"Then I'm going to the airlock. With a gun."

"I'll go with you," Kaylee said. "You need looking after. You've been shot."

"Nice of someone to notice," Jayne said, and he offered Wash a wide grin as he left. It was a grin that said, *However humped things get, we're here together*. Wash was grateful for it.

The whole ship was shaking. Great booms and thuds echoed all around them, and Mal wondered whether it was the sound of bulkheads failing behind them closer to the hull breach. If portions of the *Sun Tzu* were venting to space it would make Wash's job even more problematic, but perhaps Silas would be blasted out into the void. Mal wouldn't wish that on anyone, especially a victim of Alliance scientific meddling. He knew the pain and degradation River had gone through at their hands.

But if it was a choice between people he loved and Silas, well, that was no choice at all.

Another huge impact shook the ship, and they staggered and skidded into the wall to their right. River caught his gaze, wide-eyed.

"He's still coming," she said. "It's not stopping him. I'm not sure anything can stop him."

Mal pushed her ahead of him and helped Simon to his feet.

"We're close," Zoë said.

"He must be smashing his way through the doors," Simon added.

Another explosion came from behind them, and the screaming blast of decompression began. River slipped and slid toward him, and Mal caught her outstretched hand, holding on to a door handle with the other. The handle was slick metal and his hand started to slip. He gripped River harder, causing her to cry out, but he was not about to let her go. He'd let go of the handle first, tumble back with her, and even though he knew it was more likely that she would be able to save him, still that loyalty was there. That was what being crew was about.

Zoë fell toward him and braced herself against the doorframe, feet planted either side of his hand. She looked at him, looked at his hand, and he nodded.

She pressed down on the handle with one foot, then fell against the door and knocked it open. As she did so, Mal dropped from the handle to the doorframe, and then Simon was by his side, stronger than he had ever seemed and more capable. He reached past Mal for his sister and clasped her wrist, and Mal understood where his strength came from. He had just saved his sister, and despite her strange power and the abilities she had been displaying more and more lately, he probably always would.

As Simon pulled, River reached up and grasped the doorframe, squeezing hard. She held Mal beneath one arm and heaved him into the open doorway, then climbed through and pulled Simon in after her, kicking the door closed behind her.

"He's coming," she said. "He's close. He won't stop. We should go that way." She pointed to a door at the other side of the small room. It might once have been a store, but racking shelves had fallen, spilling dozens of plastic boxes to the floor. They contained bed sheets, hundreds of them folded and tied and never to provide warmth or comfort.

River pushed past a leaning shelf unit and kicked the door open. It was dark beyond, and Mal ducked through with her, plucking a torch from his suit pocket and shining it around. It appeared to be a service access, pipes and wire ducts lining the walls and ceiling. Several pipes had burst and a slick, sickly-smelling fluid dripped down and formed slippery puddles along the route.

"Careful," he said.

"We don't have time for careful," River said. "We don't have time for anything. He's so close I can… So close he can almost hear…"

"River!" Simon said. He pushed past Mal and grabbed her, and River's distant eyes focused on her brother.

"Through there," she said, pointing at a gridwork of metal panels and props. "The airlock access. But we don't have time."

"Then we make time," Zoë said, drawing her gun. Mal did the same. If Zoë was going to make a stand, he wouldn't let her do so on her own.

We don't have any time, she thinks, and River understands there and then that only she can save them. Her crew. Her friends.

Silas is almost upon them and he wants only her. He needs her to stay with him, and even though he is so much more advanced—his body strong, his mind expansive and filled with all the knowledge he has amassed while everyone believed he was asleep—his vision is blurred by his need for her. He cannot see that this ship is damaged and doomed. He doesn't understand how much carnage and pain he has caused and will continue to cause, wherever and whenever they are together, until it's only the two of them left.

River had believed she would welcome him, and to begin with she had. But now she feels so frightened being the focus of such a mind. It's even more terrifying that, given time, she might become like that, and do the things he has done. And it's this idea that she will fight and rage against the most, because she is still a human being, with friends and loved ones prepared to struggle and fight for her. No power is worth having if it means you end up on your own.

River goes at the wall of metal panels. She smashes her fist at one corner, plunges her hand through, and ignores the cuts on her hand and wrist as she grasps the metal and strains, focusing all her strength and finally pulling the panel away. Bracing against a metal prop with her other hand, she pulls at a second panel, then a third, feeling strength surging through her body and swallowing the stress and pain that rises in her muscles. Soon an opening large enough to crawl through is revealed.

I am saving us, she thinks, and she pushes her head through the hole and sees the space on the other side. The double sliding doors of an airlock stand open, the small space beyond both inviting and terrifying. One step through there and vacuum is all that awaits.

She pulls back to let the others go through first.

If he reaches them, it needs to be her that he meets.

We are no longer two, but one.

I cannot comprehend this, and the pain is so great that I'm sure it is killing me. Each time I breathe I remember us, not me. When I try to speak my voice is ours, not mine. We were never meant to be this way.

Yet I cannot give in because we would never want it that way. We came here with a purpose, and though that purpose has now changed—*everything* has changed—I will do my best to complete it.

From behind I hear the thuds, creaks, and explosions of decompression. Blast doors behind me have closed, and they'll protect me from the violence of space, as well as from him. For a while, at least. If he decides to come for me, it'll take some time for him to get through those doors.

I hope. Hope is all I can do, because what we thought we knew has proven to be very wrong. We came here comfortable in our knowledge and confident in our mission, and pride and confidence have been our downfall.

I run faster than I have ever run before. I hear echoes all around and think I can see us from the corners of my eyes, but when I pass polished surfaces I see only myself.

In time I reach the access tracks to the ship's bridge. I have been here only once before—long ago, when we came to this place to leave Silas where we believed he could never rise again, never cause damage and pain, never be a danger to the whole 'verse— and the memories of that time are imprinted on my mind.

Accessing the pod controls is automatic. I step inside and the pod takes me across the wide gap to the globe-shaped bridge. It is independent from the rest of the ship, contained within the fuselage, surrounded by a void and held in place by vast columns and connecting structures, built this way for safety against disaster or, perhaps, attack. I remember the locking codes, and soon I am inside, the doors closing behind me. I disable the pod systems as best I can, just in case he reaches this far.

He's going for her, I keep thinking, *going for River Tam*. The fear remains that he has already reached her, killed the others, and brought her back with him to finish me off. Combined, I don't dare imagine what their powers might be. I underestimated him once. I never will again.

"Silas might know what we are doing," I say, and I can almost hear our response. It's a comfort. "We must be quick."

I reach the ship pilot's chair. It's strange that a craft so massive and so important might have one single chair with one set of controls, but then I think back to who created this vessel, and I allow myself a small, brief sense of wonder.

Out of time, I shove the wonder aside and sit in the chair. The controls come alive at my touch.

They were good mechanics, those Earth-That-Was designers and builders.

"I wonder what they would think of what we've made of the 'verse?"

I close my eyes, and we face the end together.

18

"Suits on," Mal said, and they pulled on their helmets, attached to their suits by cords and service cables. Mal sealed his helmet and hardly heard the small pulse that indicated all contacts and air supplies were in the green. If they weren't, he'd have no time to attend to them.

River and Simon were already inside the airlock, pressed to the outside doors. It was small, but large enough for four of them to cram inside. It would be a different story on *Serenity*. With the ship moving it would be quicker and safer to use the airlock above and behind the observation window, and it would only take two of them at a time. That would be a problem for later.

The ship shook again, either from an impact or another decompression explosion. He'd seen this happening to big ships before, back during the war. Once a certain number of compartments went in a ship already battered and damaged, it often weakened the superstructure and started a chain reaction throughout the vessel. No matter how strong the blast doors and secure bulkheads, the pressures and stresses of explosive decompressions could put a weakness into the ship that winnowed through its core.

He went to enter the airlock, then saw Zoë looking at him wide-eyed.

"Zoë?"

She held up a tube, torn at the end. It was her air supply from the suit into her helmet.

"Put it on," Mal said.

"But—"

"No time!" he said. "Helmet on!" He shoved her into the airlock and followed, standing facing the double sliding doors with his gun in one hand. As he pressed the control panel, an explosion nearby warped and then burst the whole wall of the corridor. Debris fell and bounced, but the expected roar of decompression did not come.

Silas stepped through the ragged hole in the wall. He was bloodied, battered, his loose clothing torn, a terrible wound on his scalp dripping blood down his face, but his eyes were as wide and mad as his grin.

"Stay with me," Silas said to River.

"I don't want to be like you," River said. "I want to be like me." His smiled dropped, his eyes grew narrow and filled with rage, and he came at them.

Mal slammed the control panel and the doors slid shut.

Almost.

Silas's fingers were trapped between the doors. They tensed, curled, and pulled, and the doors started to creak open, fighting and straining against their motors.

Zoë and Simon bashed at his fingers. Mal aimed his gun at the man's fingers, but if he fired in here a ricochet could kill any one of them, and the gap between the doors was not big enough to shoot through, and—

River touched the controls and the doors slid open.

Mal fired once, his bullet striking Silas's left shoulder. He shrugged, took half a step back, and came at them again.

River kicked him, hard, sending him sprawling back into the wreckage of the corridor. Then she slammed the controls and the doors slid all the way shut. Without pause, without taking a breath, without warning, she hit the Purge button.

Instead of the pressure being gradually lowered and the atmosphere bled out, the doors behind them slid open, and the resultant venting of air carried them out of the *Sun Tzu* and into vacuum.

They drifted away from the ship, somehow managing to keep together. Back in the airlock Mal saw movement at the small viewing window.

Scratching at the toughened glass, eyes wide and furious and *hungry*, Silas was watching them.

Watching *her*.

Mal felt pressure on his arm, and saw that Zoë was clasping on. He took three deep breaths, then disconnected his air supply and locked it into her helmet's ingress port. She blinked her thanks and took several deep breaths. When she nodded he plugged the air back into his port.

We can't do this for long, he thought.

"Wash, we could do with a little help here—"

"Way ahead of you, Mal," Wash said.

A shadow fell over them, and Mal used a burst of air from his suit controls to spin them around.

Serenity floated behind them, and in a few seconds he reached out and grabbed hold of the hull. The others did the same. Simon disconnected his air supply tube and shared with Zoë, then River was crawling up across the top of the ship toward the airlock.

"Two at a time," Mal said. "River and Zoë first."

They all knew there was no time for arguing. As River pulled herself into the airlock and Zoë hauled herself in behind, the outer door slid shut, and Mal and Simon were left grasping on to handholds on *Serenity*'s outer hull.

Mal found a strange peace in the silence, even though they hung so close to chaos. The *Sun Tzu* was in a spin, and somehow Wash had managed to replicate the motion and keep *Serenity* in the same spot relative to the ship. Mal felt *Serenity* shuddering every few seconds beneath his hands, and he saw occasional puffs from her stabilizing retros as Wash kept adjusting her movements. Beyond *Serenity*, beyond the *Sun Tzu*, the view turned and twisted, alternating between planet, rings, and deep space.

Just a few more seconds, he thought. *Just a few breaths and we'll be back home.*

Simon grabbed his arm and pointed.

Back along the *Sun Tzu*, a great glare burst from its stern.

"What's happening?" Kaylee shouted.

"Nothing good," Wash said. "Nothing good at all. The *Sun Tzu*'s firing up, and we're way, way too close."

Kaylee knew Wash's concentration face. She left him alone, backing away from his chair and the console and the terrible view beyond, and she shouted back through the ship to where Jayne was helping Zoë and River out of the airlock.

"Jayne, we got maybe seconds to—"

"We don't even got that," Wash said. "Hang on to something. Hang on to anything!"

Mal and Simon, Kaylee thought, but there was no more time to think. The ship lurched, sending her tripping down the stairs and sprawling on the gangway, and then she felt the old girl thundering beneath her.

* * *

They had no time to get inside. Mal saw that knowledge in Simon's face as well, and they grasped on to handholds with both hands. Mal secured his magnetic boots to the ship's hull. He was a long, long way from being a praying man, but he sent a thought out to someone or something.

Just this one last bit of luck, he thought, and then *Serenity* turned and powered away from the *Sun Tzu*.

Wash took them fast but smooth, weaving through a debris field that was spreading from the Alliance destroyer, and Mal had a chance to look back and down at the massive old ship as its boosters kicked in and sent it out away from the planet.

It must have been those blue-handed spooks taking Silas away. A rush of anger filled him, fury at their stupidity, thinking that they could contain someone and something so strong. What fools they'd been making him in the first place. What fools, doing what they'd done to River. They didn't understand the implications of their actions. They had created something unstoppable.

Then his anger changed to something else as he realized what was happening.

Serenity continued up and away from the ship, at a safe distance now and still moving away, because perhaps Wash saw too.

The crippled Alliance destroyer was caught in the *Sun Tzu* blast, and it burst apart in a blooming ball of flame. Ordnance exploded and sent countless spears of light and fire out from the conflagration, an expanding globe of superheated gases and wreckage that would continue moving out through space for miles, and days, and perhaps forever, given velocity by violence and set on random courses into and out of the 'verse.

They were at a safe distance from that ruin, but perhaps not from what came next.

The Alliance twins were not taking Silas anywhere safe. Perhaps they'd seen their mistake, or perhaps their programming and mission had allowed for this. *If he cannot be contained, then he must be destroyed.*

The *Sun Tzu* accelerated across the face of the planet and powered into the strange rings. Already compromised, its hull could not withstand the impacts of thousands of rocks and chunks of ice for more than a few seconds. The massive old ship came apart. There were no explosions, other than countless geysers of atmosphere being released when holes were punched through its hull. Its hulk continued moving into the rings, disintegrating, growing smaller as pieces fell away, and soon the remains of the ship were indistinguishable from the clouds of debris surrounding it. All that was left was a wave of movement through the rings, some parts thrown out from the settled orbit, others joining in, and soon this wave would settle and become nothing but memory.

The *Sun Tzu* and everything in it would soon be nothing but dust.

"Mal, you okay out there?"

"Just dandy," Mal said. "We're both fine. That was some flying, Wash."

"What else do you pay me for?"

"Your repartee."

"Your…" Zoë began, but then she chuckled. "Let's keep that between you and me."

Close to Mal and Simon the airlock's outer door slid open, inviting them into the warmth and safety of *Serenity*.

"Silas has joined the stars," River said over their open comm, and Mal was not comforted by her comment. It felt not like the end of something, but the beginning.

* * *

The crew sat around the dining table, drinks in hands, food on plates. Wash and Zoë were on the bridge, spending some time together while Wash flew them away from the vicinity of the planet. They were keeping an eye out for any incoming Alliance ships. It seemed unlikely that no distress signals had been sent, but as yet there were no signs of any other ships close by.

The Doc hovered around Jayne. He wanted to take him down to the infirmary to tend to his wounded arm, but Jayne had been too eager to eat, drink, and share their stories. He looked pale from time to time, and Mal thought the gunshot wound was hurting him more than he let on. He'd go soon enough.

Mal kept glancing at River, then away again. After all that had occurred, he couldn't help himself. She was quiet, subdued, curled up on her chair with a drink on the table in front of her. As ever, Simon sat beside her. He was there to protect her, but Mal couldn't help thinking there was no protection against River. Not as she was now, and not if she decided to turn against them. He was only pleased that she hadn't. Faced with a stark choice, he'd seen no doubt in her when she had chosen them—her brother, the ship, her crewmates—over Silas.

She and her brother were established members of *Serenity*'s crew now, and Mal was pretty comfortable with that. But he was also a mite scared. It had become more clear what the Alliance had been tryin' to make of her—a soldier. He'd seen what she might be capable of, both in her own actions and in those of Silas. He figured he'd never cease worryin' about having her on board his boat, but he also understood that she might prove more handy than he'd ever imagined. And he figured it'd likely change the type of jobs he'd consider takin' on in the future.

River caught his eye, and this time he did not look away. He smiled, and she smiled back.

While Mal finished his meal, Jayne reached for the two backpacks he'd managed to bring on board with him and sat them in his lap.

"So let's see what we got in this little haul," he said. "After spending a treacherous and most non-shiny time on board probably the oldest and most priceless ship in the 'verse—which is now, coincidentally, dust—we managed to finish this trip with…" He dipped his hand into one backpack and brought out the first object.

"A bowl," Kaylee said.

"From Earth-That-Was," Jayne said.

"It looks like any other bowl I've ever seen."

Jayne shrugged and took out the next couple of objects.

"A watch and a shoe," he said. "Just one shoe. I'm sure I picked up the other one." He opened the second backpack and looked inside, rooting around but obviously not finding the shoe's partner.

"I do happen to know a one-legged collector of Earth-That-Was memorabilia," Mal said.

"Yeah?"

"Yeah," Mal said. "But as I recall he has a left foot, and that one is a right." Everyone laughed. Everyone but Jayne. He upended the second backpack across the table, spilling drinks and smashing a plate on the floor. A water bottle, a few books, one with a scary clown on the front, a mug with a weird smiley mouse's face on the side, an empty photo frame, a leather case with nothing inside, a roll of sticking tape.

"Great," Jayne said. "Such valuables."

"Hang on," Simon said. He picked up one of the books and let the cover fall closed so that he could read it. His eyes went wide.

"What?" Jayne asked.

"You know what this is?"

"No. What? Don't forget I found it."

"This is an Earth-That-Was medical book, *Diseases of the Inner Ear*. Amazing!"

"Worth a lot?" Jayne asked.

"I have no idea," Simon said, flicking through the pages. "I suspect priceless if you're stuck on a spaceship in deep space and you develop earache."

"I do have booze," Jayne said. "A few bottles made it out without smashing." He picked one up and examined it.

"Maybe it's worth something," Kaylee said.

"Maybe," Jayne said. "I reckon we'll just keep it for the ship's drinks cabinet. For... you know... special occasions." He twisted the top off and took a deep swig, before passing it around the table. "And today's special occasion is surviving."

When Wash and Zoë came to join them, Mal enjoyed the sense of the whole crew being together again.

"The ship's flying fine," Wash said.

"Good, considering what you did to her," Kaylee said. "I'll spend a few hours checking her over after we're finished here."

"Hey, what's that?" Wash said. He picked up the watch Jayne had dropped on the table beside the single shoe and held it up, dangling from his fingers by its strap. His eyes went wide.

"What?" Jayne said.

"This is a Taurus."

"A what?"

Wash glanced around at them all, his gaze settling on Jayne.

"That's ship's loot," Mal said quietly. He'd seen Wash like this a couple of times before.

"Hey—" Jayne said, reaching for the watch. Wash took a step

back, and handed the watch to Zoë. She closed the strap around her wrist and admired it. The face was scratched, the hands still, the metal strap pale and stained.

"Wash," Jayne said, and when he half-stood he had to press his hand against the table to keep himself from fainting.

"Sit. Down," the Doc said, and for once Jayne did as he was told.

"Legend has it they only made a thousand of these, back on Earth-That-Was," Wash said, sitting beside Zoë and holding up her arm wearing the watch. "I've heard of three of them in circulation, which means there's probably more."

"What's it worth?" Jayne asked, and Mal sensed the interest all around the table.

"Enough," Wash said.

"Enough for what?" Mal asked.

"A full fuel charge, stocking up the pantry, and maybe even some spare parts for Kaylee."

"For *Serenity*!" Kaylee said. "Be glad to get those lateral stabilizer foils."

Jayne sighed, tipped the bottle to his lips, and took several deep glugs. He smacked his lips, and already his eyes were glazed. He held up the bottle. "You're welcome," he said.

"Thank you, Jayne," Mal said, not altogether sarcastically. "Zoë, Wash, nothing on the scopes?"

"Nothing but the hopeless, soul-crushing silence of the Black."

"Sometimes that's how I like it." Mal smiled. "Book get back to us?"

"While we were having our *Sun Tzu* adventures, we received a message sayin' he's sold some of those old tomes for a good sum," Wash said. "He and Inara will be rejoining us once we're closing on the Outer Rim."

Mal nodded and smiled. It was almost as if a plan had come together.

"So what did we learn from our latest jaunt?" he asked.

"Never, ever follow mysterious maps that ain't meant to be followed," Jayne said. He picked up the old shoe, sniffed it, and dropped it on the floor.

"I learned I like being warm," said Kaylee, huddled in a blanket. "And we learned where we came from. It was kinda hauntin' in there, seeing all those dead folk. But it was sorta shiny too."

"How so?" Zoë asked.

"The empty pods," Kaylee said. "They were used by generations long gone. My ancestors might've been asleep in them." She pointed around the table. "Or yours. Or yours. Or…" When she reached River she paused and fell quiet.

Mal glanced around the table, and the whole crew was waiting for River to speak. Even Simon.

"I saw what I could become," River said. "And I learned that if I allow that to happen, there's nothing in the 'verse that can stop me."

ACKNOWLEDGEMENTS

Thanks to Joss Whedon for the 'verse, and to everyone at Titan for helping me fly the ship.

ABOUT THE AUTHOR

Tim Lebbon is the *New York Times* bestselling author of *Eden, Coldbrook, The Silence*, and the Relics trilogy. He has also written many successful movie novelizations and tie-ins for *Alien* and *Firefly*. Tim has won four British Fantasy Awards, a Bram Stoker Award, a Shocker, a Tombstone and been a finalist for the International Horror Guild and World Fantasy Awards.

For more fantastic fiction, author events,
exclusive excerpts, competitions, limited editions and more

VISIT OUR WEBSITE
titanbooks.com

LIKE US ON FACEBOOK
facebook.com/titanbooks

FOLLOW US ON TWITTER AND INSTAGRAM
@TitanBooks

EMAIL US
readerfeedback@titanemail.com